DATE DUE

DISCARD

The Talisman of Set

The
Talisman of Set

SARA HYLTON

St. Martin's Press
New York

Library of Congress Cataloging in Publication Data

Hylton, Sara.
   The Talisman of Set.

   I. Title.
PR6058.Y63T34   1984   823'.914   84-13278
ISBN 0-312-78427-9

First published in Great Britain by Hutchinson & Co. Ltd.

First U.S. Edition

10 9 8 7 6 5 4 3 2 1

I have been here before,
But when or how I cannot tell:
I know the grass beyond the door,
The sweet keen smell,
The sighing sound, the lights around the shore.

You have been mine before –
How long ago I may not know:
But just when at that swallow's soar
Your neck turned so,
Some veil did fall – I knew it all of yore.

D. G. ROSSETTI

One

Under the silken awning stretched over the deck a group of young girls laughed and chattered together, not taking the trouble to listen to the young harpist as her slender fingers tenderly plucked the strings of her instrument and her sweet melodious voice trembled on the notes of a love song. They were watched over by an older woman, sitting aloof but every now and again letting her gaze flick over them before it returned to the solitary figure of a girl staring out across the river from the prow of the barge.

The oars moved in unison at a steady beat and overhead the purple linen sails billowed in the freshening breeze.

Women, filling their pitchers at the water's edge, raised their heads to stare, and small children leading massive buffalo cows waved their hands excitedly, hoping for some response from those sitting on the deck of the barge. The prow was adorned with the crest of the cobra and vulture, twin symbols of royalty, for this was the barge of the Pharaoh's mother, the Lady of the Two Lands, sailing from Thebes northwards towards the city of Memphis.

A peal of laughter came from the girls clustered under the awning, only to draw a frown of admonishment from the older woman. She looked quickly towards the lonely figure at the prow and immediately the voices of the girls became hushed and they continued their talk in whispers.

The girl sat with her head averted, oblivious to the laughter of her handmaidens. She was oblivious, too, to the golden morning and the bright sunlight sparkling on the broad river. She looked with unseeing eyes at the village

7

they were passing, at the white-walled houses, their roofs covered with palm fronds, and the groups of village children playing in the dust outside their doors, surrounded by farm animals. In her happier moments she had admiringly watched the tall graceful women carrying pitchers on their heads, whilst others washed their garments at the water's edge. Today she did not notice and her ears were deaf to the ageless songs of the men who worked the shadoofs and to the songs the fishermen sang as they mended their nets.

She sat erect, staring at the river which curved in front of her, but to the older woman gazing at her with sad eyes she already seemed to be surrounded by a great loneliness. Her white lawn gown moulded her slender figure which was as yet barely formed, childlike almost, and the sun sparkled on the jewelled collar round her slender throat and the gold bracelets on her sun-kissed arms. Her handmaidens had dressed her hair in a multitude of minute plaits which reached down below her shoulders, each plait ending in its own tiny gold cup, her hair as shining and blue-black as a raven's wing. Around her forehead was a single fillet of gold from which sprang the royal uraeus, similar in pattern to the insignia that adorned the prow of the barge.

One of the girls rose to her feet and walked towards the prow, and gently laid her hand on the hand of the girl sitting there. She started slightly, although she did not turn her head.

'My princess,' the girl said softly, 'will you not join us under the awning? The sun is powerful and it is cooler there.'

The sympathy in her voice brought stinging tears to the eyes of her mistress, but impatiently she shook off her hand and in a cold voice said, 'Leave me, I prefer to sit here alone.'

The girl rejoined her companions, shaking her head sadly, and then the older woman rose to her feet and made her way towards the prow. She stood for a moment uncertainly. The princess kept her back turned, but betrayed her feelings by clenching her small hand upon her knee and by the way she raised her small regal head. The woman knew that the princess regarded her as her jailer, the Queen Mother's creature, sent to spy on her every movement until she had decided what should be done with her, and it was true that the old queen had moved quickly to have her sent away. The girl's father, the Pharaoh, was dead. Only yesterday, after the embalmers had prepared his body for forty days, they had followed his golden coffin to rest in his house of eternity cut deep into the rock in the royal valley.

She reached out her hand and laid it on the princess's shoulder. 'My princess, you should return to the awning,' she said gently. 'You are unprotected here and when the sun has gone down you will find it is cold on the river.'

The princess gave her the same answer she had given to the younger woman but still she persisted: 'I know that you resent my presence here but it was not of my seeking, Your Highness. I have left a dear husband and children to make this journey at the command of Her Majesty, and although I know you think I have been sent here to spy upon you and report my findings to the queen, I have no intention of doing so. Can we not be friends for the time we are together?'

For the first time since they had boarded the barge the princess spoke to her, and although her voice was choked with tears, it was also heavy with resentment. 'I love Thebes, all the best things in life are in Thebes. I shall hate Memphis and there is none to care. Soon I shall be forgotten, I could live and die in Memphis.'

'Oh no, Your Highness, that is not so. Your sister will be the new queen. She will see to it that your return to Thebes is not delayed.'

The princess turned her head and the older woman was appalled at the misery in her face. It was a beautiful, enchanting face, but the pain in the green eyes and the bitter twist that curved the soft red lips brought a sympathetic ache into her heart.

Taking the delicate stole from around her own shoulders, she draped it round the princess before she returned to her seat under the awning. She had no words to combat the girl's unhappiness, and meeting the eyes of the barge's

9

captain who had come forward to speak to her, she only shook her head sadly. With a firm tread he too walked across the deck towards the princess. Speaking normally, as though it was a pleasure cruise they were embarked upon, he said, 'In a short while I propose to drop anchor for the night, Your Highness. We will sail again at first light and should reach Memphis by sunset on the next day, that is, unless Your Highness has other instructions.'

'You received your instructions from my grandmother, captain. You know I shall not alter them.'

He bowed his head and was about to leave her when imperiously she asked, 'How well do you know Memphis?'

'Not well at all, Your Highness, but I am told it is a most interesting and beautiful city —'

'And old,' she interrupted him bitterly. 'So old that those who live there have forgotten what it is like to be young and need love and laughter.'

'I do not know, Highness, but there are those in Egypt who would wish nothing better than to spend the rest of their lives surrounded by the white walls of old Memphis,' he answered her.

The rest of her life! By Hathor, in just a few months she could be dead from boredom. She nodded her head by way of dismissal and watched him walk away from her, pausing to speak a few words to her grandmother's creature as he passed her chair.

She wondered what they spoke about. No doubt he was relating their conversation to her jailer, and they would then decide if it was worth repeating to the old queen at some future time.

She used the silken stole to wipe away her tears, then with a small secret smile her hand reached upwards. Underneath her jewelled collar, her fingers fastened round the amulet hidden beneath it.

The misery was with me still when I opened my eyes to the darkness. There was a sob in my throat and, dismayed, I put up my hand to find my face wet with tears and my pillow cold and damp under my head. I sat up, staring through the narrow aperture at the dark blue sky lit by stars. For several minutes I could not believe I was not on that opulent barge instead of lying in my narrow bed in a tent whose entrance flap trembled in the cool night breeze. I strained my ears for the sounds of the river, but all I could hear was the sighing of the wind and the distant barking of a jackal.

Wide awake now, I willed myself to go over my dream, for now I knew it had been a dream, nothing more, but it had been so vivid, so real, my fingers could still feel the contours of the amulet that the princess had worn under her jewelled collar. I could see the clothing of the young handmaidens, the chairs upon which they had sat, and, more than anything, the lofty columns of the temple on the river bank as they soared upwards into the blue sky, decorated with exquisite colours, the reliefs cut deep into the warm stone.

It was at that moment that I remembered the scene of the day before and my father's anger. It was the hottest part of the day and I was sitting with my mother in the large tent which served us as a living room, when my father came in and threw the English newspapers, already six days old, across the rough tabletop towards us. His face was pale, his eyes sharp and glittering, his voice clipped and cold, but he was not angry with us, he was angry at something he had read in the newspapers. Together we spread them out across the table to look at the photographs and the headlines splashed across the front pages.

In Egypt the tomb of a pharaoh had been discovered intact in the Valley of the Kings. The photographs showed beautiful inlaid chests of ebony and ivory, as well as chairs and beds, exquisite alabaster lamps and fabulous jewellery.

My father was pacing about, speaking in short agitated sentences, but my eyes were riveted on the newspapers spread out before me and only my mother listened to him sympathetically.

He strode out of the room and we heard his footsteps

marching away across the stones. My mother put her arm round me and held me close to her and I whispered, 'Why is he so angry?'

'I'm afraid he doesn't like being proved wrong, Kathryn. Your father has always maintained that there were no more important tombs to find in Egypt and adamantly refused to go there.'

'How could he be so sure?'

'I don't know. He quarrelled with Uncle Mark, who agreed with Howard Carter, and now Howard Carter has discovered this marvellous tomb and your father will be made to swallow his words.'

'Why is this tomb so important?'

'Most of the royal tombs were robbed in ancient days. This one has been discovered still filled with all the beautiful things that were buried with the pharaoh more than three thousand years ago.'

'Who was this pharaoh who owned such lovely things?'

'His name was Tutankhamun and he was only eighteen when he died, just a young boy and perhaps not very important in Egyptian history.'

'Then why can't Father go to Egypt to discover the tomb of one of the great pharaohs, a man who reigned for a long time and who was very powerful and a great warrior?'

'Because, my dear, most of them, probably all of them, were discovered a long time ago by other archaeologists.'

'What did they do with all the beautiful things they found?'

'Unfortunately they found very little. Most of the kings were not even found in their own tombs. All their beautiful things had been stolen in ancient times and the old high priests were forever moving the royal mummies to other tombs which they felt might be safer from tomb robbers. The mummies are now in the Cairo museum.'

'Why didn't they leave them in their tombs and put guards over them? It's horrible to think that people can stare at them in the museum.'

'They are treated with great respect, Kathryn. They are all under glass and they lie on purple velvet. Nobody can touch them, and even after all these years some of them are still very beautiful.'

I was sitting with my hands clenched tightly together, an angry frown on my face, and I said bitterly, 'And I suppose each has its own little cardboard ticket to say which pharaoh one is looking at.'

My mother looked at me strangely, then she laughed a little uncertainly. 'There are times when I hardly know you at all. Just now you seemed so fiercely adult about something you can know nothing at all about. There is a very strange story told about the day the royal mummies were taken down to Cairo from the Valley of the Kings. They were taken by river and the women from the villages they passed on the way came down to the water's edge and wailed just as the mourners used to wail in ancient days at a funeral. It must have been a very moving sight.'

'And now there is none left, and Mr Carter will get the credit for everything.'

'Well, no, only for this one. The other tombs were discovered by an Italian many years ago.'

'But Mr Carter could get a knighthood like my father did for finding this temple here in Mesopotamia.'

'Perhaps, but your father got his knighthood for his services to archaeology generally, not simply for the finding of a temple.'

'Did you ever go to Egypt, Mother?'

'A long time ago, before I met your father. I went with my elder sister, your Aunt Lois. We spent most of the time going to balls and garden parties. It was very exciting.'

'But you saw lots of wonderful things, Mother, things like these in the newspapers?'

'I suppose we did, but I was only eighteen and a complete little ninny in those days. Heaven only knows how I ever came to marry a dedicated archaeologist like your father.'

'Tell me what you saw,' I persisted.

'We went to the tombs and the pyramids, we saw so many temples that my head was spinning with the names of gods and pharaohs, but there we were, two English girls abroad for the first time and away from the eagle eyes of your grandmother. We were flattered and courted but I'll tell you what I remember most about Egypt – the light, the most beautiful golden light and the incredible sunsets and dawns. In Luxor we danced every night at the Winter Palace Hotel and went to bed just as the sun was rising. We used to go out on to our balcony overlooking the river to see the western hills turn pearly pink in the first light. They were so beautiful, so incredibly beautiful that I have never forgotten them.'

I moved away from her, my disappointment so intense I could have wept from sheer frustration. I didn't want to know about the balls and the sunsets, I wanted to know about those ancient monuments and the people who had built them.

I sat staring in front of me, the scene of the day before and my dream a confused jumble in my mind. I left my bed, the sleep still in my eyes, and after draping a blanket round my shoulders, because the mornings were often bitterly cold, I walked to the entrance to my tent. A short walk over rough ground led to the partly excavated temple and two miles further on lay a native village and the mission school run by nuns which I attended. All my friends were either Arab or wandering Bedouin children. Three other English children attended the school, but they lived on the other side of the village. Between the village and Baghdad lay several hundred miles of arid and desolate country.

I was born in Persia and had never set foot in England. My father was a man entirely dedicated to his study of the past, and my mother seemed entirely content to be wherever he wanted to be. Mention of my going to school in England was made frequently now, but forgotten again in the excitement of finding an old piece of pottery or the fragment of a statuette.

Yesterday I had seen my father at his worst, but there were times when some miraculous find would send him into raptures for days on end, when the sound of his laughter and his delighted enthusiasm would colour our days. He could make the past live again for us, and listening to his words, I would see the chariots of Darius sweeping across the plains of Asia, the nodding plumes on the heads of the horses, the flying arrows obscuring the sun, and galleys sailing across a morning world. That his moments of elation were often followed by bouts of black despair meant little to me. I could always escape by hiding in the ruined temple, peopling its empty colonnades with figures from my imagination.

In my bare feet I walked across the loose stones towards the ridge where I could see the temple before me, its columns just beginning to rise from the soil which had buried it for centuries. I stared at the columns with a frown on my face. They were nothing like the pillars of the temple I had seen in my dream, for those had been decorated with the figures of men and animals and birds, all painted in colours that had seemed to come alive in the golden sunlight. In my dream I had seen a huge stone gateway on which had been cut the figure of a man standing proud and tall in his chariot, pulled by spirited horses, their heads adorned with tossing plumes. My head ached with remembering. Who was that man with the exquisite profile under his tall helmet, wearing a short kilt and a breastplate fashioned like the wings of a bird?

I sat down on the sand. Obviously the photographs in the newspapers had occupied my thoughts for the whole of yesterday and it was natural that they should have coloured my dreams, but those photographs of furniture and jewellery did not tell me why I had dreamed of a royal barge taking a princess into exile. It seemed to me that I had always known that golden skin and proud red mouth, the painted eyes, green as jade, strangely slanting under the spiteful head of the cobra rising arrogantly from the front of the golden circlet that adorned her brow.

That was the moment when I began to hate my red-gold curls and the violet eyes which men one day would find so bewitching. I was still a child and had none of the princess's slender daintiness. I wept for the kind of beauty that I wished was mine and for the misery in the girl's eyes.

Two

My father did not seem to mind that I wandered the ship's decks or strayed from his side to explore the numerous lounges and public rooms. I had no power to suppress the grief that my mother's death had caused him, or the disappointment that he had been forced to leave his work half-finished to return with me to England. It had been my mother's wish that I should receive a proper education and she had asked him to take me to my grandmother's house in Yorkshire.

I watched the other English children playing their silly games without any desire to join them, nor was I invited to. My father looked like an eccentric artist and I looked like a street Arab. The nannies looked at me with prissy disdain and the children, too, were unkind enough to make fun of my unusual attire. I didn't care, and later on, when they learned who my father was and I was invited to join in their games, I tossed my head proudly, delighted to refuse their belated attempts to be friendly.

That was one of the few times I saw my father smile. 'My, but you're an imperious little baggage, always were,' he said. 'Your grandmother's going to cure all that, my girl. She'll have none of your high and mightiness.'

Mention of my grandmother brought back my strange dream most vividly. It had been the princess's grandmother who was the cause of all her misery. I asked curiously, 'Don't you like my grandmother?'

He stared ahead grimly, then ruffling my hair, 'Perhaps it would be more correct to say we don't like each other, Katie.'

I hated him ruffling my hair and I hated it even more when he called me Katie, but now I was more interested in my grandmother. 'Why doesn't my grandmother like you?'

'Because she wanted your mother to marry somebody with money and the right connections. Your mother was only nineteen when we met and she didn't have her mother's permission to marry me. So, she ran away with me and we were married in London four days later. Your grandmother never forgave either of us.'

'If Grandmother never forgave you, why am I going there? She won't want me, she probably hates me too.'

'She won't hate you if you behave. Anyway, it's high time you went to school. And at Random Edge you'll learn to ride fine horses and dance in proper ballrooms. This is what your mother wanted for you.'

'I can ride already,' I retorted with a toss of my head, 'without a saddle, too, if I have to.'

He threw back his head and laughed. 'I'm not talking about mules, Katie, or those mangy old camels of Sheikh Mamoud's.'

'I once rode Naeilla and Sheikh Mamoud said I rode her better than any of his sons.'

My father frowned ominously. 'He should have had more sense than to allow you to ride that flighty filly. She's no horse for a girl to handle.'

'Oh, but I loved Naeilla. Sheikh Mamoud said she was as beautiful as the morning and as swift as time.'

'Yes, well, the Arabs have a poetic turn of mind. Did he say anything else to make such a minx of you?'

'He said that one day I would be as sweet to the nostrils as orange blossom and that my eyes of lapis lazuli would make strong men swoon.'

He threw back his head and laughed. 'You're in for a period of adjustment, Katie.'

We were the only two people to alight at the little country station and the guard stared at us curiously, probably wondering what sort of foreigners we were. I was wearing loose sateen trousers with a sash draped round my middle, and a short velvet jacket edged with braid. I carried an old wicker basket which contained all my belongings, and my father had on a suit which he had not worn for over ten years and which no self-respecting Englishman would have worn even then. He strode along the station platform in his usual arrogant way and I had to run to keep pace with him, closely followed by the guard who was obviously under the impression that we did not have tickets. When my father produced them high-handedly, the guard grunted in surprise and followed us out to the cobbled station yard.

Shortly afterwards an ancient taxi rumbled into the square driven by an equally ancient driver. He eyed us dolefully, as if he thought we were hardly the kind of people likely to tip well, and looked startled when my father told him to drive us to Random Edge. The interior of the taxi smelled strongly of brass polish.

I huddled in my corner, shivering in the unfamiliar cold and miserably aware that very soon now I would meet my grandmother. For the first time in months I found myself remembering the stark look of acute misery on the face of my dream princess.

I shall never forget my first sight of Random Edge standing stark and grey against the white scudding clouds on that windy March day. It was a house of tall chimneys and mullioned windows, with a long curving drive leading across well-kept parkland before it reached the formal gardens laid out before long, small-paned windows. There wasn't another house in sight except for a few farms dotted here and there.

The trees were tossing in the wind which whistled through their still bare branches and my father's words were lost as he opened the door of the taxi to step down on to the drive. I looked up at the windows, shading my eyes in the sunlight. At that moment they seemed dark and unwelcoming as did the heavy wooden door against which a shiny brass knocker in the form of a lion's head provided the only touch of brightness. My father stood gazing at the frontage of the house, his expression as bitter as his memories.

18

He lifted the heavy knocker and brought it down with some force, and the sound it made reverberated in the hall behind the door. I stood beside him trembling, and brusquely but not unkindly he said, 'Nobody in there is going to eat you, girl. Hold up your head and show them that you're not afraid of any of them, just like I did twelve years ago.'

The door was opened by a young maid wearing a white cap and apron. She stared at us, and I am certain that she was about to suggest that we tried the servants' quarters when my father snapped, 'Please inform Mrs Hamilton that her son-in-law Sir Alexander St Clare and her granddaughter Miss Kathryn St Clare have arrived.'

Startled, the maid held the door open a little wider, and taking hold of my hand my father strode into the hall. It was a dark wood-panelled hall with a blazing fire in the huge stone grate. The walls were adorned with the stuffed heads of animals, stags and wild boar, and I looked around curiously, while the maid tripped away quickly towards a room at the back of the hall. I was bracing myself for the first encounter with my grandmother, who had become a grim figure in my imagination.

The woman who entered was very like my mother, except that her hair was auburn whereas my mother's hair had been dark. As she drew nearer I could also see that her eyes were hazel whereas my mother's had been blue, but her features were similar and her smile was warm and welcoming.

My father greeted her and kissed her cheek.

'Katie, this is your Aunt Dorothy,' he said.

My aunt knelt down and gathered me into her arms.

'Dear Katie, how nice it is to see you, and how pretty you are!'

'My name is Kathryn, I don't like to be called Katie.'

She laughed, and her laughter was so like my mother's that I could feel my eyes pricking with unshed tears.

'Come near the fire, both of you, I expect you feel the cold after spending so much time in a hot climate. My mother always rests in the afternoon but she'll be down for tea. How long will you be staying, Alex?'

'There's a ship going to the East, on the 29th of March. I intend to be on it. There's nothing to keep me here and by that time Kathryn will have settled down.'

Nothing to keep him here! My father never weighed his words. I had often seen my mother's eyes fill with tears at some hasty, thoughtless word and now I turned away quickly so that he would not see that I was hurt. I got up as if to look around the room, hastily wiping my eyes.

'I think I should show you to your rooms,' my aunt said hurriedly. 'Kathryn will probably want to change into something less exotic before she meets her grandmother.'

'I must apologize for her clothes,' my father said. 'There just wasn't time to get her anything else.'

'Oh, Alex, surely they would have had something on the boat?'

'I was in no mood for looking. I had other things on my mind than falderals for Katie here.'

Aunt Dorothy looked down at me and smiled. 'Never mind. We'll soon have you in some decent clothes, and you really do look very picturesque, my dear.'

She went ahead, and picking up our few pieces of luggage, my father and I followed. My feet sank into the rich red carpet that ran up the centre of the polished shallow stairs and fitted the square hall above.

Aunt Dorothy took my hand and led me towards a door across the hall. 'This was your mother's old room,' she said smiling down at me. 'It will be yours for as long as you're here. I've had it newly decorated for you and the drapes and bedspreads are new.'

I stood with wide eyes, staring at the room which was to be mine. It was the sort of room any girl would have been in raptures about. Delicately coloured chintz drapes fell to the floor from under quilted pelmets and the same chintz was gathered round a kidney-shaped dressing table and also covered the bed. A pale green carpet covered the floor and there was a chair in rose-pink velvet. To me, who had hitherto slept under mosquito netting on a low camp bed, this was luxury indeed and something of my delight must have shown in my eyes because my aunt said, 'I can see that you like it, Kathryn. Come along and we'll get you unpacked and see if there's anything else you can wear.'

I adored the feel of warm silken water on my skin as I lay in the huge white bath, and the feel of the thick soft towels my aunt handed me to dry myself. I could hear her going through the drawers and cupboards in my room, and when I returned to it with the bath towel draped round me, she was standing over my wicker case with something like dismay on her face.

'I don't know what you are going to wear tonight, Kathryn. I had hoped some of your cousin Serena's clothes might have been here, but there's only her old dressing gown.'

'I can wear the things I came in, or those in the case. They're quite clean.'

'I know, dear, but they're not really the sorts of things an English child would wear.'

'Perhaps not, but I haven't been living in England. None of the native children thought them strange.'

She opened a paper bag lying at the bottom of my case and I could have laughed at the expression on her face as she lifted up the pale blue baggy trousers and the deeper blue cummerbund intended for my waist. These were followed by a black satin bolero trimmed with small tinkling bells.

'Don't you think it's very pretty?' I asked her maliciously, knowing very well she thought nothing of the kind.

'It is certainly unusual, dear.'

'I have a three-cornered scarf for my head, edged with silver coins, but I forgot to bring it with me. In the East I would have looked silly in anything else.'

Her face softened and she put her arm round me, drawing me close to her. 'Oh, my dear, I am sure you looked very pretty in everything you wore. It's only that I am not accustomed to seeing children wearing such things. We shall have to hurry, Mother doesn't like to be kept waiting for her tea. Put these on quickly. Later we shall have to put our heads together and think about the clothes you will need.'

So, for want of something better I went down to tea

21

wearing my Eastern garb, and my entrance into the drawing
room caused the utmost consternation, both to the maid
who was carrying in a silver tray heavily laden with all the
necessities for afternoon tea and to the woman sitting bolt
upright in a velvet-covered chair drawn up close to the fire.
My father left his place by the window and I missed none
of the amusement in his eyes at the shock my appearance
had caused my grandmother.

She was not at all as I had pictured her. I had thought
she would be small and slender, imperious and cold, but
this woman was stout, with a large commanding face and
white hair dressed high on her head, held in place with
tortoiseshell combs. She wore a black dress and on her ample
bosom a preponderance of jet beads. A rug covered her
knees, and her hand rested heavily on an ivory-headed stick.

I stared into her eyes across the room and after a few
moments she said, 'So this is Kathryn. The child's a ragbag,
Alex. Was it necessary to bring her to my house in those
clothes?'

My father didn't answer her. 'Come here, child,' she
snapped. 'I hope you have got a tongue in your head.'

I advanced towards her, at length standing in front of
her chair, my eyes unflinching, meeting the distaste in her
haughty stare with a composure that hid a desperately
pounding heart.

'Have you no other clothes?' she asked coldly.

'Only the ones I travelled in,' I answered abruptly.

'Are you telling me, child, that your apparel in the East
was little better than a street Arab's? Did your mother allow
you to wear such garments?'

'Of course. I wore what my friends wore. I like these
clothes, they're cool and comfortable.'

'But hardly suitable for the English climate. Alex, how
could you allow my granddaughter to appear on an English
ship wearing those clothes? What did the other children
think of her?'

'I didn't care what they thought of me,' I cried. 'I didn't
want to play their silly games anyway. Besides, they looked
ridiculous in those frilly dresses and straw hats.'

'Nevertheless, young lady, you will have to get used to wearing them yourself. Tomorrow, Dorothy, you will have to go into York or Harrogate and get her some decent clothes. Take her measurements, because it is obvious she will not be able to accompany you, not in those things anyhow.'

'I don't want to wear clothes I haven't chosen for myself,' I said angrily.

'There will be plenty of time for you to choose clothes, but not until you can go into a shop properly dressed. Those you are wearing might come in useful for a fancy-dress costume or a nativity play, but you will not wear them again as a matter of choice.'

There was antagonism between us, but it was an old and bitter antagonism, not born at that moment. This woman, I felt, was my old enemy, implacable and demanding, commanding my unquestioning obedience, and here as always she would stand between me and my desires. I looked at my father watching us as though he had no part in anything but the cynical amusement that our first clash of wills had provided him with.

'You are not saying anything, Alex,' she said. 'Kathryn is your daughter.'

'I have had other things to worry about than the girl's clothes. I have lost my wife, I have had to leave my work just when I was most needed, and Basra is hardly a city where I could have demanded crêpe de Chine and a flowered hat.'

That night for dinner I wore my cousin Serena's dressing gown, which Aunt Dorothy had quickly shortened for me. It was a silent meal. My father made no attempt to enter into conversation and Aunt Dorothy floundered nervously from one subject to another to break the uneasy quiet.

Immediately after coffee I asked my father if I could be excused, and with some relief I escaped to my room. I did not go immediately to bed. The room was warm from the fire that had thoughtfully been lit in the grate and I went to stand at the window, pulling back the drapes so that I could stare outside. It was a black, moonless night and not

23

a light glimmered anywhere. The wind had risen again and I could hear it mournfully circling the house, but then above the wind I heard voices and there was no mistaking the fact that they were raised in anger. They were my father's and my grandmother's but I could not hear the words, only the tones of their bitterness.

Quietly I tiptoed along the landing and down the shallow stairs. I sat down four steps from the bottom with my ears straining to hear the words they were flinging at each other in hard, hostile voices. They hated each other, those two people behind that closed door, and the cruel, vindictive words they were hurling at each other was indicative of that hatred. Something old and bitter also stirred in me and I clenched my hands over my ears to shut out the sounds of their anger.

How could two people who had both loved my mother hate each other so terribly? Sobbing wildly, I ran back to my room to cower before a dying fire knowing that my young puny strength would falter before the cold authority in my grandmother's eyes. My father would leave me in this house and even if he thought about me at all in all the years that followed, it was certain I would have to remain here.

I lay on my back looking up at the ceiling, watching the last dying embers from the fire fall into ashes before the room was plunged into deep, impenetrable darkness. I was thinking about the scene in the room downstairs, picturing their faces filled with hostility as they hurled angry accusations at each other across the space between them, and then, almost imperceptibly, the room changed and I was looking at another room, a large beautiful room touched by the colours of the setting sun.

There was no carpet on the floor. Instead it was covered in smooth cream alabaster and there were pillars of alabaster decorated with softly tinted birds and flowers. Beautiful inlaid chests stood against the walls, and chairs made out of gold, whose legs were carved to represent the legs of lionesses. At the long windows open to the terrace, delicate pale green drapes fluttered in the cool breeze. A girl stood on the terrace outside the windows, looking out to where the gardens sloped down towards the river, and I knew who she was even before I saw her face. The scent of jasmine was heavy on the air and it was the hour of sunset when the figures of men and beasts became merely black silhouettes along the river's banks, set against a sky that flamed with colours of rose and violet, gold and tragic crimson. Across the river, the barren hills of the west were lit by a purple iridescent glow.

I was one with the girl, one with the fears in her heart as she waited in the last dying light of the sun while, behind her, her grandmother's women lit the alabaster lamps. Then almost immediately she heard the sound of her grandmother's quick light footsteps in the corridor outside. She turned and walked back into the room, squaring her shoulders and lifting her head proudly so that the woman she was to meet would not know that she was afraid.

How small her grandmother seemed in her dark draperies, with the shine of amethysts around her throat. On her head she wore the winged headdress of the queens of Egypt from which the eyes in the raised vulture's head seemed to gleam wickedly in the lamplight. Gracefully she sank into the cushions on her gold chair, and after dismissing her women, she turned to the girl and said, 'Come nearer, Tuia, where I can see you.'

The girl complied, bowing her head respectfully, and the older woman watched her out of narrowed eyes, taking in the slender graceful figure in her white pleated gown and the straight white parting in her shining dark hair.

'You know why I have sent for you?' she begun.

'I am not sure, Your Majesty.'

'Then we must make sure that you know.' Her jewelled fingers drummed irritably on the arms of her chair and her voice was unmistakably cold as she said, 'There is more to being a royal princess than following the hunting parties and tantalizing the senses of the young nobles who flatter and flirt with you. It is time you learned to justify your existence. You are sixteen years of age, an age when many young girls are married and have responsibilities.'

The girl looked up sharply as the rich red blood coloured her face and delicate throat.

'Now you understand me,' the older woman said pointedly. 'It is time you gave some thought to the future which has been planned for you.'

'I know of no such future,' the girl answered, but her voice trembled with uncertainty.

'Your father should have explained it to you, but it is too late for that now. The fact is that a husband has been found for you, a most advantageous marriage which will benefit two nations, our own and that of the Hittites.'

The princess stared at her in disbelief, her eyes wide and dark with anguish. 'My father spoke to me of no such marriage,' she murmured.

In a voice designed to lull her into acquiescence, her grandmother continued: 'A royal marriage can do much to cement the friendship between two countries. More than trade, infinitely more than war. Besides, it is time you married. Your father spoiled you when he should have been firmer.'

'Are you telling me that my father found this man for me?'

'I am telling you exactly that, Tuia, and even though he is dead you will obey him.'

'I do not require any man to find a husband for me. I am a princess of Egypt, I marry where I choose, not where the Pharaoh dictates.'

'It is because you are a princess of Egypt that you do marry where the Pharaoh dictates. It is the way with all royal persons. If they love, so much the better. If they do not, they acquiesce.'

'It is not my way,' the princess answered her proudly. 'I will go to no man who cannot put me on the throne of Egypt, for that is the only throne I shall sit upon.'

Her grandmother was watching her through narrow, gleaming eyes and her hands tightened on the arms of her chair.

'So they have been right, the stories they have told me

26

about you and the prince, and you, my girl, have been more foolish than I believed possible. Let me put it to you plainly. Your father is dead and the prince you profess to love will be the next pharaoh. As such, by the law of the land, he will marry the royal heiress, your half-sister Asnefer. Even if your father had been alive he would not have altered the law to accommodate your desires, remember that.'

The girl dropped to her knees, and with the tears streaming down her face, she looked into the implacable dark eyes of the woman facing her. 'But I love him,' she cried. 'I have loved him since I became old enough to understand love, and he loves me. Why should we not be together? Why is it suddenly so wrong for us to love each other?'

Her grandmother's face did not soften at the sight of her distress.

'Your sister Asnefer is the daughter of your father and the pharaoh's great royal wife who was also his queen. I know that you were your father's favourite child but only because you resemble your mother, that Syrian princess who died before he tired of her. Only the purest blood in Egypt is ever permitted to sit upon the throne and you, Princess Tuia, will go to marry the prince of the Hittites to whom your father affianced you these many years ago.'

'If death be my portion I would choose it before I leave Egypt to give myself to some foreign princeling. I would rather be a priestess of Isis and enter her service in the temple. Not even you, Grandmother, could take me from the service of the goddess.'

'That is your choice, of course,' the older woman said caustically, 'but you are young and warm and passionate. Can you vow so adamantly now to cut yourself off from all earthly joys to follow the goddess of so many sorrows?'

'When he returns with his troops from Syria, the new pharaoh will never allow my marriage to stand. He will tell you with his own lips that he loves me and that it is I whom he will marry.'

She met her grandmother's eyes bravely but there was no compassion in them. The old queen rose to her feet and stood looking down at the girl with haughty contempt, and

27

although she was only small and very slender, there was no denying the majesty in her fragile frame.

'When the new pharaoh returns from Syria he will honour his pledges as he has sworn to do. He will take as his queen the Princess Asnefer and he will be too preoccupied with his coronation to have any thought for you. The world is full of beautiful women, Tuia, while you will be far away and the memory of you will grow dim in the mind of the man who is master of the world.'

The princess wept as she knelt on the cool alabaster floor, pleading with her grandmother as she clutched the hem of her gown. Disdainfully the older woman turned away and summoned her guards.

'You will take the Princess Tuia to her apartments and stand guard. No one is to enter other than her handmaidens and other servants and no one is to leave,' she said haughtily. To the girl she said, 'Tomorrow you will sail on my barge to Memphis, where you will stay in the old royal palace until it is time for you to take your journey to the East.'

Tuia had no choice but to go with the guards, and like a caged panther she paced her room. Even Ipey, her old nurse, could not calm her and was ordered coldly away, only to sit cowering in a corner until the princess's anger and tears were spent.

She had only one visitor to whom the guards could not deny admittance: the Princess Asnefer. She sat on the couch beside Tuia, who had thrown her slender shapely body on to it in an agony of weeping, and in her gentle voice said, 'Tuia, what is this I hear, that you are to go to Memphis? What have you done to anger our grandmother so?'

She looked with compassion at the princess's swollen face and heard her voice choked with tears saying, 'I am to go to marry a prince of the Hittites whom I have never seen and whom I do not love. I tell you, Asnefer, I shall become a priestess of Isis or I shall throw myself in the Nile before I do this thing.'

'But that is foolish talk, Tuia. You are too young to die and too beautiful to bury yourself away for ever in the temple. Besides, you should know that those of the royal

28

house are not free to marry where their hearts dictate.'

'Why should you care? You will marry the man you love and occupy the throne of Egypt as the great royal wife.'

'But of course I care. Are you not my well-beloved sister? Even if our mothers were not the same, we have always been very close. You are very dear to me, Tuia, you know I only want what is best for you and I shall pray for your happiness.'

Tuia tossed her head. 'What good is praying when you know that the only man I shall ever love will belong to you? It is easy to speak platitudes as though they were important. You will have the throne of Egypt and the man I love while I shall be sent away, never to see him again.'

Asnefer stared at her with great sad eyes. What the princess said was true. She would have everything, even the man they both loved. Rising to her feet, she let her hand rest for a moment on her sister's head before she went silently out of the room.

The princess was aware of another hand touching her gently, an older drier hand, and she looked up, startled. Seeing that it was Ipey who knelt beside her couch, she said angrily, 'What are you doing here? I told you to leave me.'

'Oh, my princess, when hasn't old Ipey been able to dry your tears and help heal your sorrows?'

'It would take the goddess Hathor and a thousand like her to heal my sorrows. Now get you gone!'

'Spells can be woven, Your Highness. What are charms and amulets for if they are not to bring nearer the dearest wishes in our hearts? Ask any of your slaves who it is they come to when some special desire warrants some love potion or the protection of a charm or talisman.'

The princess laughed but there was no mirth in her laughter, only a great bitterness. 'Have I not a thousand amulets to protect me from every known evil? What good are they when they cannot give me the two things I long for most?'

'Things that seem impossible could warrant a stronger magic, princess. The throne of Egypt and the pharaoh who can set you upon it are not little things like a new jewelled

29

collar to wear round your pretty throat or a pair of swift horses to pull your chariot.'

'There is no magic strong enough to give me what I want. I know that for a certainty.'

'There is the talisman of Set, Your Highness.'

'What amulet is that? I know of no such.'

'But Ipey knows of it, and Ipey knows its power. It is the god of evil who has the power to give you all you desire, at a price.'

'What price? What price would the god Set ask of me?'

'That I cannot tell you, my princess, and yet you must be very sure that you would be willing to pay that price.'

'I would pay any price for the man I love and the throne of Egypt. You talk in riddles, Ipey. Where is this talisman and how can I obtain it?'

'It is kept in the innermost sanctuary of the temple of Ammon under the ever-watchful eyes of a thousand priests.'

'Then you waste my time. The amulet is unobtainable. How could it be stolen from under the eye of the high priest of Ammon and those who have access to the inner sanctuary?'

'Before we explore the possibilities of that way, would Your Highness be willing to pay the stakes if the prize were rich enough?'

'Have done with your foolishness, Ipey. The amulet is out of reach. Think instead of how I am going to bear the journey to Memphis and my life in the future that has been planned for me.'

'There is Ptahotep, Your Highness. Hasn't he loved you since you were children together? In the name of that love, cannot we ask the priest to obtain the amulet?'

'Ptahotep will not steal it for me, much as he loves me. He is a priest first and a man afterwards. Besides, the sin of sacrilege in the case of a priest would cost him his life should he be discovered. I could never ask Ptahotep to steal this amulet in order to gratify the wishes of my heart.'

The old woman's face grew sly, and with a small cackle of laughter she said, 'Why not leave all that to old Ipey? When you hold the amulet in your hands, then you shall bargain with the god Set for his favours.'

'Leave me,' the princess said haughtily, 'I will have no part in your foolishness.'

She went to stand on the terrace outside her room, gazing steadily across the river. A full moon turned the rippling water into a sheet of silver and the stars that shone in the deep blue sky seemed near enough for her to have grasped them in her hands. From beyond the garden came the sound of someone playing a reed pipe, so piercingly, hauntingly sweet that it brought the hot stinging tears to her eyes. She was not aware that, at the same moment, Ipey was trotting swiftly along the road that led beside the river, keeping into the shadows cast by the trees, with the soaring columns of the temple of Ammon in front of her.

She stood in the shadow of the temple watching the procession of white-robed priests walking in stately file along the wide avenue lined with ram-headed sphinxes. At their head was the high priest, majestic in his robes with the sheen of leopard skins around his shoulders. They appeared ghostly in the silver light. Six priests carried on their shoulders the statue of the god Ammon and behind them came other priests carrying the statues of the goddess Mut and the moon god Khonsu, the Theban trinity. Ipey had remembered that this ceremony was always enacted on the night of the full moon and she had known where to find the priest Ptahotep.

He walked alone at the end of the procession, tall and graceful in his long white robes, his head lowered as though in prayer. Cynically, Ipey suspected his thoughts to be centred on the charms of the Princess Tuia and not on the god Khonsu, whose festival they were honouring.

Still keeping to the shadows, she moved nearer to the procession until she could catch hold of his robe. He turned round quickly to see who touched him. Holding a finger to her lips, she beckoned him towards her. He looked after his fellow priests to see if he and the nurse had been observed, but they walked on with bent heads, oblivious. He followed Ipey into that part of the square where the shadows of the towering temple were deepest and where they were least likely to be seen.

'You must be quick,' he warned her in a whisper. 'I do not want to be absent when they enter the temple.'

'Have you not heard that tomorrow the Princess Tuia is to go to Memphis, from where she will journey to her marriage to a prince of the Hittites? You who are her friend should know of this.'

He stared at her in stunned silence, hardly daring to believe what she was telling him.

'But who has done this?' Then, answering the question himself, he murmured, 'Her grandmother.'

'Of course. Hasn't the old queen always hated her, particularly when her father made so much of her, almost as much as she hated her mother before her? Tuia is distraught. I have fears that she might take her life before she will submit.'

'Why have you come to me, Ipey? I have no power to interfere with her grandmother's commands.'

'But you have love for her in your heart, Ptahotep. It is too late to ask for human aid. Only the interception of the gods can aid the princess now.'

'You are asking me to pray for her, and I will do that, but surely no amount of praying will help the princess if her grandmother has set her heart on this marriage?'

'The princess is a prisoner in her room and refuses to be comforted. Tomorrow morning she sails for Memphis on the Queen Mother's barge and until then nobody will be allowed to see her. I had to sneak out of the palace through the labyrinth in the garden because the place is crawling with guards.'

'Then I can do nothing. Not even my uncle the high priest can intercede. The queen would quickly tell him it was none of his business and that he exceeded his authority.'

'You try my patience, priest. It is nothing of this world that can help the princess, but there is one amulet in the whole of Egypt that she must have and if the god demands his price, then she is prepared to pay it.'

He stared at her, and even in the dim light she saw his

32

face grow pale. In a strangled voice he said, 'Set is the god of evil, woman. It is to Hathor or Isis that the princess should be praying.'

'Don't you think she has already prayed to a thousand and one gods? But her prayers have fallen on stone ears. You can get the talisman for her, you have access to the inner sanctuary, and by the time its loss has been discovered the god will have worked his magic and it will not matter.'

He stared at her incredulously. 'Woman, you know that what you ask of me is sacrilege. If I should be discovered my life would be forfeit, and what good would that do the princess?' His eyes met hers and she saw the tortured doubt in them. Nevertheless she reached out and gripped his wrist, her thin fingers tightening round it so that he stepped back with a little cry of pain.

'Ask me what the princess would do with the amulet if she had it,' she muttered.

He stared back at her, afraid to put the question into words.

'She will ask the amulet to keep her from the marriage which is distasteful to her and to return her soon to Thebes. Then, my priest, the princess will reward you with her love. But she must have the amulet tonight before the guards come for her.'

Still hesitant, he stared at her while her eyes willed him to do what she asked. 'I may not be able to get the amulet tonight. It is not my turn to guard it and I may find it impossible to get rid of the priests who are already there.'

'But if you do not, think of the princess and that long desolate journey she must take to marry a man she has never seen, and a Hittite into the bargain. You will get the amulet, Ptahotep, or you do not love her.'

Three

Ipey waited until the first pearly lights of dawn were falling upon the lofty columns and pylons of the temple of Ammon and the mist was drifting eerily about the river as she made her weary way along the wide promenade that lined the river bank. The Theban hills were tinted gloriously in colours of pink and mauve, but she had no eyes for their beauty. She was wishing she was not so old and she shuffled painfully in sandalled feet towards the white palace on the low hillside.

The princess's body was stretched out on a long couch. She had dismissed her women early, and still in the gown she had worn for her meeting with her grandmother, she had thrown herself wearily on her couch after a night of restless pacing up and down her chamber. In vain she had appealed to the small statue of the goddess Isis set in a niche in the corner of her room, asking her plaintively but with little faith that her prayer would be answered to hold back the dawn. Now its rosy fingers edged their way into her room, falling upon her sleeping face robbed of its anguish but still bearing the stains of her tears.

Ipey roused her urgently, and blinking in the half-light, the princess said, 'It is only just dawn. Surely they have not come for me already?'

'No, my princess, it is Ipey. See what I have for you.'

Tuia sat up on her couch looking down with frightened eyes at the enamelled gold amulet the old woman thrust into her hands. She stared at it curiously. It was not beautiful as so many of her amulets were. It showed the figure of a fabled animal, neither horse nor antelope, and engraved around it

34

were charms and hieroglyphics only a priest could have understood. It seemed to burn into her fingers as she held it, almost as though it possessed a life of its own. She gasped and dropped it quickly. 'I had thought it would be beautiful but it is not.'

'The god Set is not remarkable for his beauty, princess, only for the power he brings.'

'But what must I do with it? How can I be sure I shall get what I want? And what is the price I must pay?'

'Ptahotep says in time you will be aware of that price, but for now, what is the one thing that prevents you from obtaining the man you love and the throne only he can place you upon? Who is the one person that keeps him from you?'

The princess stared at her with wide frightened eyes, then in a soft awed whisper she murmured, 'The Princess Asnefer.'

'Well then, my princess, you know what you must do. Go to Memphis and there in the north land you will find the temple of Set where you can make sacrifice in order to obtain his help.'

She stared at Ipey, hardly daring to believe what her heart told her was true. Then, remembering her grandmother's contemptuous disregard for her tears and with a vision of the life planned for her, she raised her head defiantly. 'You are right, Ipey. Tomorrow I will go to Memphis and when the time is right I will sacrifice a hundred white doves to the Lord of Evil and ask him for the life of the Princess Asnefer. I shall not be afraid to pay his price.'

They both started as firm heavy footsteps could be heard outside. Her handmaidens ran into the room with frightened faces.

'It is the guards, princess,' one of them cried. 'They are here for you already.'

It was Ipey who went outside telling them that they must wait, that the princess was only just awake and would need time to bathe and prepare herself for the journey.

They were a solemn and sad procession as they walked down to the river where the queen mother's barge lay waiting for them. The princess led the way immediately

35

behind the contingent of guards, followed by Ipey and her young handmaidens, most of them in tears at leaving the city they loved and people they loved also. Then followed porters bringing with them the princess's chests containing her clothes and her jewellery, as well as the luggage of the other women.

The captain of the barge waited at the gangway in the company of a woman whom Tuia instantly recognized as Impetra, one of her grandmother's women. She stepped forward and, bowing before the princess, said, 'I am to accompany you to Memphis, princess, at the command of Her Majesty. You are allowed to take with you your handmaidens but not your nurse Ipey.'

'But that is monstrous! Ipey has been with me since I was a child. I must take her.'

'Your grandmother has said you may not, princess. If you insist, she is to be taken away forcibly by the guards.'

The princess looked back and saw that the guards stood around Ipey, and the nurse's screams of anger followed her as she boarded the barge. Through her tears she watched them take Ipey away, struggling like a wild thing, her screams dying on the breeze that swept along the river.

Why had her grandmother forbidden her to have Ipey, she wondered fearfully. Could it be that already they had discovered the theft of the amulet? She shuddered. They would know how to make Ptahotep talk, she had been told what hideous tortures they could wreak on those who had sinned, but not so soon, surely? Besides, Ptahotep was an aristocrat, the high priest's kinsman, they would not treat him like a common thief. She could feel the amulet heavy under the collar of cornelians and turquoises. She would ask the god Set to protect Ptahotep and Ipey, she would sacrifice a hundred white doves and two hundred head of oxen if need be, and when she was queen, she would see that her grandmother and others like her were made aware of it.

I was sobbing, great heart-rending sobs that tore my body apart, and then I was screaming as firm hands were laid upon me. Through my terror I became conscious of a woman's voice saying, 'Kathryn, Kathryn, wake up. It's only a nightmare, darling.'

I opened my eyes and stared wildly round the room, at first not taking in anything of the morning sunshine falling on the chintz counterpane or the figure of my aunt shaking me into wakefulness. Her face was anxious as I fought against her restraining arms. I heard another voice, a man's, saying, 'What ails the child? I've never known her to have nightmares before.'

Gradually my fears subsided, and hardly daring to believe that I was not still back in some remote past, I struggled to sit up, taking in my aunt's agitated face and my father's puzzled frown.

'I heard you screaming as I passed your room. What on earth were you dreaming about?' my aunt asked gently.

'I don't remember,' I lied in a tremulous whisper. My father, in his usual brusque manner, said, 'Come along, Katie, time to get up.'

Suddenly I remembered, with a thrill of anticipation, that this was going to be a special day. My father had promised that he would take me to see my godfather, Mark Ensor, who lived within reach of Random Edge, and Uncle Mark knew Egypt. I was more interested in Egypt than in anything my relatives could tell me. Uncle Mark lectured all over England as an eminent Egyptologist; he undertook the training of students, and according to my father, he even kept a sort of museum in his house. I couldn't wait.

My father was in high spirits as we drove in my grandmother's expensive Daimler along the winding lanes and through dale villages with quaint high streets and majestic churches, past village greens and rippling streams where the pussy willows were already sprouting silvery furry buds and where ducks splashed gaily in the water. Narrow rustic bridges crossed the streams, and the cottage gardens were bright with spring flowers. At one place we had to pull in to the side of the road to make way for a body of men and women riding horses, preceded by a pack of hounds and a large man on horseback whose bright coat rivalled his ruddy cheeks and who carried a brass horn in his hand.

The horses they rode were larger than the Arab horses I was used to. Most of the men wore white breeches and bright red coats, which I was later to learn they described as 'pink', and many of them wore tall silk hats. The women were all clad in black with white lace ruffles at their throats and long black skirts worn over riding boots. They sat their horses side-saddle, which gave them an elegant air, and there were children younger than myself riding ponies.

'That's a spectacle you're going to see and hear a lot of,' my father said. 'That's the local hunt out for an airing. It's mostly composed of members of the gentry but there will be one or two local farmers and their wives and daughters riding. The gentry suffer the farmers so that they can gain permission to hunt over their lands. Without the farmers there would be no hunt, but it's the gentry who keep it alive with their hunt balls and point-to-point races, as well as their arrogance.'

'What are they hunting?' I asked curiously.

'Foxes. Those are foxhounds specially bred for the job.'

'Does it take so many people to catch one little fox?'

'Oh, they're out for the chase and so are the dogs. They might raise a fox if they're lucky, but old Reynard's a mighty crafty and wily animal. He usually leads them a merry dance and he knows what he's about. One day, Katie, if you do what your grandmother tells you, you could be dressed up in a long skirt, and riding one of those fine horses.'

The hunt passed, and we continued on our way. As we climbed steadily out of a small village, my father pointed to a square-towered church on the hillside. 'Your godfather's house is at the top of that hill. You will be able to see it when we round the bend.' We drove through open wrought-iron gates up a small curved drive to the front of the house. A man working in the garden raised his cap as we drove by. The door was opened by an elderly white-haired woman wearing a large white apron. There was flour on her fingers.

'Is Professor Ensor at home?' my father asked her.

38

'Perhaps you would tell him that Alexander St Clare is here to see him.'

We followed her across the hall which was covered in dark red tiles over which several foreign-looking rugs had been laid, and into a sunlit room, pleasantly furnished with faded chintz-covered furniture and a soft green carpet, and I could see no signs that there was anything approaching a museum in this house.

Professor Ensor came into the room, smiling broadly. He wore an old velvet smoking jacket and stooped a little. Although his hair was snow-white, his face showed a boyish exuberance at meeting my father again. His eyes strayed to me and he smiled, holding out his hand to me. I went forward and he said gently, 'My goddaughter Kathryn, whom I have never met. I'm delighted to meet you now, child.'

'May I see your museum?' I asked him politely.

He threw back his head and laughed, as did my father. 'She's desperate to see your museum, Mark. I don't know what she's expecting but I did warn her it wasn't very large.'

'You shall see my museum, as you call it, as soon as you've eaten lunch. I expect you're both very hungry.'

'I'm not at all hungry,' I said a little untruthfully. 'I'd really much rather see the museum first.'

'Lunch first,' my father said firmly. 'The museum won't run away, and your Uncle Mark and I have a great deal to talk about.'

Lunch was a delicious meal served in a small dining room at the back of the house. Afterwards over coffee I listened to Uncle Mark and my father talking about the temple my father had been excavating when my mother died. I burned with impatience, but it ceased immediately their talk changed and they began to discuss the discovery of the pharaoh Tutankhamun's tomb.

'You always said there was another one, didn't you, Mark?' my father said regretfully.

'Yes, I couldn't reconcile the gaps that were left, but I could have been wrong, of course. That period in ancient Egypt was a time of unrest and internal struggle. It was fortunate that Carter stuck to his guns. Of course the tomb exceeded his wildest dreams – he had never thought to discover it intact.'

'Have you seen any of the things that were taken from it?'

'Oh yes, I went out there at once, I couldn't rest until I'd seen the tomb and its contents for myself. Newspaper photographs can't possibly give you any idea of the beautiful things that were found in that tomb, but it's like a rabbit hutch compared to the tombs of Seti I and Amenhotep. I should like to have discovered one of those before the tomb robbers got at them. It's anybody's guess where the contents of the largest tombs have ended up.'

'The Egyptian government is clamping down on any antiquities leaving the country now, I hear.'

'Yes, but it's rather like closing the stable door once the horse has bolted.'

'I don't suppose you get much now?'

'Only small things that are smuggled out by John Strickland, things that he wants help with. He comes to see me when he's on leave. He's not a very high-principled Egyptologist, I'm afraid, but he says if he didn't take the stuff, the workmen certainly would.'

'I hope you chastise him suitably, but I don't suppose he's far wrong. How is Strickland?'

The professor frowned, weighing his words carefully before he spoke. 'I'm not too sure, Alex. I think he's started drinking again and he doesn't get on too well with Dalton.'

'Well, he wouldn't, would he? Dalton's a stickler for orthodoxy whereas Strickland's very much his own man. Where is Dalton now?'

'At Sakkara. There's still a lot to do there.'

'And Strickland?'

'Off on his own somewhere with a new bee in his bonnet. The last news I had from him was from Luxor so it rather looks as though he's sniffing around Thebes, hoping for another great discovery perhaps.'

My father laughed somewhat cynically. 'I can't see Strickland having the dedication Carter had. He was like a dog

40

with a bone, but Strickland's too erratic, hasn't got the stamina.'

'Are you bored by all this, Kathryn?' the professor said, suddenly remembering me. 'I expect you've had enough of tombs and temples to last you a lifetime.'

I had been listening to their conversation with the greatest interest, but I smiled politely. 'I would like to see your museum now, please.'

Both men laughed and the professor said, 'And so you shall. You could have been wandering about there on your own while your father and I talked about all those people you have never heard of. Are you coming with us, Alex, or do you prefer to stay here and finish your cigar?'

'Leave me here, I've seen your museum countless times – unless you've added to it?'

'Nothing that would interest you, mostly one or two small Egyptian things.'

'In that case I'll stay here. I'm out of countenance with Egypt. Pure envy, Mark, you know how much I hate to be proved wrong.'

I followed my godfather up the stairs and along a narrow passage towards a closed door at the end. There was a padlock on the door and I waited while he hunted in his pocket for the key. As we entered the room he switched on the light and I stood in the doorway looking around me. It was nothing like the museums I had seen pictures of, where everything was kept in glass cases. This was more like a treasure room where I could willingly have spent all day.

Ranged round the room were ornamental stands on which rested beautiful vases and dishes of exquisite porcelain and figures of Chinese jade and ivory. Swords and daggers with jewelled handles adorned the walls and against one wall stood a massive many-coloured mummy case covered from head to foot with hieroglyphics. I went to stand in front of it, looking up at the carved face of a man. It was a stern austere face, without any indication that once it might have relaxed into a smile or perhaps even laughed a little. His hands were crossed upon his breast but his legs were held together by bands of glazed enamel. I looked at my godfather curiously. 'Is the mummy still in the case?'

'No, the case was empty when it was discovered. Perhaps the mummy was found wearing jewels which the robbers took. Heaven only knows what they did with it, probably burned it.'

'Who was he?' I asked in some awe.

'A scribe who lived in the north land, around Memphis or Avaris, possibly two thousand years ago, which is comparatively recent for Egypt.'

I looked around the room. 'I thought all the things would be Egyptian.'

'The things I have collected have been Egyptian. The others were collected by my father and his father before him.'

I looked up at the mummy case again. It towered over both of us and I shuddered a little at the finality of death.

'I should hate to keep a mummy case in my house,' I said fearfully. 'He was once a man.'

'Yes, Kathryn, perhaps that makes it rather sad.'

'Why didn't they want to keep it in Egypt?'

'Maybe he wasn't anyone of great importance and they already have enough of them. Mummy cases like this can be manufactured in Egypt and made to look old, although I believe this one is authentic enough.'

'Do you have any amulets, Uncle Mark?'

'I can see your father did a good job with your education.' He laughed. 'Come over to the window. There is a bench where you will be able to pick them up and look at them.'

Amulets there were in plenty but not one like the amulet in my dream. I could have wept with disappointment. I picked them up one by one, gazing at them curiously. Some of them were quite beautiful, particularly the hawk with his graceful outstretched wings, and there were a great many scarabs and strange-looking crosses which the professor explained were symbols of the word *ankh*, which meant 'life'.

Something of my disappointment must have shown in my face because he said curiously, 'You are looking for one amulet in particular, Kathryn, and it isn't there?'

'No.'

'Can you explain to me what it is like and where you have seen it?'

'I think I must have seen a photograph of it somewhere,' I lied. 'It is an animal surrounded by charms.'

'The Egyptians deified a great many animals in the name of the attribute they admired them for. What kind of an animal are you looking for?'

'I'm not sure.'

'Well, there is Horus the hawk, Anubis the jackal, Thoth the ibis, and a hundred others.'

'I don't think he was a real animal. He was like one that never really existed, like a dragon or a unicorn, and I think he was very wicked. Can you think of some animal like that?'

'Oh yes, indeed I can, my dear. You are thinking of the god Set, the lord of the underworld. He took many forms, but a fabled animal was one of them and, like you said, he was considered to be very, very wicked.'

'What did he do that made him so evil?'

'He invited his brother Osiris to a great banquet where he murdered him, then he cut his body into many pieces and scattered them the length and breadth of Egypt. The goddess Isis, the wife of Osiris, searched for those pieces of her husband's body for many a year until at last she found them all. Breathing magic over them, she restored his body and he was whole again. Never again, however, could he take his place in the land of the living, so he became the god of the dead and is represented by the form of a mummy. It is said that he was finally buried at Abydos, which is possibly the most holy place in Egypt.'

'What happened to Set?'

'The son of Osiris and Isis set out to kill his wicked uncle Set, but I am not very sure if he ever really managed it. This god's name is Horus and you will see him represented as a hawk. I believe in later years the god Set was vindicated or forgiven, at least in the north land. Two pharaohs, Seti I and Seti II, were named after him, so perhaps he was not all bad after all.'

'Why would somebody want to own an amulet of the god Set if he was the Lord of Evil?'

'Very much as people in medieval times wanted to own waxen images of those people they wished to injure. If an ancient Egyptian possessed the talisman of Set he, or she, would ask it for help in obtaining something forbidden, something so wicked the normal gods would have little sympathy with it.'

My heart was racing and I hoped fervently that he would not notice the trembling of my fingers as I replaced one of the amulets I had been holding in my hand. I no longer had any real interest in the museum although I made myself walk slowly round the other exhibits, and once or twice I found him watching me curiously.

I felt sure he would inform my father about the questions I had asked him concerning Egypt, but to my relief he did not. Once, across the room, he smiled at me, a smile that somehow seemed to make us conspirators, and I think after that my godfather became one of my favourite people.

We left in the afternoon after he had extracted a promise from my father to write to him more frequently, and saying to me that, now he had found me, I must feel free to visit him whenever it was possible.

I was quiet on the way home, absorbed entirely with my own thoughts. The day had turned colder and there were soft flakes of snow in the air, the first snow I had ever seen. My father seemed content to concentrate on his driving, and I sat huddled in the corner of the huge front seat while the car ate up the miles and overhead the thunder rolled ominously over the fells.

The long country twilight was strange to me. In the East the darkness had come suddenly, almost as soon as the sun had sunk beyond the rim of the low hills that edged the Arabian desert, but here the half-light lingered and I learned to love sitting in the windowseat that overlooked the park, watching its last fading glow.

My grandmother sat with closed eyes in her chair. There

44

was an open book on her knees but she had not turned the pages for a considerable time. My father smoked his pipe and read his newspaper. The wind had dropped and it felt so still that even the sounds of the ashes dropping in the grate were intensified.

From my place by the window, I could see the solitary figure of a woman walking quickly up the drive towards the house. She was tall and angular and her clothes seemed shapelessly shabby, her long skirts flapping above her ankles and a battered felt hat pulled down over her hair. In one hand she carried a small suitcase and in the other an umbrella. She hardly seemed like the sort of woman who would come to my grandmother's house, yet she walked purposefully towards it, looking up at the windows for any sign of life.

I stared at her curiously. She was a stranger to me and yet my heart was racing oddly, as though I had been anticipating the arrival of this strange woman who was one more piece in the chain of destiny. For one moment her eyes met mine and she stood still, staring at me, then with a brief nod of her head she marched round the side of the house.

My throat felt so tight that I could scarcely breathe and then, as swiftly as it had come, my anxiety subsided and I stared at the room behind me, surprised at its normality. The woman had gone to the back of the house. There was evidently no need for her visit to concern me; she was obviously a friend or relative of one of the servants. It was dark now so I returned to sit on the rug in front of the fire. My father had switched on the lamp on the table beside his chair and now went over to the window to pull the curtains. My grandmother opened her eyes, and after staring round the room, her gaze returned to the book in her lap.

'Shall I put on the other lights?' I asked her dutifully.

'Thank you, Kathryn. The lamp will do quite well.'

I jumped to my feet and switched on the lamp near the chair. The room looked charming in the lamplight and the glow from the fire, but the next moment the door opened and my aunt switched on every light in the room. She seemed faintly agitated as she advanced towards my grandmother's chair, and my grandmother looked up sharply at the intrusion.

'Bridie's back, Mother. She's just walked into the kitchen as though we were expecting her.'

'What is her excuse this time?' my grandmother snapped. She was sitting bolt upright in the chair and it was obvious that she was displeased.

My father looked up from his newspaper. 'I thought there was something missing but I couldn't think what it was,' he said, smiling. 'Of course it was Bridie. What has she been up to?'

'She walked out just before Christmas,' Aunt Dorothy answered him. 'She said she was going to look after her sick father, but since then we've not had a letter to say if she expected to return here. It has happened all too frequently over the years. Either it's her sick father or one of her sisters. We've been wondering how much truth we can place in her excuses.'

He chuckled. 'I've heard a lot about old Bridie from Margaret. If she goes away to nurse her old father, he must be well over a hundred.'

'Exactly,' my grandmother snapped. 'See that she has a decent meal and tell her I wish to see her immediately afterwards. She can't have her old room, Mrs Marriot has moved in there.'

'You can't send her away tonight, Mother. Where would she go?'

'You surely can't send her away at all,' my father said firmly. 'She's been a member of this household since she was little more than a child. If I'm wrong about that, it's only what Margaret told me.'

'She came here as a kitchen maid when she was thirteen. She told my mother that she was the youngest of a very large family and that most of them had come over here from Ireland to find work. Bridie was always a very good worker but she was unreliable,' my aunt explained. 'When she was eighteen she went off with one of the tinkers who had been at the fair in one of the villages and we didn't see her for three years. Then back she came, pleading to be taken on

46

again. I can't begin to tell you how often that has happened over the years.'

'But not to run off with tinkers, I hope,' my father said, smiling.

'There's nothing amusing about flighty servants,' my grandmother snapped. 'I suppose there is another room we could put her in?'

'Yes, although the bed won't be aired and will need making up.'

'I don't suppose that will pose any problem for Bridie. If her stories are to be believed, she is accustomed to sleeping rough. Remember, Dorothy, I wish to see her as soon as she's had her meal.'

I strolled out into the hall and made to go up the stairs. At one side of the hall was a huge mirror which stretched from the skirting board to the ceiling and I hesitated before it, staring at my reflection ruefully. I hated my little-girl's face with its violet eyes and gold-tipped lashes, my red-gold curls, and once my tan finally faded, I thought miserably, the pink-and-white English skin over which my mother had taken such care would begin to show through. Most of all I hated my dimpled knees and my shapeless form in the lumpy unimaginative clothes bought for me by my aunt in the village. As I turned away in disgust, a voice close by me said, 'To be sure the divil 'imself will be at the ither side o' that mirror.'

I spun round and found myself staring at the strange woman. She had taken off her hat and outdoor clothing and I could now see that her grey hair was thin and wispy round her thin angular face, and her eyes were sharp and filled with a sly humour. Haughtily I pulled myself up to my full height and said, 'I suppose you must be Bridie?'

She chuckled. 'That's roight, and you be Miss Kathryn. Well, we'll no doubt be seeing plenty o' each ither from now on, allus supposin' the divil 'imself doesn't get you from the ither side o' that glass there.'

I passed her with my chin in the air and she chuckled unabashed. I would have none of Bridie's insolence, I told myself. All the same, there was something about her that disquieted me. She seemed like another part of that chain which stretched out into infinity, but how or why I did not at that time know.

I had little patience with my school years. I wanted them to pass quickly, seeing them only as stepping stones towards that closed door behind which I should find other years in which all my questions concerning the past, present and future would be answered.

I was considered a very lucky girl to be accepted at the boarding school where my cousin Serena already was. My father wrote spasmodically from China where he was busy excavating and, when he remembered, he sent me birthday cards and picture postcards. In the early days my godfather came to speech days, and on several occasions he took me into York where we happily wandered its medieval streets and museums, or into Harrogate where we ate delicious teas in fashionable restaurants. Then, to my utmost dismay, he returned to Egypt, from where he sent me postcards and photographs which I pasted meticulously into a scrapbook.

I became no closer to my grandmother than I had been on the day I had arrived at Random Edge but I learned to obey her even if I could not love her. I was very fond of Aunt Dorothy, liking her humour and her views on life in general, even though I disliked her dependence on my grandmother for money and the way she allowed her entire life to be manipulated to suit the old lady's ends. That, of course, was her affair, just so long as it never happened to me.

I went home to Random Edge for school holidays and it was then that I entered the life of the community, scattered though it was. I had been given a pony soon after my father had returned to the East and some decent riding clothes had also been bought for me. I became a junior member of the local hunt and, because of my age, at first I was permitted to ride my pony astride. When I became old enough to own a horse, I was expected to ride side-saddle, which was considered to be more appropriate to my sex.

The first day I rode with them as a new member, a fox was killed, and when they attempted to smear my face with its blood, I became hysterical. Consequently, I was frowned upon by all and sundry as a difficult and unnatural child, particularly as I had accused them of following a sport that was both bestial and cruel. It took me many years to live that episode down, and although I continued to ride with them for pleasure, I was never there at the kill. I much preferred to ride down to the copse where I could lie on the grass beside the river, watching the pale sunlight filtering through the trembling beach leaves.

My reports from school were good, giving my grandmother little cause to complain. In my last year I collected the main history prize as well as the English one, and as I wandered among the groups of teachers and pupils on prize day there were many who stopped to congratulate me on my success, whereupon my grandmother said caustically, 'Her father is Sir Alexander St Clare. It would have been a disaster if the girl had not done well in history.'

For the first time I realized that she was snobbish enough to take pride in his title even if she deplored his work and disliked him as a man. She had no reason to complain that either of her granddaughters had disappointed her. Serena, too, had collected several prizes, and as head girl, she came in for a great deal of flattering attention and adulation from the younger girls.

I should have felt very close to Serena, who was always kind to me. She had smoothed my path at school and had welcomed me into her circle of friends, but it was I who was always difficult. Serena was pretty with dark brown hair and soft brown eyes. She was popular because she possessed a real and generous interest in those around her, and although I recognized and admired those qualities, I held myself aloof from her, responding to her overtures of friendship with ill-concealed doubts and caution. In spite of her charm and her kindness to me, I could not rid myself of the feeling that, one day, Serena would be my enemy and that it would not be for the first time.

I should have forgotten the strange dreams of my childhood, for it had been many years since they had come to haunt my sleep and trouble my waking hours. Although I was considered to be something of a beauty, I found little delight in my appearance. I had grown up to be tall and slender, with the short bright curls now shoulder-length. My eyes were described as being as blue as the pansies that skirt the grass borders in the garden and my skin was that delicate pale variety that goes with auburn hair. Why was it then that I always compared myself with that other face, whose jade-green eyes stared so proudly out of a delicate painted face, as exquisite as porcelain? Each night when I brushed my hair I longed for that raven-black hair round which the golden cobra wound its sinuous coils, raising its hooded, spiteful head above the pure line of her brow.

Four

The morning of Boxing Day dawned blustery bright and the household was astir early. In the hall, long tables had to be laid out with crockery and cutlery. Plates had to be piled high with all kinds of sandwiches, great pork pies and veal and ham pies, cakes and trifles and cheeses for midday when the hunt would meet at Random Edge. I could hear the sounds of activity long before I left my bed, and soon after nine o'clock, horse-boxes could be heard trundling along the drive and the sounds of voices and many feet. People would travel from far and near to follow the hunt on foot, and already an atmosphere of excitement seemed to have invaded the house.

My grandmother had employed waiters and barmen from several of the inns in the area, all of them familiar with the needs of the hunt because, on other days, the riders would meet at many of those same inns. All the local gentry would be riding as well as most of the farming community. This was the circle we moved in, from hunt balls to dog shows, from point-to-point meetings to three-day horse trials, but my social life was not entirely connected with sporting pursuits. There were concerts in York and Harrogate as well as in the music rooms of great country houses. My father had been right when he told me that a whole new world was waiting for me, although there were many times when, like him, I found the talk of dogs and horses and racing irksome and without purpose.

There was a light tap on my bedroom door and Serena came in. She was wearing a pale pink, quilted dressing gown

51

over her night attire and she ran quickly to the window where she stood looking out.

'Gracious, they're arriving already!' she exclaimed. 'I can't see very much from my side of the house. Aren't you excited?'

I shrugged my shoulders indifferently. 'You forget I've seen this every year since I came to live here. That's nine years ago so I should be used to it by now.'

'Of course, but I'm always excited by it. I expect they're too busy to bring us tea this morning.'

There was another tap on my door and Bridie came in bringing a tray containing my morning tea. 'I've brought another cup and saucer for you, Miss Serena,' she said. 'Will you be havin' your cup o' tea in here or in your own room?'

'Oh, in here, thank you, Bridie. How did you know I was in here, anyway?'

'There's not much escapes me notice in this 'ouse, Miss Serena. You ask your mither. Didn't I always know where they were and what they were up to, and didn't I always say to them, "Leave it to old Bridie"? Oh yes, Bridie always had the answer.'

Serena laughed, but I didn't. Words that to Serena were amusing seemed singularly sinister to me. 'Leave it to old Bridie!' Centuries ago, in a room tinted with the colours of the sunset, another woman had said, 'Leave it to old Ipey,' and I shuddered as though someone walked over my grave.

'You'd better hurry, Bridie, before they start looking for you downstairs,' I said to her sharply and Serena stared at me doubtfully over the rim of her cup.

Irritably I got out of bed, walked over to my dressing table and started brushing my hair.

'Your tea will get cold,' Serena reminded me. 'Is something wrong, Kathryn? You were very sharp with Bridie.'

'Bridie pretends to know everything. How does she think Random Edge ever managed when she went away from it?'

'How long is it since Bridie did one of her disappearing tricks?' Serena asked.

'She's not disappeared since I came here.'

'My mother says Grandmother wouldn't have stood it from anybody else. Why Bridie, I wonder?'

'I don't know, but not out of sentimentality, surely.'

'You don't like her, do you?'

'I neither like her nor dislike her. She is a servant in this house.'

'Oh, Kathryn, we did away with slavery years ago. You talk as though you still subscribe to it.'

I went to the tray to pour myself a cup of tea, hoping that she would not see how my hands trembled. I needn't have worried; she was back at the window with her eyes glued to the scene below. She appeared to be looking for some person in particular, eyeing each new arrival hopefully, and somewhat sharply I said, 'Who are you looking for, Serena? You haven't simply come in here to watch all that lot arriving?'

She blushed and moved away. 'I was hoping to see some friends of my parents. They live in the West Riding now and I thought that if I saw them I could go along and tell my mother they'd arrived.'

'Do I know them?' I asked her.

'I don't think so. I've known them most of my life, and it will be nice to see them again.'

She seemed embarrassed as she moved towards the door. She did not want the conversation regarding her parents' friends to continue, and because I was not very interested in them I didn't prolong it. At the door she turned and said, 'I'd better go and get into my riding clothes. You too, Kathryn, or Aunt Dorothy will be along here to find out why we're not dressed and helping downstairs.'

'I suppose so. You know what it will be like, all the same people riding the same horses chatting about the same old things. Aren't you sometimes bored by it all?'

'Not really, but then I don't live here. I enjoy coming to Yorkshire to see Grandmother and Aunt Dorothy, I always have, and the country life is such a complete change for all of us.'

I shrugged my shoulders noncommittally. Serena's father was a civil servant who had spent most of his young life overseas and was happier within easy reach of theatres, cinemas, and his golf club. I always believed he accompanied Aunt Lois to Yorkshire with bad grace and regarded these visits as a duty. Once on leaving he had remarked to me, 'Well, thank goodness that's over and done with for three months,' and after giving me a conspiratorial wink, he had gone out to the car. Consequently I kept my own counsel when Serena spoke of enjoying her visits to the North.

'I'll see you downstairs,' called Serena and then she was gone, closing the door quietly behind her. I heard her talking to someone in the corridor outside and then Aunt Dorothy appeared, dressed in good country tweeds and a cashmere twin-set. It was a sort of uniform worn by the women who did not ride, but she looked pretty this morning with a blush on her cheeks and her eyes bright.

'Oh, Kathryn, you're going to be so late. You're not even dressed yet.'

'No, but it won't take me long. Besides there are enough people helping downstairs without me.'

'Peter Hardcastle has been looking for you already. He asked me twice if I'd seen you.'

'All the more reason to dawdle then,' I snapped.

'Peter's a charming boy. He's good-looking and popular, and he comes from a very good and wealthy family. Why don't you like him?'

'I don't dislike him, I suppose he's very nice. I just don't want to encourage him, that's all.'

'There's nothing to say you wouldn't like him a lot more if you encouraged him a little. I sometimes wonder what exactly you do want out of life, Kathryn.'

I laughed across the room at her. 'I shall know what I want when I see it, but I know exactly what my life will be like if I encourage Peter. It will be a succession of days exactly like this one, and I just know I couldn't stand it for the rest of my life.'

'I thought you were happy with the life here.'

'I am happy, but it isn't going to be for ever. There's much more to life than he's going to be able to offer me.'

'There are a great many young women in Yorkshire who would be glad of the chance.'

'I know, so why doesn't he shop around?'

'Your grandmother would like to see you well married, you know.'

I was silent. I didn't see Aunt Dorothy leave the room and I only dimly heard her insistence that I should hurry. I was back in that other room in a world I had only dreamed of, looking into the cold implacable eyes of a small regal woman in dark draperies, with the gleam of amethysts round her throat, and I was hearing her voice falling like drops of ice in the stillness of the room as she banished me from a familiar beloved world, and for ever more from the life of the man I adored.

Only dimly the sounds of the morning reached me, and I have no memory of how long I sat on the edge of my bed staring at the carpet without seeing it. It was the creak of the door opening that made me look up suddenly to find Bridie staring at me in astonishment.

'Everybody's here, Miss Kathryn, and you not even dressed yet. It's a fit your grandmother'll be 'avin' and no mistake if you don't get down those stairs sharpish. Shall I be stayin' to help you dress now?'

'No, Bridie, I can manage. What time is it?'

'Nigh on eleven, and will you listen to them dogs barkin' their silly 'eads off?'

I could hear them barking excitedly underneath the window as I fled into the bathroom, and I could hear Bridie going about my room putting my things away, for I was not a particularly tidy person. It did not take me long to dress. The black riding clothes and white silk shirt were flattering to my colouring, and the long skirt over black leather riding boots gave my figure a slender grace. Bridie came to stand behind me, and meeting her gaze in the mirror I said, 'I know, Bridie, the divil himself will get me one of these days.'

'That he will, Missy, and what's more he'll demand a forfeit if he's to let you go.'

'You appear to be very familiar with the devil and his needs, Bridie.'

'That I am now. Me old father always said I should fear

the Lord and give the divil his due, and sure I 'ave a healthy respect for both of 'em.'

Our eyes met in the mirror and she smiled. There were many times when her sense of humour made me laugh. It could be gay and sly, malicious and witty, but there were occasions in her dealings with me when I sensed an underlying insolence and desire to inflict some sort of hurt. I had heard Serena laugh happily when Bridie told her one of her stories, but she never told them to me. Her only contact with me was to point out my shortcomings in no uncertain manner, and to threaten me with the miseries I might have to bear as a consequence.

I turned away from the mirror irritably and, picking up my riding crop from the top of a chest, I let myself out of the room. The noise was louder now as I ran downstairs, pausing at the top of the first flight to look down on the hall below. It was crowded with women in dark riding clothes, and the men in their hunting pink gave a cheerful note to the occasion.

The waiters and barmen were filling up glasses and handing round refreshments, and I could see Aunt Dorothy busy at one of the side tables, assisted by Serena. In one corner Major Danvers was already the centre of a large crowd who were listening to him singing one of the ribald hunting songs from his repertoire, while in another, two women were arguing fiercely about the pros and cons of a particular saddle. The children sat together at the end of the room, all talking at once so that the noise was deafening.

I ran down the stairs and was immediately accosted by a voice behind me saying, 'At last! Where on earth have you been? I've been looking for you all morning.'

I turned round with a smile on my face which did not exactly match the irritation I was feeling. Peter Hardcastle was good-looking, tall and well made, although looking at his father I could tell that in only a few years Peter would resemble him. The older Mr Hardcastle was also tall, with a round, bright-red face and eyes which it was difficult to see within the rolls of fat on his cheeks. He was corpulent and liked his whisky, and when they were together, Peter's youth was the only thing that seriously divided them.

Peter placed a heavy arm round my shoulders and said, 'Now about next Saturday at Wetherby. You'll be joining our party, won't you, Kathryn?'

'I'm afraid not. I've promised to go into York with my aunt on that day.'

'But you can't do that, old girl. York's miserable at the weekend, it's full of trippers doing the shops. If you don't want to go to Wetherby, there are other race meetings. Take your pick.'

'I'm sorry, I've already promised.'

'Then I'll have to talk to your aunt. She won't keep you to that promise, I'm sure.'

'But I want to go into York and I don't want you to talk to my aunt. I must go, Peter, there are some people over there I want to see.'

Somehow I escaped from his restraining arm and fled towards Aunt Dorothy and Serena who were talking to a tall distinguished man and his wife who had just arrived. Before I reached them, they were joined by Serena's parents and another man who stood with his back to me. I could tell that he was young and there was something about him even then that made my heart lurch sickeningly in my breast. He was talking to Serena and she was laughing up into his face, more animated than I had ever seen her.

His was the face she had been looking for earlier that morning from the window of my room, and from the expression on her rosy face I knew that she was in love with him. I turned to walk away but Aunt Dorothy saw me and called me over. Introductions were performed but I shall never know the words I murmured. His name was David Laurenson. I had never seen his face until that moment, but if I had met him on a crowded street, I would have been instantly aware of the current of awareness that passed between us. He was good-looking, dark and tall, and he stood smiling down at me, taking my hand in a firm grasp.

I have no memory of what we talked about as we moved out of the house towards the horses waiting outside. I only knew that he moved with a lithe grace and there was a strange puzzlement in his eyes in keeping with the awareness in my heart.

'Did you have something to eat, Kathryn?' Aunt Dorothy asked solicitously.

I wasn't hungry. I wanted to get to my horse quickly, and although I was surrounded by excited talk and laughter, I went straight towards Saunders, the groom, where he waited with my horse in front of the house. I hung back as David and Serena rode together down the drive. She rode a mare, gentle and predictable, and he was riding a large chestnut with a mind of his own. They waited for me beside the gates and David said, 'I've been admiring your stallion, Kathryn. Isn't he rather a handful for a girl to ride?'

I had often been warned that Demetrius was no mount for a girl, but we had a rapport and with me he was gentle and obedient. I was glad of his beauty and his proud high-stepping grace. I knew that we looked well together and I was glad, too, of the admiration in David's eyes although I knew it was nothing more than admiration for a striking girl on a beautiful horse.

I rode with them until we reached the high meadow, then I set Demetrius off towards the river and the copse I called my own. I felt disturbed and anxious and needed to be alone. It was beautiful even on this cold winter's day with the hedgerows etched in silver frost and the bare branches of the trees standing like silver skeletons against the red sky. I dismounted, took the reins and walked with Demetrius until we could look down to where the narrow stream lay still under a coating of ice. There was a scurry in the hedge-row and suddenly a cock pheasant came into view, his feathers glowing brightly against the grey and silver branches. I watched him, hardly daring to breathe, as he sauntered majestically along the edge of the river.

There were a great many times when I felt I had no ties with Yorkshire, when I hated her dark rolling moors and the great skies that covered her vast acres, but at moments like these I warmed to her. I loved the beautiful horse which had shied nervously at the sight of the bird, and I loved the bird which moved so colourfully in a grey and frozen scene.

From where I stood I could hear the sound of the hunts-man's horn and the baying of the hounds and I knew they had sighted a fox. I clenched my hands in anger, willing that small rust-coloured animal to lead them a merry dance and then run to ground, and I was glad that I was not with them.

By the time I rode my horse back to the stable, most of the horse-boxes had been driven away and only a few of the foot followers remained to eat and drink all that was left.

'You're late back, Miss Kathryn,' the stableboy said to me as he took the reins from my hands and helped me down on to the cobbled stable yard.

'Yes, I hunt by myself, Peters. Did they make a kill?'

He grinned from ear to ear. 'No, miss, they followed him all over Four Acres and back down to Edgecombe, then the fox just disappeared. One of the horses arrived back lame and Major Digby had a fall.'

I tried not to look too pleased.

My grandmother had kept a distance between herself and the hunt, preferring to sit in the drawing room all day rather than subject herself to the noise. She received an account of the day that evening over dinner, and retired early. Serena was happy, I could tell from her bright eyes and her often absent answers to questions that were put to her. Her thoughts were not on the day's hunting but on the man she was so obviously in love with.

As we walked together up the staircase to our rooms she whispered, 'May I come into your room to talk to you for a while?'

The excitement was still there when, later, she perched on the end of my bed, watching me brush my hair at the dressing table.

'We lost you this afternoon,' she said. 'I know how you hate to see the fox caught so I thought you had ridden back through the village.'

I didn't want her to know about the private lonely place I had found. It was my own place where I could be alone with my thoughts and I was quick to turn our conversation away from my absence.

'I'm surprised you can stand to witness the spectacle of the fox being killed. You're supposed to be the sweet gentle one and yet you can stand all that and I can't.'

'We didn't keep up with the leaders so I didn't see what happened to the fox. But you know that foxes are a nuisance. They can kill every single fowl in a chicken roost and they do an awful amount of damage, ask any farmer.'

'I know what they do, but there must be a better way of killing them than to make it a day of sport for adult men and women. Shoot them by all means, but to hunt the poor creature until he's demented! What sort of sport is that?'

'Well, if you marry Peter Hardcastle you'll be expected to enjoy that sort of thing.'

'I have no intention of marrying Peter Hardcastle. I can see now why my mother fell in love with my father. He must have seemed like manna from heaven to a girl hemmed in by the sort of people who were here today.'

'What are you going to do with your life, Kathryn?'

'I don't know yet. Perhaps I'll go out to my father and take up archaeology. I got a good history result, I'm not too stupid to learn more.'

'Grandmother wouldn't agree to your doing that.'

'It has nothing to do with Grandmother, it concerns my father more.'

'But he's never here, he's simply dumped you on her so she's bound to have some say in your future.'

I hated the word 'dumped'. It made me feel like some sort of parcel to be handed around from place to place, and seeing my annoyance, Serena was quick to apologize. 'I'm sorry, of course you haven't been dumped, but you will only antagonize Grandmother if you start talking about joining your father abroad. She has always maintained it was that sort of life that killed your mother.'

'She believes what she wants to believe, but my life is my own to do with it what I please. I won't be pushed into anything, least of all matrimony. Why are you looking so happy tonight? Ever since you caught sight of that young man from that window this morning, you've been floating around in a pink cloud.'

60

The bright rosy colour flooded her face as she sat against my pillows, her arms encircling her knees in an attitude of delighted complacency.

'Isn't he nice, Kathryn? He's so good-looking and charming, he made everybody else look so ordinary.'

'How long have you known him?'

'Practically all my life. His parents are friends of my parents but David has been abroad so that I haven't seen him for a long time. He's a water engineer and has been working in Egypt, but I was already in love with him when he left. I don't think I've ever wanted anybody else. I wrote to him when he was away and when he had the time he wrote to me, but I don't suppose he ever thought of me as anything but a schoolgirl.'

'But you're not a schoolgirl now.'

'No, that's true, and in the New Year David and his parents are coming to stay with us in London. That will give us a chance of getting to know one another much better.'

I could feel my palms grow hot as I clenched my hands together, my throat tightening until I could scarcely breathe, and all the time I was watching her with an intense stare. She prattled on, unaware that my heart was racing with a strange sort of envy.

Quite suddenly I wanted her to go, to leave me alone to my bitterness, and as if she read something of my thoughts she said, 'You're tired, you should have said something.'

'Perhaps I am a little,' I said. 'We can talk again tomorrow.'

'Of course. It's so lovely to be able to talk to you about David. I don't want to talk to my mother about him, not yet at any rate, but you're like a sister to me.'

She leaned over and kissed my cheek. 'Good night, Kathryn. Perhaps we could go riding tomorrow, just the two of us, and we can talk some more.'

I didn't hear her go. I was thinking of David and Serena together in London. Walking through the parks, the trees silver with frost or dining in intimate candlelit restaurants. I thought of them sitting side by side at the theatre or

61

dancing in each other's arms. That night the dream was back with me, but more real than it had ever been before.

Once the Princess Tuia had been a being outside myself, a creature of my dreams and I only an onlooker, but now it seemed that we were one and it was I who waited anxiously in the white-walled city of Memphis for the future to unfold.

I had been in Memphis for a month, a month when every day I had paced my terrace staring at the pyramids standing stark and lonely on the edge of the desert, or walked the colonnades surrounding them to gaze upon the enigmatic face of the Sphinx wearing that strange half smile that promised nothing. A month when I had stood every morning on the banks of the river staring disconsolately southwards so that every barge that rounded the bend in the river would set my heart racing, leaving me sick with despair when it was not the barge I had been expecting.

They came for me at night while I was still sleeping and my women roused me, their eyes wide with apprehension, telling me that it was the Pharaoh's own guards who had come for me. I only felt exultation in their coming and I had my women robe me as though already I wore the queen's crown.

The night was dark as we walked through the gardens towards the barge and a low mist drifted eerily about the river as we stepped on board. It was the Pharaoh's own barge we were sailing in and I stood alone on the prow looking upwards at the billowing purple sails as we left the harbour wall and pulled into midstream.

There were none to see us depart and I amused myself by speculating on how long it would be before I returned to Memphis as the Pharaoh's queen. I did not doubt that the lord of the underworld would listen to my prayers and that soon the streets of Thebes would be filled with the cries of mourners because Asnefer lay dead. I tried to imagine who would meet me on my arrival, or if I must go to the palace secretly under cover of darkness, but I asked no questions of the officer in charge of the guards or of the captain of the barge.

It was the hour before the dawn when we arrived in Thebes on the fourth day, and the shadows in the streets were still dense. There was no rosy light in the eastern sky, Ammon was still safe in the arms of the goddess Mut, it was not yet time for him to pull his golden sun chariot over the rim of the eastern desert, and across the river the western hills rose in sombre splendour untouched by the rosy glow of dawn.

Another contingent of guards waited for us on the quayside and they fell into step on either side of my litter. The great white palace of the Pharaoh gleamed like alabaster through the morning mist, but it was to the palace where I had spent my youth that they carried me. The corridors were silent, with sentries standing as rigid as mummies in their coffins outside the stateroom doors, and for the first time I realized that during all these days when we had sailed from Memphis to Thebes no words had been exchanged between myself and the officers of Pharaoh's guards. Now it was Impetra, my grandmother's woman, who came to attend to me.

I asked haughtily after my own handmaidens, but to all my questions she said she knew nothing, and now I was beginning to see something sinister and terrifying in the silence that surrounded me. The absence of my servants, the lack of any official reception, in all this I suspected the hand of my grandmother and I became desperately afraid.

When I went out on my terrace I found that other sentries had been posted there. Impetra glided in and out of my room like a shadow, attending to my needs, but I knew that I was a prisoner. It was on the second night that she asked me to follow her to the queen mother's rooms on the other side of the palace. She had put aside my queen's finery and now I was clad in a simple white gown, wearing on my head the single fillet of gold from which the cobra raised his hooded head, and somewhat savagely I thought, this at least she cannot take away from me. I am the daughter of the

63

man who was pharaoh even though my mother was only his secondary queen.

Impetra left me to wait in my grandmother's room alone. The bright moonlight filtered through the delicate drapes stirring in the soft breeze that came from the river, bringing with it the sweet scent of jasmine, and from her niche in the corner of the room, the lapis lazuli eyes of the goddess Isis stared back at me. I turned away. How could I, who had sacrificed to the god Set, meet the eyes of the goddess whose husband he had murdered? I shivered as though a cold hand had been placed over mine, and then I found myself staring into the colder eyes of my grandmother, black narrowed eyes that stared back at me, pitiless in the accusation I read in them. I bowed respectfully before her, remembering bitterly that I had expected *her* to bow the knee to *me* when next we met. I followed her down the long corridors of the palace. Her face was cold and proud under the vulture's headdress and although she only reached my shoulder there was majesty in the set of her regal head and her upright carriage.

We left the palace by a side door and entered the temple by a gateway not used by any but those from the royal house. I had never been more aware of its imposing vastness. We made our way between gigantic columns on which the lamplight fell, throwing into sharp relief the delicate colours of birds and beasts, gods and pharaohs, which had been carved over the centuries by skilled temple craftsmen. Our sandalled feet struck sharply on the alabaster floor and I willed myself to look straight ahead and not at the statues of gods which towered over me from the niches where they had been placed. Ahead of us glowed a stronger light.

We were in the great hypostyle hall. Standing under the massive columns were many priests and dignitaries, but my grandmother marched straight towards the royal dais and, taking her place on her own special throne, indicated that I should take the gold chair which had been placed beside it. Three steps above us were the two royal thrones, and behind them the great statue of the god Ammon sat calmly staring down the length of the hall, his hands resting on his knees, his expression one of cold majesty. I had little time to speculate about our reasons for being here, because almost immediately the trumpets sounded to announce the arrival of the pharaoh.

All those standing in the hall knelt with lowered heads and my grandmother and I followed their example, waiting with bent heads until the pharaoh took his place on the throne. I turned my head to look into his face. He did not look at me. He seemed like an image in gold sitting there in his robes of state, holding the crook and the flail in his hands. His face, touched by the lamplight, was remote and coldly handsome, as though it had been sculpted out of marble.

I could not believe that this was the face of the man I had laughed with, and that I had explored with him the tender passions of love which had left us shaken and drained in the hours before the dawn. I was trembling, I longed to run to him, to fling myself on the steps before his throne, asking him to look at me once more with eyes of love, but I dared not move. By an effort that took the remainder of my courage I tore my eyes away from him only to meet the eyes of my grandmother watching me with cool speculation.

From one side of the hall came a procession of priests in their white robes. The priest walking in the midst of them made my blood run cold. He walked with his eyes on the ground, looking neither to left nor right, and I could see that his wrists and ankles were chained. Before they reached the centre of the hall I could hear the sounds of a woman screaming and cursing, then she was dragged forward into the light. It was Ipey, thrown to the floor where her terrified eyes roved round the room, meeting mine without recognition.

Ptahotep stood calmly, oblivious to her moans. Once I saw him rub his wrist where the chains bit into the flesh, and once also he lifted his eyes and looked upwards at the god above him. Another priest approached the royal dais carrying a cushion, and as he passed my chair I could see what lay on it. I shall never know what stopped me from crying out, but I clenched my hands so tightly the rings on

65

my fingers bit into the flesh and the pain brought the hot salty tears into my eyes. Lying on the purple cushion, small and gleaming, yet bristling with the power of revenge, lay the talisman of Set.

I sat staring as though in a dream at figures that moved and gesticulated and spoke, until Ipey's screams of denial startled my senses into sharp reality.

Ptahotep stood like a granite statue, unmoving, stoically calm as the high priest accused him of stealing the amulet, and he answered him never a word.

Another priest stepped forward and gave evidence that he had seen Ptahotep speaking with Ipey, the servant of the Princess Tuia, outside the temple, and later that night Ptahotep had exempted him from his duty as guard in the innermost sanctuary saying that he personally would take his place. The priest's suspicions had been aroused, and next morning he had decided to see for himself that everything was in its proper place. It was then that he had found the talisman of Set to be missing.

I had not thought how drastic the evidence against Ptahotep could be. Another priest reported seeing Ipey hurrying back towards the palace just before dawn, and although my name was not mentioned again, they told how the talisman came to light six days later in the temple of Ptah at Memphis. I could feel the colour leave my face while my hands trembled on the arms of my chair. Ipey had not gone to Memphis but I, her mistress, had, and although I could feel my grandmother's eyes upon me, I stared resolutely ahead while Ipey's screams of denial filled the hall.

There were priests who spoke in favour of Ptahotep, extolling his virtues as an honourable and good man, and there were others who spoke against him, saying he was too ambitious and was a man who would adopt any method or means to rise high in the service of the temple. All the time Ptahotep stood as though in a dream, his calm face registering neither grief nor anger.

I heard the pharaoh's voice speaking calmly to Ptahotep, cautioning him to defend himself, but to the pharaoh he merely replied, 'I have nothing to say, Your Majesty,' and then once more his eyes were on the ground and the high priest was looking at him with ill-disguised frustration.

The pharaoh too waited, as though he could hardly believe that here was a man who refused to defend himself or implicate some other. At last he spoke and his voice showed a reluctance to involve himself further.

'The fate of this priest is in your hands,' he said to the high priest. 'He will tell you nothing more and you must apply your own methods of persuasion. As for the woman screaming on the floor there, unless I am mistaken she is the property of the Princess Tuia. I suggest that she should be returned to the princess so that she may administer the proper chastisement.'

For the first time our eyes met and I was instantly aware that he knew who the real culprit was. There was no softening of his stern features, no hint that once that cold remote face had grown warm with tenderness. He rose to show those present that the proceedings were at an end and once more we knelt with bowed heads until he had left the hall. Dimly in the distance I could hear the sounds of trumpets and the cheers of the people, and I could picture him in my imagination, acknowledging those cheers from the platform of his golden chariot.

I followed my grandmother from the room and it was only when we were once more in her apartment that I faced her, asking with tears in my eyes what would become of me. She looked at me coldly, and in a voice designed to give me little hope, she said, 'His Majesty will decide in the morning what is to become of you. You seem singularly uninterested in what is to become of the priest Ptahotep.'

'But they will release him, surely? After all, he did not want the talisman for himself. They must release him.'

She looked at me with pitying scorn. 'If you think so, you are more naïve than I imagined you to be. To release a priest who has committed an act of sacrilege and stolen from the inner sanctuary for whatever reason would be folly beyond words. It is a sin punishable by death and Ptahotep knows it. I do not understand, Tuia, why men should love you more than life, or even more than honour, nor shall I ever fully comprehend why Ptahotep forfeits his life to protect a woman who has eyes for one man only. It is an act of madness.'

'The high priest must know that he stole the amulet for me. They have not openly accused me because I am of the royal house, but all those standing or sitting in that hall today knew that I took the amulet from Thebes to Memphis. How can they punish Ptahotep for my wickedness?'

'They can and they will. He stole the amulet and he was a priest who knew full well what he was doing. The high priest dare not be lenient with his kinsman. It would open the floodgate to all kinds of transgressions.'

Her women came into the room to remove her finery and I watched as she took off her rings, dropping them one by one into the jewellery chest they had brought for her. She paid no more attention to me standing miserably before her and I hated her proud cold face and air of detachment.

At last they left her sitting without her royal raiment, wearing a simple robe of pale blue lawn and with her hair released from under the heavy crown she had worn earlier, and I could not help thinking that much of her majesty had gone with it. Her once black hair was streaked with grey and the lines on her thin aristocratic face seemed more prominent. By Hathor, but she is old, as old as a dried-up fig tree, I thought to myself, and as if she could read my thoughts, she rose from her chair and drew herself up to her full height, saying, 'You may go now, Princess Tuia, but remain in your apartment until His Majesty sends for you.'

My heart fluttered with relief as I made my obeisance, and the fact that she did not look at me troubled me not at all. Only one ray of hope sustained me as I walked back to my apartment. The pharaoh himself would decide my fate and surely he would not have forgotten so soon that once we had been lovers.

I had forgotten Ipey but she was waiting for me, crouched on the floor in a corner of the room muttering to herself. As I looked at her, I was gripped by a feeling of revulsion so powerful that at that moment I could have killed her. She with her love potions and her charms. I had not known of the talisman until Ipey had told me of it, and now Ptahotep would die and only the gods knew what would happen to me. Ignoring her, I walked out on to my terrace; the sentries were still posted at a discreet distance. There were tears in my eyes as I looked at the familiar scene. I loved the river with the graceful palms lining its banks and the western hill beyond. How soon, I wondered, before their sombre beauty hid all that was left of me, although it was not to a queen's tomb that I would be taken? I shrugged off such melancholy thoughts when I felt Ipey's thin clawlike hand clutching at my arm.

'None of this is worth dying for, my princess,' she whined. 'You will be a great queen in the land of the Hittites, as great a queen as your sister in Egypt, and if you are clever you will know how to bend this foreign prince to your will. Men are creatures of stupidity, haven't I always said so?'

I shrank away from her and the distaste she read in my eyes sent her scuttling back to her corner where she remained staring at me fearfully. After I had spoken with the pharaoh, I would know what I must do with Ipey.

It was late in the afternoon when he sent for me, and as I stood outside the entrance to his reception room, I thought tearfully of my father, who once had occupied the suite beyond, and how I had often run to him, expecting him to embrace me regardless of who was with him. The man who waited in that room was not my father. He was a man whose cool glance of amusement could reduce me to the stature of a nonentity, but whose charm, when he cared to use it, could bring me trembling to his knees. With my head held high, I followed his chamberlain into the room.

He was alone, standing outside the room on the terrace that overlooked the royal gardens, and when he did not immediately turn round, I went to stand beside him. Asnefer sat in the gardens surrounded by her ladies and she was laughing at the antics of a leopard cub who rolled on the grass with a jewelled bauble between his soft paws.

I could feel my throat tightening with anger, or despair, I could not tell which was the stronger emotion. He turned and walked back into his room and I followed him, standing before him with bent head. It seemed an eternity before I dared to raise my eyes to find that his were stern yet strangely sorrowful. His first words told me that he knew everything.

'Why did you ask Ptahotep to steal the talisman, Tuia? And do not play at words with me, I want the truth.'

My voice was a choked whisper in keeping with the pain in my heart as I answered him. 'I could not believe that you would send me to the Hittites. I believed it was my grandmother's doing, so I sacrificed to the god Set and asked him to bring me back to Thebes and to all those I loved.'

I was telling him only half the truth, but I could not bear to see his eyes look at me with hatred or even anger. It was not possible to tell this man who was master of the world that I had asked the god of evil for the life of his queen so that I could take her place at his side.

We stared at each other and I had never been more aware of his air of sovereignty. It sat upon his shoulders like a mantle and I became afraid. This was not the boy who had loved me. The careless years of his youth had been eradicated at that moment when he knew he would be pharaoh.

He gestured to a chair and somewhat irritably he said, 'Come, Tuia, I cannot have you standing before me like one of my servants I have had cause to chastise. What I have to say to you is better said quietly and while there is still friendship between us.'

Friendship! I did not want this man's friendship if I could not have his love. I sank on to the chair he indicated and he spoke to me as though he lectured a child.

'You know that for centuries there has been much strife between the people of Egypt and the Hittite nation, and that it is only now, since I was victorious in the last battle, that we have some sort of peace between us?'

I nodded miserably.

'If we have peace, we should try to maintain it. It does no good that we spill the blood of our soldiers along our frontiers when we would be better employed sending trade delegations. Your own father and mine spent their strength and their youth in waging war against the Hittites and they too came to see the futility of such encounters. Egypt is tired of unrest, and there was so much you could have done, Tuia, to cement the friendship between our two nations and bring a lasting peace.'

The silence between us seemed interminable. A strange hatred seemed to hang on the air until it became a tangible thing, a spectre, at once ethereal and obscene, a thing conjured up by the fear in my heart.

His voice was very gentle when next he spoke to me, and in it I was aware of a compassion and tenderness that brought the hot despairing tears into my eyes.

'Have you not always known that one day such a summons would come for you? Had your father lived, it would have fallen upon him to administer the blow, for such I can see it to be. But is not this a sacrifice that is expected from the daughters of kings, for when have the princes and princesses of the royal house been free to choose the men and women they would marry?'

With my eyes bleak with misery, I looked at his face to find that it too was sad. At the same time I had never been more conscious that behind that calm impersonal mask was power unlimited, power to bend me to his will as easily as he bent a bow, and my voice trembled in spite of myself.

'Your Majesty, I cannot marry the son of the Hittite king who was my father's enemy. How can you ask this of me? I love Egypt, I cannot leave this land when I feel I have so much to give her. There are other women, far too many, who call themselves princesses but are only relics of long-dead courts and forgotten romances, yet all jealously guarding their right to wear the royal insignia above their brows. Can you not command one of these so-called royal persons to do something at last for Egypt? Why should we of the royal house be treated like prize stallions or brood mares in the name of diplomacy? I tell you now, I would rather die than give myself to this prince.'

He rose from his chair and walked round his desk. Then he pulled me to my feet so that we stood facing each other.

'Look at me, Tuia,' he commanded sternly, 'and do not

71

think that I do not know your thoughts. What you asked of the lord of evil was an impossibility that not even he could grant you, and now a brave man must die for it and you must be asked to choose. Do you go willingly to Kadesh or do you enter the temple of Isis to serve the goddess for the rest of your life?'

I could not believe that it was his voice asking me to choose between life in an alien land and the life of a priestess. Never to see the dawn striking the obelisks with rose and gold, lighting up the western hills with tints of gentle mauve. Never to see the swallows skimming the waters of the Nile or watch the kingfisher's bright plumage as he waited on the branches of the tamarisk tree for his prey. Never to see the lotus blossoms opening to the sun in the pool outside my window, but to live the rest of my life listening to the sounds of chanting priests and priestesses. To live for ever in the dark confines of the temple in the company of women who had never known love, sad, lonely, disappointed women, as I would become. How could I bear it, knowing that in the land of the living the man I loved ruled Egypt with Asnefer by his side? I would rather be dead.

I lifted my head and met his gaze bravely, then in a voice which trembled only slightly I said, 'That would be my wish, Your Majesty, to serve the goddess Isis in the halls of her temple.'

Not even he was quick enough to disguise the spasm which crossed his face, but almost immediately it was replaced by the calm mask he showed to the world.

'Very well, Princess Tuia, I shall accept your wishes. You will leave the palace twenty-four hours from now, leaving behind you all your private possessions, your jewellery, your royal garments and diadems. You may take none of your handmaidens with you. The high priestess will come for you and you will leave the palace by the private doorway where none will see you go. Is that understood?'

'Yes, Your Majesty.'

'It is farewell then. The courts of the temple of Isis are filled with a great many priestesses, but there was only one princess who could have properly fulfilled her role as a

72

future queen of the Hittite nation and thereby serve her country.'

As if to show me that our audience was at an end he opened up a scroll of papyrus that had been lying on a chest and started to read it. I bowed my head acknowledging the rebuke and left the room. I shall never know if he looked up to watch me go.

Ipey stared at me anxiously as I entered my room, but I had no intention of telling her what had transpired between the pharaoh and myself.

I allowed her to serve my evening meal and then I had her massage my limbs with cool lotions as only she knew how. She brushed my hair with a silken pad until it shone like polished ebony under the lamplight and then I bade her robe me in my most royal garments and bring me the jewels I loved. I fastened a collar of lapis lazuli and gold around my throat, armlets and bracelets round my arms and my favourite rings on my fingers. Then, last of all, I chose the winged headdress I loved more than any other. The exquisite curve of the wings followed the contours of my face with graceful accuracy, and when I looked in my mirror, I knew that I was beautiful.

Ipey was happy as she helped me to choose my finery. I stared at her in my mirror where she stood behind me, well pleased with her handiwork.

'Now you may leave me, Ipey, but in the quiet of your room you will prepare for me one last potion.'

'Oh yes, my princess, anything, anything. One that will bring the man you love back to you, one that will make sure that you will be the queen.'

'There is no potion in the world capable of fulfilling those two wishes. No, Ipey, the potion you will make for me is one that will bring me death. See to it that it is one which will not destroy my beauty and will bring with it as little pain as possible. I know that you have prepared such potions before and I have heard how effective they have been. You did not know that I knew about them, did you, Ipey? It is

73

no longer important. Do this thing quickly before they come for me.'

She stared at me out of horror-filled eyes, then on her knees she started to plead with me, her thin hands clutching my gown, the tears coursing down her gnarled old cheeks. 'Oh, my princess, do not do this terrible thing! If you do, what will become of me?'

I stepped away from her and, disdaining her pleas, said, 'Can you prepare this potion or must I seek death in some other way?'

'Oh yes, my princess, there is nothing to the mixing of a potion that will bring a swift and painless death, but what is to become of me without your protection?'

I did not care what was to become of her. I had known this woman since I was little more than a child. She had been taken prisoner in one of my father's wars against the Mitanni and had been placed in the service of my mother soon afterwards. Quick to ingratiate herself into the life of the palace, she had always been relied upon to listen at doors and skulk along the corridors. She had a malicious tongue and delighted in repeating court gossip that would not have reached my ears if she had not kept her own so close to the ground. I had found her amusing but devious; now I looked upon her as something infinitely more sinister. She was the evil genius who had destroyed me, and not only me, Ptahotep also.

I looked down at her and, with a contemptuous shrug of my shoulders, I said, 'You will have the opportunity of returning to your own people. See, I give you your freedom. Has not that always been your dream, to go where you will and call no man your master?'

'But I have been too long away, princess. I no longer know where to find my people for they are wanderers over the face of the earth. Even if I found them, it is unlikely they would receive me. I have served the Egyptians for so long.'

'Then, Ipey, that would be your misfortune, but it would not be so great a misfortune as that which awaits Ptahotep and the one I have planned for myself. Now hurry with the

74

potion or I might forget that I have given you your freedom and command that you follow me into the long corridors of eternity.'

I heard her scuttling away and I sat staring into my mirror until the sounds of her shuffling footsteps could be heard no more in the corridors outside my room, then I went to stand on the terrace looking out across the gardens and the gleaming waters of the Nile.

It was the hour of sunset and already the western hills were alight with all the magical tones of rose and amber, crimson and gold, and my heart ached to think that this would be the last time I would ever see them. The figures silhouetted against the sky on the river bank seemed like a frieze in black basalt. Women carrying pitchers of water on their heads and children leading heavy buffalo cows, men riding small pattering donkeys, and priests in long robes carrying effigies of their gods. My eyes filled with tears so that people and colour became mingled as though an artist had thrown his paints haphazardly against an alabaster wall, and shivering in the cool breeze that came from the river, I turned my back on the splendour of the evening sky. Slowly I walked round my room, handling the ornaments that had been dear to me over the years. Then in the creeping darkness I sat in my chair to wait.

Five

I lay staring at the unfamiliar ceiling for several minutes before I accepted that the dream was over and that I was back in the present, in a room which seemed unreal and alien, my bedspread already touched with the first pale light of dawn. Wearily I left my bed, and shivering a little in the cold morning air, I shrugged my arms into my dressing gown and went over to the window.

The branches of the trees outside my window were white with frost, and it shimmered across the parkland as though some wizard had waved his magic wand, turning the grey dismal colours of winter into a sparkling field of diamonds. I felt drained, as though the events of the night had happened to me, Kathryn St Clare, instead of the Princess Tuia in a land I had only heard of. I sank into a chair reliving the dream. Shivering in the cold morning light, I asked myself why this dream should have haunted my life, continuing its story so that the fate of that long-dead princess reached out with icy fingers to shape my own life.

Somewhere there had to be answers to the question and I needed to find them, but where was I to look? How was it possible to reach out across the crumbling centuries into another life?

I sat down to breakfast, weary-eyed and listless, and all eyes turned towards me when my grandmother snapped, 'Are you sickening for something, Kathryn? A girl of your age shouldn't be tired. Serena isn't tired, she looks full of life.'

Serena did indeed look full of life and bitterly I knew why.

76

Serena was in love and she was in love with a man who fascinated me as no other had ever done. All morning I mooned about the house until I could stand it no longer, so I dressed myself in some warm outdoor clothing and set off across the park. By lunchtime some semblance of colour had returned to my cheeks and no further comments were made about my appearance over the luncheon table.

The dream was not done with me yet, however. On the Sunday evening after Christmas, a carol service was to be held in the village church and it was one that all the family, including my grandmother, liked to attend. It was a beautiful Gothic church, large for such a tiny village, and the entire family as well as the servants set out in cars after eating an early dinner. The church was decorated with the usual Christmas holly and mistletoe and the service was conducted by candlelight.

The family took its place near the front of the church. I was miserably aware of David's dark head among the party in the Edgecombe pew. It was only when the lights were extinguished and candlelight took their place, however, that something old and terrifyingly real crept up on me. The flickering candles lit up the lofty stone pillars and suddenly I was remembering the glow of lamplight on other pillars, far greater pillars on which exquisite reliefs were carved. I felt strangely light-headed, but it was only when the choir began their long procession towards the altar in their white robes that I had to clutch in front of me for support. I remember that Serena looked at me anxiously, and then I remember nothing more beyond the sudden darkness.

I had never fainted in my life before, I was not given to such weaknesses, but when I opened by eyes I was lying on a couch in the vestry surrounded by anxious faces. Aunt Dorothy was twittering about getting me home immediately, saying I hadn't been like myself for several days.

It was David who drove me home, listening to my apologies politely, assisting me from the car and waiting inside the hall until I assured him I was perfectly well and would go immediately to bed.

Our words were commonplace but underneath them I felt

again that strange undercurrent of awareness. It was there in the concern on his face, in his fingers as he took my hand in farewell, in his long, lithe grace as I watched him walk to his car. I stood with my back to the door until the sound of the engine had died away into the night, then I ran quickly up the stairs to my room, trembling with the pain of loving him.

For the next few days I was fussed over by both my aunts and Serena, and I watched the doctor scratching his head as he diagnosed too much over-indulgence at Christmas time. Consequently, for the next few days I lived on lightly poached eggs and fish and I became so hungry I could have eaten a horse.

Only one good thing emerged from my enforced isolation: I didn't need to meet David before he departed with Serena and her parents for London early in the New Year. It was only when I learned that they had gone that I declared myself sufficiently recovered to join in the everyday events of country life once more. I was restored to a world of race meetings, and dog shows, and long rides across the moors. In January I heard from my godfather that he was coming home.

I had been giving serious thought to my future and I knew I could not go on living for ever the sort of existence I was experiencing now. I wanted to travel, but more than anything I wanted to take up archaeology and I believed my godfather was the one to help me. I said nothing to my relatives about my ambitions, but when my godfather returned at the beginning of February, I rushed over to see him.

Nothing about my godfather's house seemed to have changed, and he opened the door to me with a smile lighting up his tanned face.

'I have something very important to show to you,' he said immediately our greetings were over.

'Something you've brought back with you?' I asked excitedly.

'Yes, something that should interest you very much.'

He insisted that we ate before revealing anything of his

excavations, and remembering his housekeeper's cooking I was prepared to do full justice to the meal. We talked a little about my father, neither of us having heard anything from him for months. Suddenly he asked, 'What do you propose to do with yourself now, Kathryn? Are you quite happy to settle down to country life like your Aunt Dorothy?'

'Oh no, I don't want that at all. I want to work and I want to work abroad. I've been giving a lot of thought to a career in archaeology but I need to know a lot more about it and I was hoping you might be able to help me.'

'Your father could help you, too, and he might not like it if I interfered. I'm an Egyptologist, and you know that your father prefers to work in other countries. For years, he's maintained that Egypt is clapped out.'

'I know, and look how wrong he was.'

'Don't you fancy going out to China to work with him?'

'No. I have no interest in China, which perhaps is a silly high-handed thing to say, but I am interested in Egypt and I need to learn a lot more. I was hoping you would coach me like your other students, and I want to learn to read hieroglyphics. I'm prepared to pay for my tuition, I have my mother's money now and what better way to spend it than on my education?'

'I would prefer to get your father's blessing first, Kathryn.'

'I'll write to him tomorrow, but whether he says yes or no will make no difference to me. Somehow or other I shall go to Egypt.'

'Yes, well, perhaps now is the time for me to show you what I brought back from Egypt. You must tell me if it is what you were looking for the first day we met.'

My heart was thumping painfully against my ribs as I followed him up the stairs and along the corridor towards the museum. Feverishly I watched him insert his key into the padlock and then the doors swung open to a familiar scene. Nothing seemed to have changed. The mummy case still stood against the wall, although now it did not seem so tall against my advanced stature. My godfather went to the end of the room and took something from the bench where the amulets lay. I felt light-headed as I walked towards him, and then he was placing in my hands the talisman I had seen so many times in my dreams.

My chilled fingers curled themselves round its smoothness. It was as familiar as the brooch I had fastened to my blouse only that morning, and as in my dream it seemed to scorch my fingers so that I dropped it hurriedly on to the bench where it clattered and lay still. I was staring at it like a frightened bird stares at the snake that is contriving to hypnotize it, until Uncle Mark's voice shattered the feeling and returned me to sanity.

'That is the talisman?' he inquired.

'Yes,' I replied hoarsely. 'Where did you find it?'

'It was brought to me in Upper Egypt and I asked if I might keep it for you. Now I am not so sure I should give it to you when it causes you such obvious distress.'

He was watching me closely, holding my arm to steady me. My legs felt shaky, trembling as though they no longer belonged to me. The amulet corresponded in every detail to the one I had seen in my dreams and I felt confused, as though at any moment I would cease to be Kathryn St Clare and that long-dead princess who had so desired the amulet would face my godfather in my place.

I was afraid of it. It seemed to have a power which reached out and held me with strong, tenacious fingers, bringing with it all the desires and yearnings of a people who had trusted in its power to fulfil the most secret longings of their hearts, however evil, however tragic, but at a price. My desires now were greater than my fears, and holding out my hand I said, more calmly than I felt, 'How can I refuse when you have brought it such a long way?'

Still he did not give it to me. Instead he slipped it into the pocket of his waistcoat and, holding my arm tightly, he drew me away from the museum and down the stairs. In the room overlooking the church, he pushed a glass of brandy into my hand, and with a strange feeling of relief I began to tell him the story of the dream that had begun when I was still a little girl in Mesopotamia. He listened without interrupting me, his face betraying a keen interest, his eyes gleaming with an inner excitement.

He did not speak for a long time after I had finished my story. He seemed to be pondering, searching for explanations. My eyes searched his face for reassurance, or perhaps even amusement that I should have the audacity to endow my dreams with such meaning.

'Do you think in some other life I could have been that princess?' I asked him intensely. 'When I dream about her I become her, I feel her anger as well as her despair, I even suffer for the love she believed she had lost. Do you think it is possible that we ever live again? But why am I the only one who seems to remember? Why don't we all have such feelings?'

'I haven't any answers for you, Kathryn, but how can I discount a theory that half the world believes? Philosophers, prophets, wise men throughout the ages have had all sorts of theories about reincarnation. Poets too, but wait. . .'

He went across the room to where a huge bookcase covered the length of one wall and took from it a small leatherbound book which he brought back to where I was sitting. He turned the pages until he found what he was looking for. 'This is from the New Koran, and is perhaps more potent than the words any poet wrote: "I tell you, of a truth, that the spirits which now have affinity shall be kindred together, although they all meet in new persons and names." '

'But what good is it to live again if most of us don't remember the steps we have wandered from the beginning, and how can we atone for past sins if we can't even remember making them?'

'That, my dear, is a question a mere professor of Egyptology is unable to answer. Have you told others about your dreams?'

'No. They would laugh at me, say I had too much imagination or blame my father for filling my head with too much ancient knowledge when I was young and foolishly impressionable. My grandmother would probably say I had eaten too much supper.'

'And yet you say your father never talked to you about Egypt. Knowing his feelings on the subject, I believe you.'

'Now please tell me about the amulet. If you didn't find it, how did you get it?'

'It was brought to me by another Egyptologist, John Strickland. He'd been doing some excavating on his own at some little distance from the site we were working on. He had a few native diggers with him and one Egyptian who was a personal friend, a very serious, reliable man who had worked with both Strickland and myself on a great number of occasions. They came to me one very dark night, carrying lanterns. I was reading in my tent for a little while before putting out the light, and you can imagine how surprised I was to find them looking for me. They had walked several miles over rough terrain, and the lanterns were hardly adequate to guide them along the narrow paths and over the rocks. I got out the whisky bottle for Strickland and made coffee for myself and Ahmed Sadek – being a Muslim he doesn't touch alcohol.

'I could tell that Strickland was ill at ease. His eyes were bloodshot and he seemed restless. His hands were shaking round his glass and I wondered if he had taken to drinking again. It had been his downfall most of his working life and his friend, too, seemed anxious.

'Strickland told me that they had decided to give up the dig they had been working on since it had brought very little to light, but then he fished in his pocket and brought out the amulet. I had never seen its like before but I recognized it from your description and was amazed. I remembered your disappointment, that spring morning long ago, when I did not have the amulet you were seeking.

'Strickland said they had unearthed what appeared to be the entrance to a far larger tomb, but on entry it had proved to be merely a simple square chamber cut into the solid rock in the centre of which stood a plain sarcophagus. Neither of them had been able to understand why it was so plain. It bore none of the usual charms and prayers to assist the dead through his journey into the "Land of the West", and after breaking the seal on the sarcophagus they found that within it was a plain wooden coffin in which the mummy reposed. Here again the usual texts and charms were missing. Later that day they removed the mummy and the coffin to their workroom.

'There were no signs that the chamber had ever been entered. There were bare footprints on the floor but Strickland firmly believed they were the footprints of the last Egyptians to leave it centuries before. Their Arab workmen shrank away from the mummy and refused to enter the tomb.

'During the days that followed the workmen left the site one after another and returned to their village. Sadek went to visit the head man of the village but he refused to send the men back. Strickland and Sadek decided to go ahead without them. They searched the burial chamber for another outlet but found none. Then they decided to unwrap the mummy to see if it contained any clues to what was becoming a mystery. They started to unwrap it in the morning, very carefully in case it contained jewellery or rolls of papyrus between the bandages. There have been cases when a mummy, suddenly exposed to air and light, simply disintegrates before one's eyes, and Strickland had the strangest feeling that something like that might happen to this one. They came at last to the amulet which had been placed over the mummy's heart under cover of the last few wrappings.

'He immediately recognized it as being an amulet of the god Set and his suspicions deepened. The god of evil was never represented in funeral rites and they began to believe that this person must have sinned grievously to have been buried so coldly with only his amulet to keep him company through the long, dark centuries. Carefully they went on with their task until at last they uncovered the dead man's face. They both recoiled in horror at the expression of extreme agony they saw there. Later they discovered the body was not eviscerated or embalmed but merely swathed in mummy cloths. This told them quite plainly that the man had been buried alive.'

I gasped with horror, shrinking back in my chair and trembling so much that he looked at me with concern.

'I should have warned you that it was not a pretty story,' he said anxiously.

'No, please go on, I have to know.'

'I asked Strickland if I could keep the amulet, there was someone I wanted to show it to, and he said he didn't want it, he loathed the sight of it. Soon after that he left Luxor and returned to Cairo. I tried to find him before I came home but he seems to have vanished off the face of the earth, and at that time I did not know where Sadek was either. I have learned since that Sadek is working on a new site near Sakkara. He is the only man who might know what has happened to John Strickland.'

'Did they discover who the mummy had once been?'

'No, although only an act of extreme sacrilege would merit such a fate – not merely burying him alive, but also the punishment of sending him into death without the usual prayers for the survival of his soul. When you go to Egypt, you will see that the tombs are lined with texts for the soul's survival, that the deceased is assisted along this last lonely journey with every god and goddess to aid him, and every prayer known to man to make sure he is received in the "Land of the Blessed" kindly and with joy. In this tomb there was nothing.'

'They must have been a very cruel and unforgiving people.'

'No, Kathryn, they were not. In Egypt there are no monuments to demonstrate the cruelty of men towards other men or to beasts. There is no ruin like the Colosseum to remind us that once a crowd of men and women grew wild with delight at the slaughter of Christians or the pitting of a br ve man against the brute strength of a bull or lion. In Egypt one is only aware of how much the ancient Egyptians loved life in the valley of the Nile, of the closeness of families and the staunch conservatism of principles. The ancient Egyptian loved life so much he desired only that death should be a joyous continuation of that life, and although many would say they were morbidly obsessed with death, this wouldn't be true. They were obsessed with life and a desire that its beauties should continue.'

'And yet they were capable of doing this wicked thing.'

'Yes, but we are thinking like people of today, failing to understand the laws and penalties of yesterday.'

'You said you had brought the amulet for me.'

'Yes, and now I am wondering if I should give it to you. Its history is not a pretty one and the part it played in those dreams of yours should make you want to shun it rather than keep it.'

'I know, and yet I would like to have it. There is no danger that I shall put it to the test.'

He took it out of his pocket and held it out to me. 'No, you are not likely to sacrifice a hundred white doves to secure the love of some man you have set your heart on. I think I can safely leave it with you in peace.'

As I drove home across the moor in the fading twilight, with the sound of the rain beating against the windscreen, I could not tear my thoughts away from that lonely man in his lonely tomb, unable to breathe for the tight bandages that covered his face, and with no prayers to guide him through the terrors of that last solitary journey. I dared not openly ask myself if this man could have been the priest Ptahotep, although I did believe that the past was alive and potent, and I feared that in some way its tragedies and dramas were about to be played out in the present.

That night I lay in bed turning the pages of a book my godfather had lent to me. I found again the passage he had read to me earlier in the day but I could not rid myself of the feeling that the beliefs held by intelligent and responsible people were hardly proofs.

I was about to close the book and lay it aside when one verse leaped at me from the white pages, and as I read, my fingers trembled so that the book shook in my hands.

A Presence, strange at once and known
Walked with me as my guide,
The skirts of some forgotten life
Trailed noiseless at my side.

If only I knew for sure. I put the book aside and switched off the light. For a long time I lay staring up at the ceiling, watching the play of shadows and listening to the sound of the rain driving steadily against the windows.

*

85

I wrote to my father and waited feverishly for his reply. The mail from China was notoriously bad and he was a poor correspondent. Even so I expected my letter to provoke some reaction, whether anger, disappointment or approval. In the meantime I went on with my life. Peter Hardcastle became less persistent in his attentions for want of any encouragement from me. Soon I heard that he was escorting another girl, a girl who would prove far more suitable for him than ever I could have been.

I visited my godfather's house constantly and sat with his other students while we struggled with the difficulties of reading the ancient Egyptian hieroglyphics, and I discovered in myself a dedication to this ancient civilization that surprised even Uncle Mark.

I was garaging my car after one of those visits when a gay voice hailed me from the gardens and I turned round to see Serena. I had always thought her pretty in a gentle English rose sort of way and today she looked beautiful, her rosy face and laughing brown eyes confirming her inner happiness. She ran up to me, catching me round the waist and kissing me happily.

She talked to me of London and David, mostly of David, expecting me to be happy for her. The words I should have said stuck in my throat. She followed me into my bedroom and sat on the edge of my bed, calling out to me as I washed and changed next door in the bathroom.

'Does this mean that you are engaged?' I asked her, but there was no warmth in my voice.

'Not yet, but this year's hunt ball is to be at Edgecombe at the end of March and my father intends to announce our engagement then.'

'But why Edgecombe?'

'David's mother and Sir Geoffrey are brother and sister, didn't you know?'

'No. I know very little about this David or his family.'

'We're not having a long engagement. David will be going out to the Sudan to work in the summer and we hope to get married in June so that I can go there with him.'

I stared at her through the mirror. 'So soon!'

'Well, yes. Oh, Kathryn, aren't you happy for me? I love him so much! I just hope you'll find somebody as nice for you when the time comes.'

'Where is he now, this David of yours?'

'He's downstairs in the drawing room with Grandmother and Aunt Dorothy. Do hurry up and change so that we can join them.'

'You mean he's staying here?'

'No. He's staying at Edgecombe. I'm going back to London tomorrow, there's so much to do and not a lot of time. I want a beautiful wedding at the church here. We couldn't possibly ask Grandmother to travel to London, she's far too old, and I want four bridesmaids as well as you. You will be my chief bridesmaid, won't you, Kathryn?'

My heart lurched sickeningly with every word she uttered, but she seemed not to notice as she rushed on to talk about materials and colours for our dresses. 'You look so pretty in blue, I'd thought of a deeper blue for you and the others in very pale blue. I'm having two little girls, David's nieces actually, and I've asked two of my friends in London to be the other two. June is such a lovely month for a wedding and I love roses, don't you?'

I was hunting through my wardrobe looking for something that would do me justice when Serena jumped off the bed and came to stand behind me.

'Wear that one, I've always thought it was your prettiest dress and so right for your colouring.' It was a fine woollen dress in subtle shades of green, ranging from the palest eau de nil to jade, and although it was quite plain, it was so beautifully cut that it gave my slender figure an exchanting grace.

'I wish I was as pretty as you,' Serena said wistfully.

'You know what Miss Richardson said to us at school,' I reminded her. 'She said I was the beautiful one but you were probably the nicest one. It was a long time before I forgave her for that statement but she was probably right.'

'She should never have made the remark at all,' Serena said staunchly.

She appeared not to notice my preoccupation as we

walked down the stairs together, she did not know that my knees were trembling and that there was a dull sick feeling in my heart. I wanted to be wrong, silently I pleaded, oh please please let me be wrong, because by being wrong I believed I would be defeating the past which seemed to have such a terrifying hold upon the present.

The sound of voices came to us from the drawing room and Serena said, 'Grandmother'll be asking David all sorts of things. I warned him to be ready for her.'

She threw open the drawing-room door and I followed her into the room.

All the faces in that room turned towards us but my eyes were on the man standing at the window. As I looked into his eyes I saw again the puzzlement in his and I felt again the enchantment that drew me towards him like a magnet.

I have no memory now of what we talked about that afternoon over the teacups. I suppose I must have answered questions, perhaps even volunteering some conversation of my own, otherwise they would have noticed and remarks would have been passed. Nothing was said so I can only assume that I behaved normally. I tried not to look at him, but every now and again I would find my eyes drawn to him only to find him looking at me with that strange air of perplexity.

That night I lay sleepless in the darkness and I thought about Serena lying peacefully asleep, her whole being warm and sheltered by love, and I asked myself bitterly how fate intended to play with us this time. I felt that we were like pawns upon a chessboard to be moved and mated and slain, and that although David and I had smiled into each other's eyes and conversed like two polite strangers, the past was shaping the present.

In the morning Serena would be returning to London, so I decided I would get up very early and drive over to my godfather's. I couldn't bear to hear her going on and on about her wedding plans as though they were the only things in the world that mattered.

Seemingly, the best-laid schemes of mice and men are

doomed to disappointment. In the morning the car refused to start and I was no mechanic. I pulled on the choke until I flooded the engine and I knew I would get no life out of it until somebody from the local garage had taken a look at it. By this time it was almost eight o'clock and the family would be stirring. I stood dejectedly beside the little car, then making up my mind swiftly, I ran back to the house and up to my room. Bridie was there, humming to herself as she dusted round. Her eyebrows shot up when she saw me and there was a sly smile on her face as she said, 'I wondered why you'd left the house so early, Miss Kathryn. Sure and I thought you'd a bin wantin' to see Miss Serena afore she goes back to London.'

I frowned at her smiling face, and taking down my riding habit from the wardrobe, I went into the bathroom to change.

She lingered on. I could hear her singing, and although I dawdled she was determined to out-dawdle me.

'Didn't I say to yer grandmither that it's a beauty you are in that black ridin' habit, Miss Kathryn? There be none o' them fine young dandies sits a horse quite like 'er, I said.'

'And what reply did my grandmother make, if any?' I asked her.

She chuckled. 'She said you were too pretty for yer own good and thet you needed a good strong arm to tame ye.'

'Just as long as she doesn't have anybody in mind.'

'Well now, Miss Serena's got 'erself a moity noice young man, 'andsome too. Didn't ye think so, Miss Kathryn?'

'He seems very nice. I didn't take particular notice of whether he was good-looking or not.'

'Oh, you noticed all roight. I said to Cook, the sooner Miss Serena marries 'im the better. She shouldn't be leavin' 'im round 'ere where loike as not he could get into mischief. There be monny a slip twixt cup and lip, an' don't think I didn't see 'im lookin' at you too, Miss Kathryn.'

'You've too much imagination, Bridie. I can get a man for myself, I don't need to take one from Serena.'

'Well, o' course, but there's nothin' round 'ere you've bin a-fancyin' so if I were Miss Serena I'd pick up me young man and off wi' 'im to London instead o' leavin' 'im at Edgecombe till she decides to come back.'

'He's not likely to be interested in anybody else if he's in love with Serena.'

'Don't you believe it, me dearie. Wi' Miss Serena gone an' you sittin' 'ere loike a spider jest waitin' for 'im, it's moi guess 'e could soon forget 'e was in love wi' Miss Serena.'

'You're ridiculous, Bridie. I'm sitting here waiting for nobody, least of all a man who belongs to somebody else. I consider your remarks to be impertinent. Just because my grandmother takes you back time and again doesn't give you the right to say what you like to me.'

There was a wicked malicious gleam in her eyes, and tossing my head, I left her. Her laughter followed me along the passage, but her remarks had filled me with a strange excitement. David was only four miles away. Running down the stairs exultantly, I said to myself over and over again that it was my turn. No hint that I was stealing from Serena came to trouble my exultation. Wasn't I only paying her back for the time when she had stolen from me? I could not think that fate would be so cruel a second time. It was only when I reached the stables that I pulled myself up sharply. I had been thinking like the Princess Tuia, not like me at all. There were codes and conventions I must observe. I was no autocratic princess observing the customs of another age, an age more cruel than the one in which I lived, an age of more primitive passions and selfish egotism. Surely something of the veneer of the century in which I now lived must take precedence over that other time of unlicensed individuality.

I waited while they saddled up Demetrius for me, then I set off at a canter along the path across the park. I loved the late February morning and the wind in my hair. I felt so alive, at one with the beautiful horse beneath me, and as we rode along the village lane, a group of men going out to work in the fields raised their hats and turned round to watch me with admiring eyes.

I rode along the route that the hunt nearly always took,

across the Langdale fields, following the bridle paths, with the scents of the morning in my nostrils and the birds twittering around me. I had not set out to ride towards Edgecombe, but at last I found myself looking down on the house and the smoke rising straight into the air from its tall chimneys. Somewhere in that house was David Laurenson, possibly at the breakfast table, discussing with his host and hostess the arrangements for the hunt ball to announce Serena's and his engagement. I saw two figures leave the house and walk towards the stables. I recognized Sir Geoffrey at once, and then with my face burning with colour I recognized David, walking with that long graceful stride, beside him. I turned Demetrius round sharply, climbing up towards the summit of the fell, hoping against hope that he would not ride my way, yet wishing we could come face to face, as if by accident, on those rolling moors.

There were rocks at the top of the fell and the grass was short and springy there. I knew a place where I could sit on the grass in the sun with my back against a rock and look out across the moorland and down on to a dozen little hamlets below, while Demetrius champed the short grass and the lapwings wheeled and dived over the tarn. I wished I had thought to bring a book with me instead of sitting with nothing else to do but dream of impossibilities. The sun was warm on my face, and there was no sound except the chirping of the birds. It was so comfortable on the grass with my back resting against a curved piece of rock that I fell asleep.

I do not know how long I slept, but the sound of movement in the grass woke me, and then a chill came over my face as though a shadow had obliterated the sun. I blinked, opening my eyes slowly and, looking up, I saw that a man sat on his horse looking down at me with a half smile on his face. I struggled to get up, and he leaped down from his horse and took my arm to assist me.

He was smiling and I thought again how attractive his smile was, and his voice as he asked, 'Do you often come up here alone to sit in the sunshine?'

I had not planned for David Laurenson to find me there,

even though I had secretly hoped for it, and now here we were again, talking banalities when there were so many words to say.

I smoothed my skirt and, after calling to Demetrius, I said, 'Have you never been up here before?'

'Oh yes, many times when I was young and spent some of my school holidays here. I thought I might have forgotten the path but it all came back to me. Nothing seems to have changed.'

'It is lonely up here, I suppose only fell walkers come this way.'

'And solitary riders. I found you here and I didn't know if I should wake you or let you go on sleeping.'

'I should be getting back. I'm afraid I keep very peculiar hours and am often chided for being late for meals.'

He laughed a low musical laugh and I remembered other laughter and words more endearing than the ones we had just spoken, although they had been spoken in an alien tongue. He helped me to mount my horse and side by side we set off down the fell. He rode well, sitting his horse easily and gracefully, and his first words were, 'I envy you that horse of yours, Kathryn.'

'Most people think he's too much for me.'

'I don't suppose many girls ride stallions but you handle yours very well. You look right together.'

I blushed under his regard, and smiling down at me, he said, 'Serena told me her young cousin was beautiful and of course you are, but when I met you at Christmas you were quite different to what I expected.'

'Oh. Why is that?'

'I had imagined you would be dark. I don't know why I got that idea. It's funny, isn't it, one hears about someone and automatically builds up a picture of how she will look. I suppose it isn't surprising that I got it wrong.'

'I always wanted to be dark. When I was a little girl, I hated my reflection in a mirror. I used to think that the mirror was lying. Bridie said the devil himself would get me because I was so vain, but it wasn't that, I looked in the mirror to see if I'd changed.'

A cold wind suddenly swept along the moor and made me shiver. I changed the subject. 'Serena tells me you've worked in Egypt. Did you like it?'

'The climate was beautiful, Cairo was dusty, busy and rather dirty, I'm afraid, but of course the Nile is unforgettable and the past was magnificent.'

'You were more interested in the past than the present?'

'Naturally. Isn't that why people go to Egypt?'

I didn't answer him. The words were not what I had wanted to hear but the sound of his voice and an undefinable something about his manner made my heart race strangely.

We rode in silence for several minutes, and then below us I could see the chimneys of Edgecombe and those of Random Edge in the distance.

'Why haven't you gone back to London with Serena?' I asked him.

'Because she'll be spending all her time around the shops hunting for things for her trousseau. I should get in the way. She's far better off with her mother. Anyway she'll be back here at the end of March.'

'In time for the hunt ball, when you intend to announce your engagement?'

'Yes. I shall expect you to dance with me, Kathryn.'

I smiled, and turning my horse towards home, I said, 'I'll leave you now. Perhaps we'll meet again one morning.'

'I hope so. I invariably ride in the morning.'

I rode down the fell towards the road, and when I reached it, I turned my head expecting to find him gone. He was standing where I had left him, and I watched him raise his arm in farewell before he too turned his horse and rode away.

It was the last time I would go riding up on the fells, I told myself. In the mornings I would return to my godfather's house and go on with my studies. David Laurenson belonged to Serena. There seemed no point in asking for trouble and I was afraid of the attraction that flared between us, afraid yet excited by it.

*

93

My godfather telephoned me that afternoon, saying he had expected me and wondered why I hadn't arrived.

I lied that I had had a headache but would see him in the morning.

'I'm afraid that won't be possible,' he said. 'I have to go up to London in the morning and will be away almost two weeks. I'll let you know as soon as I get back.'

Two weeks! Two weeks when I could die of boredom. Later that afternoon I telephoned Peter Hardcastle on the pretence of asking his advice. More and more girls were now abandoning their side-saddles in favour of riding astride and I asked him to tell me the correct sort of saddle to buy, and when he suggested driving over, I agreed readily.

I was grateful for his help. Peter knew about horses and I listened to him and the saddle-maker discussing the merits of one saddle against another most knowledgeably. At last one was chosen which Peter believed would suit me best, and on leaving Random Edge, he suggested that we ride together the following morning to try it out.

'It will seem strange to you at first, Kathryn. You should have somebody with you the first time you try it.'

'It's Saturday tomorrow. Won't you be going racing?'

'Oh, I can always cry off that.'

'But won't your latest girlfriend be very disappointed?'

'I shall be leaving her with the crowd. Besides, you know, there's nobody like you, Kathryn.'

'I shan't go with you if you keep that up, Peter. I'm very grateful for your help and your friendship, but there can't ever be anything more than that between us.'

'Why can't there be anything more? Is there somebody else?'

'No, but I'm a funny girl. I've told you I want to go out to Egypt and work there. Nothing and nobody is going to stop me doing that, so I can't afford to get serious with any man.'

'What do a lot of old ruins and dead pharaohs matter? It's the here and now that should be important.'

'But not to me, I'm afraid it's the there and then with me.'

94

He stared at me dolefully, and then kissing me lightly on the cheek, he said, 'I'll be here about ten to help you saddle up Demetrius. You'll soon get used to the new saddle.'

'When I was a young girl, I used to ride an Arab mare without any saddle at all. I don't suppose that a new saddle will pose any problems.'

I walked with him towards his car and stood on the front doorstep until it turned out of the gates on to the road. I was halfway up the stairs when Bridie, leaning over the balustrade above, said, 'That poor young man's willin' to let you lead him like a lamb to the slaughter, and you with not an ounce of feeling in yer heart except for . . .'

'Except for what, Bridie?'

'I saw you up on the fells this mornin', ridin' with Miss Serena's young man, an 'er only just left the house.'

I ran up the steps and flounced past her but she followed me to my room on the pretext of turning down the bedspread. 'One o' you's goin' to get hurt, me fine lady, and it's my guess it'll be you. Sure and there's all the county to choose from and you've got to pick on Miss Serena's young man.'

'Can't I go riding with some man without you thinking I'm setting a trap for him? I didn't arrange to meet him, we met by chance. Besides, it's none of your business.'

She was lookimg at me through narrowed eyes and irritably I sat before my mirror brushing my hair. Our eyes met in the mirror and hers were filled with a strange sort of compassion. I looked away quickly, annoyed with the treacherous tears that threatened to fill my eyes.

'Oh, Miss Kathryn,' she said sadly. 'Roight from that first day I saw you starin' in the hall mirror there as though you couldn't believe your reflection, I thought to meself, poor mite, and her without her mither and a father who's goin' to go away and leave her in this great house wi' that martinet of a grandmither and an aunt who's never bin able to say boo to a goose. Miss Serena 'ad everythin', even then. Don't go 'ankerin' after her young man, lassie, there be only heartache in that for thee.'

'Oh Bridie, just because you've seen me riding over the fells with him.'

'It has to start somewhere and that's a fact.'

'So tomorrow when you see me riding with Peter Hardcastle, you're going to be pleased then?'

'No, he's not for you either.'

'Why not?'

' 'E's too ordinary, 'e thinks o' nothin' but horses and 'untin' and in a few years time he'll 'ave run to fat just like 'is father. No, it's a different kind o' man for you, an' like as not 'e's not appeared yet.'

'In the meantime, I can't speak to a man without your thinking I aim to get him.'

'You've never bin as kind to Miss Serena as she's bin to you. It's allus been as though you've resented 'er somehow just like you've resented me. Almost as though you've bin expectin' us to do something bad to you. You shouldn't be envyin' Miss Serena, it's a rare sweet lassie she is and she thinks the world o' you.'

'Oh, Bridie, I don't envy her. Besides, even if I did, haven't you ever envied somebody and wished you had what they had?'

She sat on the edge of my bed with her brow furrowed and I knew that she was thinking. Then suddenly she said, 'That I did now. I envied me sister Mary, particularly when she married that old farmer and 'im with a field full o' cows and a goat or two.'

'Well then!'

'It were only the farm I envied, not the farmer. I wouldn't a given twopence for 'im. A roight old loife she 'ad with 'im and no mistake.'

I spun round on my dressing stool and laughed. 'How many sisters do you have?'

'Well there were me sister Mary and me sister Martha just loike those two in the Bible, an' there was Fanny and Geraldine who went into a convent and we've niver seen 'em since. I were the eldest so I 'elped me mither to raise the others. I 'ad four brothers, too, but I 'aven't clapped eyes on 'em in years.'

'Nine children!'

'Sure, and two that died when they were chillun.'

'Did you never want to get married?'

'I did get married once, it were a tinker I met at local fair, but then I found out 'e 'ad another wife back in Doncaster and I upped and left 'im. Sure and 'imself told me I were the only woman he'd ever loved. I weren't bad looking in them days and me hair was as red as copper and me eyes nearly as blue as yours, Miss Kathryn. Men an' their promises. Loike pie crusts they are, meant to be broken.'

'All men are not like that, Bridie.'

'Find me one as isn't an I'll set me cap at 'im tomorrow. I must get on wi' me work or 'erself will be after me scalp an' no mistake. Ye mustn't mind old Bridie talkin to ye, lassie, but there's no call for ye to get hurt. Loife'll do that for ye without ye looking for it.'

Oh, Bridie, I thought miserably, you don't know what it's like to be two people. It's best not to remember, better by far to go on throughout a hundred lifetimes making mistakes and forgetting them, starting afresh with no memories of other years so that each little lifetime is complete and unique in itself and not tormented by old sins and the passions that stirred us before.

Six

I soon adapted to sitting Demetrius astride and during the next two weeks I rode often across the fells but not the fells near Edgecombe. Approval shone in Bridie's eyes but I had not needed her advice. I knew myself the dangers I faced in meeting David too frequently during Serena's absence.

It was the day before her return when I rode with Peter and a few others across the fields, following the route the hunt often took. I grew restless with their familiar chatter so I left them and rode towards the copse alone. It was nearly March and all around me was the promise of spring. I dismounted from my horse, allowing him to champ the sweet new grass while I sat on the stile staring into the river.

The crackle of twigs under a horse's hoofs made me spin round. I expected to find that Peter had followed me, and there was a frown of annoyance on my face. I could feel the frown become a blush and David smiled, saying, 'I'm sorry, Kathryn, I can see that I'm intruding on your solitude.'

'I thought you were somebody else,' I said.

'Somebody you evidently didn't want to see.'

'Yes.'

'Well, I won't ask who that someone was but I have the strangest feeling that you've been avoiding me these last few weeks. Why?'

He had dismounted from his horse and stood looking down at me and I raised my eyes to meet his intent stare. His eyes were grey, unlike those dark brown eyes that had gazed at me sternly across a sunlit room. There was no sternness in David Laurenson's eyes, only a whimsical

98

friendliness, and I looked away quickly in case he insisted on an answer.

'I had hoped you and I were going to be good friends,' he said, still smiling. 'Now I have to face the prospect that you may not even like me.'

'Oh, David, what a ridiculous idea!'

'You've been busy with your studies then?'

'No. Professor Ensor is in London.'

'I see.'

I looked up at him and suddenly the teasing look left his eyes and he was looking at me as a woman, not just Serena's cousin. I moved away from him to walk to my horse. He followed me and lightly, as though he must speak of every-day matters and ignore more serious things, he said, 'It's very beautiful down here. I remember this copse as a favourite of mine when I was a boy. I used to come here with a jam-jar and fish for minnows.'

'I come here when I want to escape from the hunt, particularly when a fox has been sighted.'

'You don't like to see them killed?'

'I hate it.'

'Then why do you ride with them?'

'Because it's the thing to do. Because it's expected of me. I enjoy the chase, I loathe the kill, it's as simple as that.'

'And what do you dream about here on your own, with the hounds in full cry and the rest of them pelting across the fields?'

'Sometimes nothing at all, sometimes a great many things. It's beautiful here in the summertime, and even in the winter it's quiet and secluded, and I love it when the frost is on the trees and the river is still and frozen under ice. I like to think that this is my place where I can come to be alone.'

'And now I have intruded and it can never be your own again.'

'Oh, it will be. You will marry Serena and go away, and if ever you come back to it, neither of us will be the people we are today.'

We stared at each other, and perhaps because I had mentioned Serena, he became suddenly circumspect, helping me on to my horse and leaving me with murmured words of farewell. I felt shaken by our meeting so that when I returned to the house I was sharp with Peter, who was waiting for me.

'Wherever did you get to?' he complained.

'Oh, I rode off on my own. I suddenly didn't want to ride with the crowd.'

'You might have called to me, I'd have ridden with you.'

'I just felt I wanted to be by myself. In a couple of days the house will be turned upside down because of the hunt ball. There won't be a single minute when we're not thinking about ball gowns, and then wedding clothes, and there'll be all the invitations to send out. I suppose I shall be expected to do my share.'

He grinned. 'You'll save the supper dance for me, I hope.'

I laughed, squeezing his arm affectionately. 'I'll see you before the ball, Peter, but right now I'd better get back to the house and get changed in time for tea. My grandmother insists on the niceties and afternoon tea is quite a ceremony.'

I had not seen David Laurenson since the afternoon when we had met in the copse and I felt a pulsing excitement as I dressed for the ball. I had bought my gown in Harrogate, a pale blue confection in chiffon which draped round my slender finger like a gown some Grecian goddess might have worn. Serena, who of course had done all her shopping in London, was wearing pale apricot that flattered her brown hair and brown eyes.

As we drove past the drawing-room window towards the gate I could see Bridie staring after us. Somehow her presence had a sobering effect on my excitement and, shivering a little, I leaned back into the dark anonymity of the Daimler.

Edgecombe was ablaze with light. Large cars were drawing up in front of the open entrance doors and disgorging a throng of people looking gay and festive in evening dress. As we walked up the wide shallow staircase to leave our wraps, more than a dozen girls descended upon Serena to wish her well. I walked behind, strangely light-headed, until a voice beside me said, 'When is it your turn, Kathryn, and who is it going to be?'

I looked up sharply to find myself gazing into the eyes of Joan Martingdale, my old headmistress. I had not known that Serena had invited her, and blushing a little, I said, 'I have no man in mind. Instead I hope to go out to the Middle East to work.'

'That doesn't surprise me, my dear, and perhaps there you will meet some nice man who thinks like you do and likes the things you like. You have both grown up to be very lovely girls. I was sure you would.'

'I don't think I was ever a very good pupil, Miss Martingdale. I was often rebellious and undisciplined.'

'You were always one of my most exciting pupils, though. If you do decide to go abroad, please let me know. I would like to see you before you go.'

'Yes, of course.'

I was looking at her hesitantly and she leaned forward and patted my arm. 'You were a strange girl in many respects, Kathryn. I sometimes thought you lived in a world of your own and were not greatly interested in things around you. I was pleased when you did so well in your examinations. It proved you were with us even when you appeared not to be.'

She smiled warmly at me and left me.

Most of the girls had left their wraps and were about to go downstairs when I entered the bedroom that served as a ladies' cloakroom.

'Do hurry, Kathryn,' Serena cautioned me, 'or you'll miss some of the dancing.' I watched her run down the stairs lightly and before I turned back into the room I saw David come forward to meet her. He looked very tall and distinguished in his dark evening dress and Serena's face turned up to his was alight with happiness. I dawdled in the bedroom, and from downstairs I could hear the haunting refrain of a waltz and laughter from the terrace outside.

I couldn't stay there indefinitely, so leaving my wrap, I

101

made my way slowly downstairs. The waltz had finished and a slow foxtrot was being played. Serena had been claimed by her father, and from my place at the edge of the floor, my eyes met David's. Something so incredibly intense passed between us that I could feel my legs become like jelly underneath me, and I would have fallen if a firm hand hadn't grasped my arm. I looked up into Peter Hardcastle's fair, open face. 'Shall we dance?' he asked in a light tone that belied his expression of concern.

I don't remember anything about that dance except that I followed his steps without being aware of it, and all the time he looked anxiously into my eyes so that I looked sharply away with the warm colour flooding my face. There were other dances after that with a great many men, but none of them mattered until, finally, after the supper dance, I was dancing with David.

I have forgotten the tune we waltzed to, only that it was slow and haunting. He danced effortlessly as I had known he would. I felt light and ethereal in his arms, and once, when two other dancers came too close, he pulled me near to him and the top of my head brushed against his cheek. We danced in silence and it was only when the waltz came to an end that he said, 'You're looking very beautiful tonight, Kathryn. I suppose men have been saying that to you all evening.'

'I don't know. If they have, I haven't been listening.'

'But you're listening now?'

'Yes.'

I had no subterfuge for David, no arch or airy reply that teased and flattered but meant nothing. There was a stillness around us and I felt that people were looking at us strangely but I could no more have moved than the marble statue in the corner of the room.

He was the first to recover and, taking my arm, he drew me towards the corner where a crowd of young people were standing, including Serena. She came to my side, asking a little breathlessly, 'Are you all right, Kathryn? You seemed a little strange just then.'

I nodded, unable at that moment to trust my voice. David

came to my rescue. 'I think it's the champagne, Serena, she isn't accustomed to it.'

'My, but she's drunk plenty at one time or another,' Peter said, and a laugh went up from those around us. It sobered me up as nothing else would have done, and laughing in their direction I said, 'Perhaps I've developed an allergy. People can, you know.'

The music had started again and I was glad to be in Peter Hardcastle's arms again, trying to follow his none-too-perfect steps through the intricacies of a quickstep.

'I think we were all a bit embarrassed just then,' he said lightly, 'even Serena. David was looking at you as though you were the only person in the room. I was glad when you decided to come to life.'

'What rubbish you talk! In just half an hour my uncle will announce their engagement.'

I remember very little of the events of the next few hours. Toasts were drunk and there was much talk and laughter. Through it all, Serena floated sublimely happy while David stood enigmatic beside her responding to well-wishers automatically with a set smile on his face.

I had never been more miserable in my life but I made myself dance and laugh and chatter. I flirted with too many men and drank too much champagne, and if my laughter was forced and my flirting so dangerous that it earned me looks of disapproval from those present, I didn't care. After tonight they would refer to me as the wild one, and none of them would ever know that it had been because my heart was breaking.

The atmosphere was very tense as we drove back to Random Edge and I sat between my grandmother and my aunt. Neither of them spoke and I was glad. It meant that I could hug my misery closer to me so that it became a searing ache in my heart. I wanted to suffer, I deserved to suffer. When we reached the house, Aunt Dorothy took my grandmother's arm and assisted her out of the car and up the stairs. Neither of them wished me good night.

*

The first light of dawn was already creeping across the sky when I crept between the sheets. It was Bridie who roused me much later with my morning tea.

She went to draw back the curtains, then she returned to the side of my bed and stood looking down at me.

'Did you 'ave a good time at the ball then?' she asked me.

'Yes, thank you, Bridie.'

'I heard that you 'ad.'

'News travels fast.'

'Sure but 'adn't you forgot that some o' the servants were over at Edgecombe to 'elp out? I've 'eard 'ow you were the life and soul of the party, flirtin' with all those young gentlemen an' lookin' up at Mr David in a way you should niver a done.'

'I would have thought the servants would have had enough to do at Edgecombe without gossiping about me. I suppose it was Vickers and Mrs Greenway, they're the ones with the vivid imaginations.'

'So you reckon there's no truth in it then?'

'Haven't you anything to do this morning besides gossip? If you have, why don't you get on with it?'

'I shall, I jest wanted ye to know what the talk is in the servants' quarters.'

'I'm not interested.' I reached over for the clock on my bedside table. It was eleven o'clock and, meeting her amused eyes, I snapped, 'I shan't want any breakfast. If the servants are interested, I will be riding over to the Hardcastle's place.'

She tittered and removed the tray from my bed. I was relieved when I heard the door of my bedroom close behind her.

The day stretched in front of me and I wondered how soon I would be made aware of my grandmother's displeasure and the hurtful, disappointed glances of Aunt Dorothy. I had to get out, although I knew that I would have to face them some time.

That evening, my grandmother summoned me to the library. I entered the room reluctantly, feeling like a child about to be chastised, and closed the door behind me. Two bright spots of colour burned in my cheeks, but raising my head proudly I waited for the censure.

The old lady was sitting stiffly upright, regarding me without pity. 'What have you to say for yourself?' she snapped.

'I don't know what you mean, Grandmother.'

'You know very well what I mean. Aren't there enough men in Yorkshire, or anywhere else for that matter, without you setting your cap at your cousin's fiancé?'

I didn't answer her, but stood biting my lip. I wanted to storm at her, to tell her things that would have astounded her, but I couldn't speak. For ten long years she had more or less ignored my existence and now there seemed nothing to say.

'I don't know what to do with you, Kathryn. You certainly made a spectacle of yourself in front of all those people.'

'I don't care about those people,' I said defiantly, holding back the stinging tears in my eyes.

This provoked a long tirade from my grandmother on how abysmally she had failed in my upbringing. I was accused of unseemly behaviour, of flirting with all the men at the ball and especially my cousin's fiancé, and she finished by saying, 'I look for dutiful and respectful behaviour in my granddaughters. I have found it in Serena, but I have never found it in you. Now go to your room.'

I left the library and ran straight into Aunt Dorothy, who didn't know whether to comfort or scold me, but her advice was the same.

'David Laurenson is not for you and the sooner you realize it, the better it'll be for your peace of mind. Has he given you any encouragement?'

'I haven't been seeing him, not intentionally, anyway, and he hasn't encouraged me. Anyway they'll be so busy between now and June I don't expect to see anything of David anyhow. By that time I shall have found somebody else perhaps.'

I said it without conviction. There was nobody else. Aunt Dorothy gave me a doubtful look.

'Did Serena say anything to you? You know she thinks a lot of you, she's been very kind to you.'

'She has been kind to me. I'm to be her chief bridesmaid, and I don't know how I'm going to bear it.'

My shoulders were shaking with sobs and she was trying to comfort me, holding me against her, saying over and over again, 'Kathryn, Kathryn, no man's worth it,' and all I could do was weep miserably against her shoulder.

I wept until there were no more tears left and she put me away from her, her face concerned, looking at me sadly.

I kissed her cheek and walked towards the door. At the door I turned to find her watching me sorrowfully. 'You needn't worry,' I told her. 'I'm young and resilient. By this time next year it could be somebody else I'm crying over.'

'I hope not, Kathryn. I'd rather think that by this time next year you'll be as happy as Serena instead of hankering after a man who can never belong to you.'

Never belong to me! Those words would keep drumming in my ears for the rest of the night. But I walked up the stairs with my head held high. Nothing that had been said would alter in any detail the pattern of my life. Only destiny would do that and I had the strangest conviction that whatever happened to me in the future had been ordained centuries before.

Seven

Serena was in London again and her wedding was finally fixed for early June. It was April and the days were lengthening. There were fat buds on the beech trees and primroses in the woods. Spring, which in the past had always seemed to me to be a time of renewed life and expectancy, had become for me a season of hopelessness, bringing me ever nearer to the day when Serena and David would marry. The hunting season was almost at an end and I could not think beyond that day early in June.

She wrote long ecstatic letters to us and embarked upon long telephone conversations that irritated my grandmother beyond words.

'Why can't she come up here and we could talk matters over? London is too remote. If she wants to get married from Edgecombe then she should be here.'

'She's doing most of her shopping in London,' Aunt Dorothy said reasonably. 'You have to admit, Mother, that there is probably more choice there.'

'Fiddlesticks!' retorted my grandmother. 'The shops in York and Harrogate are splendid. I suppose the next thing will be for her to want Kathryn down there. Serena isn't usually so thoughtless.'

Serena and I were much the same size although I was slightly taller. I was hoping she could choose my bridesmaid's dress without any assistance from me. Her final choice was blue and I knew it was a colour that suited me very well, and I had no feelings either way about the flowers she wanted me to carry.

I felt lethargic. Day by day, the wedding was coming nearer and I began to wonder if my dreams hadn't been a huge hoax engineered by fate.

I decided I would turn out with the hunt on the next meeting. It was a glorious day with white scudding clouds across a bright blue sky, but I was late arriving at the village inn around which they congregated. One of the stableboys had cut his hand badly and everybody seemed to be rushing around trying to find a doctor who would stitch it for him. The two local doctors both rode with the hunt, so in the end I volunteered to take him to the village hospital which was roughly fifteen miles from the house. Demetrius was saddled and waiting for me when I got back, and by the time I joined the rest, there was no time for conversation before we rode out down the narrow lanes towards the fields.

I rode alongside three or four children on their ponies and couldn't help hearing their chatter. They were desperate for a fox to be sighted and even more anxious to be in at the kill. I moved away from them, thinking that they were loathsome little brats, so young and so bloodthirsty. Other adults riding nearby smiled approvingly, no doubt thinking how game and courageous the children were, but after that I had little heart in following the hunt whether a fox was raised or not. I held Demetrius back, and soon after we passed over the Langdale field, I turned off to ride towards the copse. I was surprised to see another rider well ahead of me and I frowned with annoyance thinking it was Peter who had anticipated my withdrawal. I was of half a mind to turn back but the other rider was now out of sight. I hoped he had ridden on instead of entering the copse.

I soon realized I would not be alone in my favourite place. A large bay horse stood cropping the grass, and although I was tempted to turn away, my curiosity got the better of me. I rode deeper into the shade to find a man standing motionless, looking into the stream where it gurgled and splashed among the stones. The brittle twigs snapped under my horse's feet and the man turned his head sharply so that I was looking into David's eyes with the smile dying on my lips at the sight of his serious face.

I felt safe and filled with courage with the warmth of the horse's body between my knees, the reins held loosely in my hands, mounted and ready for flight, but he left his place by the stream and came over to stand beside me, looking up into my face. Even then I felt secure sitting so far above him, but I allowed him to take the reins and assist me to dismount until I stood at last with the horse against my back and David looking down into my eyes. It was the moment I had dreamed of, yearned for and now I was afraid of it. We should have been greeting one another like friends, like two people who were soon to be related and who had met accidentally on a golden afternoon. Instead I was clasped in his arms and he was bruising my lips with his kisses.

I had no thoughts for anything outside ourselves and the time and place. It seemed to me that we were two people that fate had brought together from the ends of the earth and from the limits of time, that we had stood together from the dawn of the world as we would stand together in lives as yet unknown. I laid my hand gently against his cheek, almost as though I asked my fingers to remember the contours of his face which my eyes might one day forget.

Time had no meaning for us as we lay together on the warm spring grass with the horses calmly champing the short grass and I realized that not even in my hunger had I fully understood the pain and anguish and power of love. It was only later, when a young crescent moon rose high above the beech trees, that I became aware of the time and the fact that, apart from our being together, nothing was solved.

'What will you do?' I asked him in a whisper.

'I don't know.'

He looked bemused in the fading light, as though what had happened to us had little bearing on the future. Then he laid his head in his hands and said, 'Oh God, what a mess! But I couldn't get you out of my mind, Kathryn. From the first moment we met, I could think of nothing but you.'

'But you loved Serena,' I reminded him gently.

'Yes. God knows I loved her when I asked her to marry

me, so why has this happened? I'd rather die than hurt Serena, but if I can't have you, nothing matters, I might as well be dead.'

'What will you do?' I asked him again, waiting with bated breath for his answer.

'I'll have to tell her, but you must be patient in case it isn't possible to tell her immediately. I never loved Serena as I love you but the breaking of her heart is not going to be easy, and even without love she is very dear to me.'

'You realize that after she knows there will be no place for me at Random Edge or you at Edgecombe?'

'You don't think our love is strong enough to withstand that?'

'Oh yes, I do, strong enough to withstand a thousand such places.'

'They will talk to me of duty, Kathryn, and honour, but neither of these things matters when I look at you. When I hold you in my arms nothing else matters except the here and the now.'

My heart was beating furiously against his and at that moment I thought I would have cried out with remembered pain. Once, a long long time ago, I had heard those words, and at that time I had been so sure of my happiness, so confident that it could never be taken away from me, and now, hearing them again, a strange feeling of fatalism made me draw away from him. Those words long ago had been meant as sincerely as now, but I was no longer confident of my future, I knew it could be changed. Happiness was not a captive bird that one could cage, but something that must fly free to seek whatever destiny fate had planned for it.

'What is it, Kathryn?' he asked urgently.

'I don't know. They will try to make you change your mind, they will try to make you see that Serena is real and that this is only fleeting and unimportant.'

'How can they make me change my mind about something which I know is good and right? How can they ask me to marry Serena when I love you? That would be more cruel than what I am already going to do.'

'Serena will hate me. She will think I have deliberately

110

set myself out to steal you from her, and she will hate me without knowing the truth.'

He gripped my shoulders, staring fiercely into my eyes.

'What sort of courage do you have, Kathryn?' he asked sternly.

'The sort that will match yours, I hope,' I answered him, and then once more we were in each other's arms and the night closed in around us.

There was consternation at Random Edge as I rode Demetrius slowly along the drive. I could see that the front door was open and lights streamed out across the park. Round the stables lights also blazed, and as I rode nearer to the house, stable hands came out to meet me, their faces pale and frightened.

It was the head groom Saunders who met me first. 'Lor, Miss Kathryn, but you've given us a turn and no mistake. The rest of 'em came back hours ago, and when you didn't come, Miss Dorothy started telephonin' everybody she could think of. We thought you'd 'ad an accident and nobody seen it 'appen.'

'I'm quite all right, Saunders. I didn't stay with the hunt, I decided to ride across the fells. I sat in the sun and I must have gone to sleep. By the time I awoke it was quite dark and it was a fair way to ride back.'

'Dinner's bin waitin' for over an hour and the old lady's in a state, I can tell you.'

'Will you see to Demetrius, Saunders? I'd better go inside and try to placate them.'

Aunt Dorothy met me at the door, her face pale and streaked with tears, almost collapsing with relief at the sight of me.

I gave her the same excuse I had given Saunders but almost immediately we heard my grandmother's voice calling out to us from the library. 'And what excuse has she to offer this time? Bring her in here, Dorothy, I want to hear what she's got to say for herself.'

I followed my aunt into the library to find my grand-

111

mother sitting in front of the fire with a shawl round her shoulders for it was a draughty room at the best of times and I suspected she only sat in it now so that she could hear me coming in.

'You seem absolutely oblivious of the trouble you put other people to, Kathryn,' was her opening gambit. 'I don't suppose you gave a thought to the worry your failure to arrive home at a reasonable hour caused your aunt and myself.'

'I'm sorry, Grandmother. I fell asleep. I didn't realize it was so late.'

'Why ride with the hunt when you have no intention of staying with them?'

'From almost my first moment in this house I was told what would be expected of me. I must hunt with the gentry because I must never forget that we were gentry. I do not enjoy hunting although I love riding. Today I left them because I heard some children enthusing about killing a fox and I couldn't bear to see the delight on their arrogant little faces when a group of inane adults streaked their faces with the animal's blood.'

'But to go riding on the fells alone! The fells are dangerous. Suppose you'd fallen into a bog or your horse had gone lame. There would have had to be a search party sent out, but I don't suppose you are the least concerned about causing trouble for others.'

'I didn't fall into a bog, Grandmother, nor did Demetrius go lame. I've said I'm sorry, can't we leave it at that?'

'I am beginning to think that the best thing you could have done was join your father in China. My heart won't stand these constant upsets. I sincerely hope this will be the last of them.'

It won't be, I told myself savagely as I stalked upstairs to my room. I wonder how your heart is going to stand Serena's engagement being broken, particularly when you know the reasons for it.

I met Bridie on the staircase, looking at me expectantly, her small bright eyes inquisitive in her sharp face. Before she could speak, however, I said to her, 'Not one word,

112

Bridie. I don't have to explain my absences to you.'

I left her staring after me as I went into my room, closing the door sharply behind me.

I wished I didn't have to eat dinner with them. My grandmother would be distant and Aunt Dorothy would be tearful, but I made myself take extra care with my appearance. That at least would not give rise to bitterness. I opened my jewel casket in search of a gold pendant when my eyes fell upon the ancient Egyptian amulet staring up at me from the blue silk lining of the casket, the eyes in the fabled animal's head gleaming wickedly.

I picked it up and held it tight against my breast. How did its magic work? The Princess Tuia must have sacrificed extravagantly in the temple and yet it had not fulfilled her desires. Those old priests had known how to work their spells and I wished with all my heart that I knew the invocations that would set in motion the events that would leave David free to marry me. Tuia had asked for the life of Asnefer. I did not want Serena's life, only that she might go away and leave her memory a dim shadow in David's mind, soon to be forgotten.

I was afraid of the amulet and yet my fingers were clenched around it as though they could hardly part from it. A strange stillness seemed to have settled over the house so that the normal sounds of early evening were silenced. Outside in the parkland the wind had dropped, when before it had been sighing through the trees outside my window, and in my terror I peopled the shadows at the edge of my room with vague unhappy shapes who stared at me with hollow haunted eyes. With a sharp cry I wrenched my hands apart so that the talisman fell on to my lap, then picking it up swiftly I flung it into the back of the drawer and slammed it shut.

I was shivering as though with cold and my teeth were chattering. My heart was thumping painfully against my ribs and my throat ached as though with unshed tears. I shall never know if this reaction was brought about by my own fears or if the amulet did possess some ancient power, because at that moment the door was unceremoniously flung

113

open and Bridie stood on the threshold looking at me. I stared back at her in the mirror, my eyes large in my white face, and it seemed to me at that moment that I was looking at Ipey reliving that other moment when I had commanded her to mix that one last potion.

She spoke and the illusion was gone.

'They're waitin' dinner for ye, Miss Kathryn.'

I couldn't speak. I had to drag my mind back from the past to face the future. She walked over to me and stood looking down at me in such a way that I felt sure she knew the secret of the amulet that the drawer contained.

I willed myself to pick up my hairbrush and start to brush my hair. I knew that my fingers were trembling because I could hardly manage the strokes, and she reached out and took the brush from me and began to do my hair. Gradually the colour returned to my face and my heart stopped its mad relentless fluttering.

'I don't know what you've bin up to, Miss Kathryn, but I've niver known you to get so worked up afore. Comin' 'ome at this time, you moight a known herself would be as mad as the divil.'

'I won't be treated like a child,' I snapped back, glad that my teeth had stopped chattering and the colour was back in my cheeks.

Bridie only looked at me sorrowfully before she went about setting the room to rights, then without another word, she let herself out of the door. Before I followed, I was careful to lock the drawer containing the amulet.

The following morning I was out of the house and over at my godfather's place before Serena arrived, but somehow I was not following his lessons with any enthusiasm. He remarked upon it as I was leaving.

'You don't seem yourself today, Kathryn. Are you becoming bored by Egypt?'

'Oh no, how could I be? Serena arrives today, I expect I was thinking about her.'

'Of course, and the wedding is not far off. Suppose we

give the tuition up until later? You can telephone me when all the excitement is over.'

I agreed. Things were closing in on me. One half of me wanted to go to Egypt with my new knowledge but the other half told me all that was past and now only the future mattered and my future lay with David Laurenson.

I listened to Serena going on and on about her wedding. The materials for her gown and her bridesmaids' gowns were spread across my bed, and her talk of flowers for the church and the reception afterwards went round and round in my head until I felt dizzy with their repetition. I hated myself. I was so sure that all her plans would come to nothing, and I had to keep on remembering that other, older hurt that had destroyed me. Fortunately the rest of the family made up for any lack of warmth on my part.

I arranged to be constantly out during the next few days so that I didn't have to be in her company, but whenever I did see her, she appeared puzzled and faintly unhappy. I felt sure that David was preparing her for the breaking of their engagement by a growing coldness, and when I looked at her shadowed eyes, I pitied her, realizing perhaps for the first time that I loved her. What was there about me that destroyed the people who loved me? I asked myself.

The two little girls who were to be her bridesmaids were visiting Edgecombe and she had gone over to meet them. On the following Saturday the last meeting of the hunt would take place. Serena informed me that the two little girls wished to ride and it was her intention to ride with them from Edgecombe. The end of the season would attract a large following and I hoped desperately that David and I would be able to slip away without causing too much notice.

'Will David be riding?' I asked her.

'Oh yes, I'm sure he will. I'll ride over on the mare and stable her at Edgecombe so that we can all ride over together on Saturday morning. You'll be turning out, won't you, Kathryn?'

'Oh yes, I expect so.'

I hadn't seen David alone since Serena had returned but he telephoned me late one night long after the others were in bed. I could say very little in case I was overheard, but he told me he loved me and intended to break the news to Serena some time over the weekend.

I begged him to tell her on Saturday night. 'Please, David,' I urged him, 'I can't stand it much longer. Please tell her on Saturday night and then drive over to tell me. It doesn't matter what time, I'll wait up until you come.'

He gave me his promise, and after that, every minute seemed like a little lifetime. Although it was April, Saturday dawned cold and windy with a promise of rain in the air, and Demetrius lashed his tail savagely as we rode down the lane towards the inn where a crowd had begun to congregate. I chatted feverishly with a group of people on the forecourt of the inn until I saw Serena riding along the bridle path that led from Edgecombe. Two small girls on ponies rode beside her and behind were David and Sir Geoffrey on their big bay horses. Serena looked pale, her eyes without sparkle, and there was a lethargy about her. Once I saw David look at her anxiously and I knew he was hating himself for what he was doing to her.

She raised her hand and put on a brave smile when she saw me, so I rode across to her, noticing for the first time that she was not riding the mare but another, smaller animal. He was wiry and dark and he trembled with nervous excitement so that it took all her attention to curb his restlessness.

'What's happened to Amanda?' I asked her, 'And whose horse is that you're riding?'

'Amanda's cast a shoe and we couldn't get her shod until later this afternoon. This is Castillion. I think I'm going to find him a bit of a handful. David didn't want me to ride him,' she went on after speaking to the horse soothingly and quietly, 'but the children begged me to ride with them and I didn't want to disappoint them.'

'He seems very nervous. Has he hunted before?'

'I don't know. Sir Geoffrey only bought him at the beginning of the season but I didn't want to ride David's horse, he's far too skittish, and Sir Geoffrey won't let anybody else ride Major. I'll be safe enough. I'll just have to keep a tight rein on him.'

116

We had no sooner left the Langdale fields than a fox was sighted, running like a mad thing against the hedge, and then like a cavalry charge they were after him. The sounds of the horn, the baying of the hounds and the shouts of the followers became a clamour to my ears, and I turned away. David followed me and together we reached the copse and the peace of the afternoon closed in upon us.

We stood together with my head resting on his chest, his chin on my hair, but there was no passion between us. It seemed by mutual consent that we must contain our passion until the wounding of Serena was over and done with, but the peace of those moments in his arms became more beautiful than passion, more binding and enduring.

'You go, David,' I said to him. 'I'll wait a little while and then I'll ride back towards the inn. I don't want any of those people to miss us both.'

He bent his head and for a few moments our lips clung together. Then he mounted his horse and I watched him ride up the hill until he disappeared over the summit. I rode slowly across the fell in the opposite direction to that which the hunt had taken until the mist came down cold and damp and I was glad to leave the moorland and ride towards the lights of the village. It was dusk, a grey dismal dusk, and I decided not to go down to the inn but to ride on home instead. When I arrived, a stableboy came forward to take my horse and wearily I took off my riding hat, shaking out my hair on which the damp had settled. The rooms downstairs were in darkness and I was surprised, knowing how early my grandmother liked to put on the lights. Only the fires blazed. There were no sounds of life from the large rooms at the front of the house and no sounds from the kitchens that the evening meal was in progress. I switched the lights on in the hall and over the staircase thinking that I would have a bath before the rest of them returned, and as I walked up the stairs, I wondered idly where my grandmother had gone. Aunt Dorothy and Serena's mother I could understand. They had probably gone into York or Harrogate to do some shopping, but my grandmother never went to the shops and had absolutely no interest in the hunt meeting. I wondered if she was asleep in her chair in front of the fire, but I had no wish to disturb her, and I made my way along the corridor above, my feet making no sound on the thick carpet.

I felt relaxed after my bath and I occupied my time by manicuring my nails, reading and dozing in the chair. I slept, but for how long I do not know. It was completely dark in my room when I awoke. I fumbled for the light switch so that I could see the clock by the bed. I stared at it in amazement. It was ten o'clock and nobody had come into my room to see if I was in or to tell me that dinner was being served.

I dressed hurriedly, snagging my stockings in my haste but I couldn't bother to change them. I wore the first things my hands encountered, a long black velvet skirt and a soft mohair sweater. After a swift dusting of powder on my face and a bright splash of lipstick, I opened the door and ran down the stairs. The lights still blazed in the hall, but my search of the rooms on either side of it showed me that they were in total darkness. Where was everybody? For the first time, a vague hint of fear seized hold of me.

I was convinced that David had told Serena that they could not marry and now they were all at Edgecombe endeavouring to persuade him to change his mind. My grandmother would waste no opportunity to tell him of my misdemeanours against Serena's sweetness, my pride and her gentleness, my waywardness and Serena's stability. I paced those downstairs rooms like a tigress fearing the unknown. It was only the thought that soon David would come to me that sustained me with any sort of courage.

Midnight came and went and there were many times I went towards the telephone only to turn away. He would come, I thought confidently, he would come before they could get to me and we would face them together, but as the long night wore on my courage deserted me bit by bit. By this time the servants would be in bed, and I was beginning to think it strange that they had not gone into the dining room to lay the dinner table or stoke the fires. It was as though they knew the family would not be returning and that I was probably with them. I wanted to ask, but my pride would not let me, so instead I curled up in a chair after adding logs to the fire.

It was warm in the room but I was shivering, my heart filled with a nameless dread. I poured out a large glass of sherry, more to steady my nerves than anything else, and after a while I must have drifted off to sleep because, when I awoke several hours later, I felt cold and cramped. The fire had gone out and I could have cried out with the pain when I attempted to rise on my stiff and cramped limbs. I stared at the clock on the mantelpiece and my eyes in the mirror registered my surprise. It was almost five o'clock and I knew that he would not come now.

I couldn't believe it. I had been so sure of his love, had never doubted for one moment that he would come. Now I was suddenly seized by such a surge of anger against all those people who had conspired to prevent him from coming that I would willingly have killed any one of them. I had expected my grandmother to be against me, but not Aunt Dorothy, not even Serena when she realized he loved me and not her. How dare they leave me waiting in an empty house without a message of any kind? It was more than cruel, it was torture.

I went to the window and drew back the drapes. It was still dark and the parkland was shrouded with a mist that swirled and drifted, forming obscene shapes that appeared like disoriented wraiths, ghostly enough to have escaped from the nearby churchyard. He would not come now. I would have to wait to see what the morning brought. I went to my room and lay unsleeping in my bed. Once I heard the sighing of a night train speeding through the darkness. The sound of the clock on the cabinet beside my bed seemed unnaturally loud, and miserably I thought to myself that every second was ticking my life away, taking me nearer to what?

Dawn came, cold and damp on that April morning, and gradually the furniture in my room took shape. I made myself deliberately dawdle over my toilet, bathing and playing with my hair, but long before seven o'clock I was

119

dressed in a tweed skirt and sweater and ready to face the day.

I left my room and went downstairs. I could hear sounds in the kitchens which told me that at least there was some form of life in the house. The drawing-room door was open and I could see Agnes busy with the fire but I went towards the morning room. It was there I hoped breakfast would be set but as yet there was no fire there and the table remained unlaid. Making up my mind suddenly I went to the cloak-room and taking a scarf and a warm coat from the rail I let myself out by the side door and set off across the park. It was still misty, but I kept to the paths, walking briskly and trying with all my might to keep my thoughts on ordinary mundane things, but without much success.

I had to find out why the family was absent and why David had not kept his promise, but whether I should telephone or ride over to Edgecombe I didn't know.

As I neared the house, I saw Saunders and one of the stableboys walking towards the stable yard, and when they saw me, Saunders came over to speak to me.

'I don't suppose you'll 'ave much news yet, Miss Kathryn?' he asked quietly.

I stared at him. 'News, Saunders, news about what?'

'Why, Miss Serena.' He was staring at me. 'Do ye mean ye 'aven't 'eard? But ye were out wi' the hunt, Miss Kathryn, didn't ye see it 'appen?'

'I don't know what you're talking about, Saunders. See what happen?'

'She should never a ridden that 'orse, he were too much for 'er. Miss Serena were never an 'orsewoman like you, Miss Kathryn, she never 'ad much practice except when she come 'ere and she'd never set eyes on that 'orse till yesterday. I knew as soon as I saw 'im that 'e were highly strung, 'e should never a bin 'unted. I 'eard Mr David askin 'er to stay behind but the chillun went up front and she would go wi' 'em.'

I was watching him feverishly, wishing he would tell me what had happened to Serena instead of prattling on about the horse, but I didn't speak. Finally, he became aware of my eyes watching him, willing him to stop, and he said, 'I'm sorry, Miss Kathryn. I shouldn't be goin' on like this but I thowt ye knew. Miss Serena came off 'im near 'olbrooks farm. They put 'er on a five-barred gate and took 'er over to Edgecombe. She were unconscious and they thowt the 'orse must a kicked 'er. 'E took off down the field and it took three of 'em to catch 'im and take 'im back. They came 'ere to break the news to 'er mother and the rest of 'em and then they all piled into 't car and went off theer. I thowt ye'd gone wi' 'em, Miss Kathryn.'

'I didn't stay with the hunt, Saunders. You know how I hate it when a fox is sighted. Have they taken Serena into hospital? Is she badly hurt?'

'I know no more than I've told ye but no doubt they'll be back wi' some proper news this mornin'. Mr David were as white as a sheet, he were.'

'If I have any news, Saunders, I'll be sure to let you know.'

He raised his cap and went back towards the stables, shaking his head sorrowfully. I hurried back to the house and went straight to the morning room. There on a side table I found an envelope addressed to me in Aunt Dorothy's writing. I tore it open to find a brief note inside telling me that Serena had had a fall and they were all driving over to Edgecombe. She didn't say if they expected me to follow them, or if they would telephone me later in the evening, but I imagined she would have been in quite a state when she wrote the note. I thought bitterly that I would have saved myself a lot of unnecessary worrying if I had discovered it sooner.

I returned my coat to the cloakroom in the hall and started off up the stairs. My heart was racing in my breast, I could feel it thudding mercilessly, so that by the time I reached my room I was gasping for breath and I knew that it was fear that was taking its toll of me. Serena was hurt and I wondered agonizingly how badly. Would this mean the end to my plans for the future? I didn't want Serena to be badly hurt, I wanted her to be well and strong so that she could face losing David, and I hated myself for the selfish thoughts that prompted my cravings for her well-being.

I sat down in front of my dressing table to regain my breath, and almost immediately there was a light tap on the door. Without waiting for me to call, Bridie came into the room. I would rather have seen anybody but Bridie at that moment, and one look at her sharp, mischievous face made me think suddenly of Ipey's face when she had something entirely poisonous to report.

'So it's 'ere that you are, Miss Kathryn, and not over at Edgecombe, an' 'ere's me thinkin' you'd be over there trying to comfort Mr David over Miss Serena's accident.'

I met her narrow twinkling eyes without flinching.

'I have only just heard of Miss Serena's accident. My aunt would have done better to have left her letter with one of the servants.'

'Oh but she probably thought ye'd know, Miss Kathryn, an' you out wi' the 'unt an' all.'

'Well, I didn't know, and nobody thought fit to telephone me during the evening. I'd like some tea, Bridie. Perhaps you could get me a cup, but I shan't want any breakfast.'

'I suppose you'll be goin' over to Edgecombe. You'll be anxious to know 'ow the poor dearie is farin'. Ah but it's a roight pity it is, an' 'er with all her weddin' plans made. Thet poor Mr David'll be in a roight state, out o' 'is mind I shouldn't wonder, poor lad.'

'She isn't dead, for heaven's sake. Bridie, please get the tea.'

I glared at her balefully and not even Bridie was proof against my anger at that moment. She returned with the tea in minutes and curtly I told her she could leave me to myself.

'What did you do all night on yer own in this great 'ouse, an' you not knowin' what was 'appenin' loike?'

I forced myself to pour out my tea, trying to keep my hands from trembling, aware that she watched me with vindictive humour.

'What does one usually do in a country house when one

122

is alone? I read and listened to the radio and wondered why I was alone.'

'It's a pity neither you nor Mr David was around when it 'appened. There was poor Miss Serena lying on the grass near the fence an' you an' Mr David somewhere off on yer own. It's a good thing Doctor Seaten were there to 'elp 'er.'

'What do you mean, me and Mr David off on our own?'

'Jes' what I sez, Miss Kathryn. I saw ye roide down fro' the top o' Langdale field an' I saw 'im follow ye, neither o' you wi' any thought for Miss Serena up wi' the 'ounds there. An' what will they do now? I asked meself when I 'eard about the accident. He moight think 'e loves 'er but 'e's a gentleman an' gentlemen don't behave loike my tinker did. 'E won't go off into the blue at the soite of a pretty face, 'e'll stay an' do 'is duty, 'e'll put 'onour afore Miss Kathryn, that much I said to meself.'

'Did you, Bridie? And what other significant assumptions did you arrive at while you skulked and snooped up there on the hillside?'

Suddenly the malice seemed to leave her eyes and instead she was looking at me sorrowfully, and in a soothing voice that brought treacherous tears to my eyes she said, 'Eh, lass, must ye make a rod to break yer own back? Fro' the first day ye clapped eyes on 'im I knew this'd 'appen. Ye've got to learn to let 'im go. If ye don't it'll spoil the rest o' yer loife.'

I put my head in my hands and sobbed so that the tears ran between my fingers and on to my sweater.

Clumsily she came to put her arms around me, and her voice was gentle and soothing. 'There, there, lassie, the world's full o' young men who don't belong to anybody else. Why torture yerself over one that does?'

'You don't understand, Bridie, nobody does. I love him, he belongs to me. Why shouldn't we be together? It would be wrong for him to marry Serena when he cares for me.'

'He loved Serena first, though, didn't 'e? If 'e didn't love 'er why did 'e want to marry 'er, answer me that? Oh, sure an' we make mistakes we're sorry for but there be different

123

shades o' lovin'. There be love loike you 'ave for 'im an' 'e for you, 'eady and passionate loike wine, an' there be another love that's gentle an' carin', the sort that grows wi' the years. If ye take this man you'll loike as not break Miss Serena's 'eart. 'Ow are ye goin' to live wi' that then?'

'Doesn't it matter if my heart gets broken, David's too if he loves me?'

'There be other things in loife for ye, luv. Didn't ye say ye wanted to go away an' work at the sort o' thing yer father does? Well, then ye should go. Maybe it's not meant that ye should give it all up for luv. Loife's never loike we think it should be. Why don't you foind the answers to all them questions you've been askin' yerself all these years?'

I lifted my head and stared at her. My eyes searched her face and my hands gripped hers fiercely, willing her to look at me. 'What do you mean, Bridie, what do you know?'

'Nay, lass, I know nothin'. I'm only a poor country girl who's 'ad little or no larnin'. Now drink up yer tea and let me get back to me chores. There be little or no love lost atween me an' cook as it is.'

She gathered together the things on the tray and without looking at me again she shuffled out through the door. There were a thousand questions I wanted to ask her but she would tell me nothing more, she had said too much already. Whatever memories Bridie might have about another time and place, she would keep them to herself. She was a good Catholic in spite of her sharp tongue, which was often levelled at the parish priest and his flock, and whatever her secret thoughts or moments of recall she would not disregard the teachings of her faith.

I restored my tear-stained face to some semblance of normality, then I went to the window to stare out at the day. It had turned dismally wet. A light rain was falling, dripping monotonously from the branches of the trees, collecting in puddles along the paths, a day completely in keeping with my own dismal thoughts. I heard the sound of a car's engine approaching the house and my eyes strained to see through the gloom. Then my heart leaped with excitement. It was David's long powerful tourer that came to a halt in the centre of the courtyard, and I left my room and flew down the stairs to meet him.

I was at the door long before he reached it, and as I opened it, my eyes searched his face for the signs I wanted to see but his face was severe, stern almost. I stepped back to allow him to enter the house.

'Oh, David,' I murmured, 'thank heaven you've come. I've been so miserable, I didn't know about Serena until this morning.'

'We must talk, Kathryn. Are you alone?'

'Yes. We'll go into the drawing room, there's a fire in there and the day's so cold.'

David was wearing a white trenchcoat which I took from him to place in the cloakroom, then together we walked into the room. A glowing fire burned in the grate and the room looked lived in and cheerful. Stiltedly I asked him, 'Can I get you a drink or anything or would you prefer tea?'

'Nothing, thank you, Kathryn. I said I wouldn't be long.'

'They know you've come here?'

'Yes. I told them I would drive over with the news. Your aunt left you a letter.'

'I know, but I didn't find it until this morning.'

'Then you didn't know last night, you didn't know that they were all over at Edgecombe?'

'No, I sat in here all night waiting for somebody to tell me something, waiting for you to come to me.'

He sat down on the couch with his head in his hands and I stood watching him, willing him to come to the point quickly so that I would know one way or another what I must do. Somehow I seemed to have discovered a strange sort of courage, a fatalistic courage that would make me accept what I could not change, and as his eyes at last met mine and he rose to his feet and came towards me, I looked at him bravely. I wanted the truth, without subterfuge, without any glossing over of the hurt if hurt it was going to be, and reading the message in my eyes, he said simply, 'I haven't been able to tell her, Kathryn.'

'She was badly hurt, wasn't she?'

'We don't know yet. She is suffering from concussion, and

until she regains consciousness we can't be sure. You do understand, don't you, Kathryn? We shall have to wait a little longer.'

'I understand.'

Was that really me saying that I understood? Looking into his eyes which seemed so grave and impersonal I found myself asking silently if he might find it easier to break my heart than Serena's. I felt at that moment that I was two people: I was a woman who was hating him because he didn't love me enough to put me before everything, Serena, honour, family, and I was a different woman telling him that I understood, that he must explain to all of them waiting at Edgecombe that I was sorry, that in the morning I would ride over to see Serena. I felt I was prattling on, oblivious to either pain or resentment, but wanting him to go, desperately wanting him to go.

'I expect your aunt and your grandmother will return here tomorrow. There is nothing they can do at Edgecombe and Serena may have to go into hospital until she is fully recovered.'

'Of course.'

'Are you able to be alone in this house, Kathryn, or shall I ask your aunt to return here this evening?'

'I'm perfectly all right, David, I was here alone last night and there are the servants.'

'You'll promise to telephone if you are nervous.'

'I shan't be. Goodbye, David.'

I didn't wait to watch him drive away, instead I went straight to my room and stood looking out into the wet gloom. I wanted to die. The years that stretched ahead of me seemed empty and futile. It was as if my life until then had been waiting for something momentous to happen and now I could no longer think that David and I would have a future together. I left the window and went to sit at my dressing table, automatically playing with the objects lying on top. I stared at my reflection, at eyes that were dark with pain and lips that trembled proudly, then resolutely I raised my head and squared my shoulders. This time I would not die, I would live, I told myself fiercely. I would live and fill my days with so many things that there would be no time to think about David or what might have been. Once, centuries ago, I had asked the amulet for the life of Asnefer but instead it had cost me my life. I had not asked for Serena's life but the man I loved was as far away from me as he had ever been.

I knew what I had to do. I would go to Egypt where, please God, I would find the answers to so many haunting and bitter questions.

Edgecombe was a sad house when I visited it the next morning. Serena's mother greeted me with a sad face, and the telltale signs of tears still lingered on Aunt Dorothy's cheeks. My grandmother sat in a straight-backed chair, severe and enigmatic, receiving the kiss I bestowed on her cheek without recognition of any kind.

'David told us you hadn't seen my letter,' Aunt Dorothy said. 'I should have telephoned you but we were all so upset I don't think any one of us thought about it.'

'It doesn't matter, Aunt Dorothy. How is Serena?'

'Still unconscious, I'm afraid, but the doctor says the depth of the coma is not as great as it was yesterday. They are taking her into hospital in York this afternoon.'

'May I see her before she goes?'

'I'll go with you now but, like I said, she won't know you are there. There is a nurse with her.'

Together we walked up the shallow staircase leading to the bedrooms and entered a room at the end of the first corridor. It was a large, beautifully proportioned room, and a nurse sat close to the bed where Serena lay straight and slender under the coverlets. Her face was as pale as the pillow under her head and she hardly seemed to be breathing.

'May I be left alone with her for a few moments?' I asked my aunt.

She nodded and, motioning to the nurse, they both went outside.

I knelt on the floor beside the bed and I began to cry.

127

The tears rolled down my cheeks on to the bedspread. The tears were good for me, coming as a blessed relief after being bottled up for most of the night. I took Serena's hand in mind, such a thin white hand, almost like that of a child, and through a haze of tears I looked at her face. She seemed so peaceful, and she was beautiful, like a marble statue, so that the softness of her hand seemed strange. There was a blue bruise at the side of her head and I wondered if she had received it in falling or if the horse had kicked her. I began to talk to her even though I knew she couldn't hear me, and I asked her to forgive me for every mean and sharp word I had ever said to her, and for my envy because she was going to marry David. I asked her to love him as I would have loved him, but I knew even then that she would love him better, less tempestuously, less demandingly.

My aunt and the nurse came back into the room and I struggled to regain my composure before I faced them.

'You should go now,' the nurse said kindly. 'There isn't much point in any of you waiting here. The doctor will be here shortly and if there is any change I'll be sure to let you know.'

I smiled at her and thanked her for allowing me to see Serena, then together my aunt and I left the room.

'What are you doing now, Kathryn? Did you ride over or bring the car?'

'I rode over. I'm going to see my godfather this afternoon.'

'Of course you should, there's nothing you can do here. I expect we shall be back at Random Edge when you arrive home. David will be sorry he's missed you, he's out in the park somewhere.'

I kissed her briefly on her cheek, then left the house and ran to where Demetrius was champing the grass at the edge of the path. I knew where I would find David, and resolutely I set Demetrius off at a brisk canter towards the copse.

He was standing morosely looking down into the stream but he turned and looked up as I rode through the trees. I made no effort to dismount but rode straight up to him. I felt safer on my horse. I didn't want him to touch me. If he did I would be lost, all my courage and resolve meaningless.

128

As we stared into each other's eyes, I was reliving that other time when I stared into the eyes of the ancient David and knew that it was over, the love and the longing, the passion that had united us and the conventions that divided us.

'You have seen Serena?' he asked calmly.

'Yes.'

'And you see that we must wait, Kathryn?'

'I see that we are not meant to be together. Please, David, don't say anything now. Help me to do what I must. Don't you see we're not meant for each other, that we never were? What kind of happiness could we ever have had after breaking Serena's heart? And it would have been broken, she loves you so much.'

'But what about us? Are you telling me that we never loved one another?'

'No, but there's so much more I could tell you which I know you'd never understand. You'll love Serena again after I've gone away, and probably in time you'll come to see that she's so much better than I am. She's a much finer person, David, and she needs you so very much.'

'You're going away? Where?' he asked sharply.

'I'm going to work in Egypt. It's what I've always wanted to do. I'm going to ask my godfather if he can find me a place at some excavation there.'

'You mean you're not prepared to wait?'

'Oh, David. I'd wait ten thousand years if I felt it would work out but I know it won't, but think that if you must.'

He stepped forward and took the bridle and for a moment panic seized me when I thought he was going to lift me bodily down from my horse, then reluctantly he let go of the reins and stepped back. His face was cold, and with a sob in my throat I pulled Demetrius round and rode across the fields as though Set himself pursued me.

I told my godfather everything of the last few weeks and he listened to me without interruption, his face kind. I could not have told my father any of the things I told him as I sat curled up in a deep armchair with the firelight dancing

129

in the grate between us and the daylight dying outside the room.

'What do you intend to do now?' he asked quietly.

'Will you be able to help me? I want to get away quickly and I must go to Egypt, you do see that, don't you? I shall have trouble with my grandmother and possibly Aunt Dorothy, but I can't bear to hang about waiting. Now that fate has decided things for me, I must go out there as soon as possible. Is there any way you can help me, please?'

'I've promised to send Dalton one of my students. I didn't think of you, Kathryn, I thought your father'd make you change your mind, but you're quite knowledgeable enough. I'm just wondering how you'd get along with Dalton.'

'I don't care how he treats me, it's not important.'

'It is important, my dear. You'll be the only girl among four or five men. Most of them are dedicated to their job and will treat you like one of themselves, but Dalton never got on with your father. Any little mistake on your part, any clash of wills and you could be the loser.'

'I'll be meek as a lamb, I won't give him cause to dislike me, but I must go there, I must.'

He looked at me without speaking and I could see that he was weighing the pros and cons of my going carefully in his mind. Then he spoke briskly. 'I'll write to Dalton and tell him who you are. He might enjoy having Alex's daughter to order about. You'll have no trouble with the others.'

'Do you know them all?'

'Very well. One of them, Mike O'Hara, was a pupil of mine, one of the best I ever had. Reading hieroglyphics was child's play to him. He's never said as much but I don't think he has a lot of time for Dalton. He could be a good friend to you, Kathryn.'

'I'll meet each day and each person as they come. I feel at the moment that I never want to form an association again, either friendship or anything deeper. May I keep the talisman, Uncle Mark?'

'Of course, that is why I gave it to you.'

'I want to find John Strickland and Ahmed Sadek. I have so many questions to ask about the amulet.'

'I doubt if you'll find Strickland and I doubt if he'd talk to you even if you did. Sadek was working at Sakkara the last time I heard but by this time he could be anywhere. Do you think either of them could tell you more than you already know?'

'I don't know, but if I'm in Egypt I could try to find out.'

' "Sufficient unto the day is the evil thereof", Kathryn. I've often thought they were the truest words I ever read.'

'Perhaps, but what if that evil goes on and on?'

'I can see that your mind is made up. I'll write to Dalton tonight and as soon as I hear from him, I'll get in touch. How about your passport? Do you have one?'

'Yes, and I've kept it up to date. Shall I have to have injections of some sort?'

'Yes, but all that can be gone into when we have Dalton's acceptance. I shouldn't say anything to them at Random Edge until you know something definite.'

Fortunately I was not often in their thoughts, all their attention being given to Serena. She was recovering in hospital, and in spite of three broken ribs and a broken ankle, the sparkle had come back into her eyes and the concussion which had affected her memory was less severe. David was back at work and I did not meet him again before I left.

Only one thing sustained me during the days and weeks that followed and that was the letter I received from my father. It was a letter of reproach that I had chosen Egypt instead of joining him in China, and in it he reaffirmed his belief that Egypt had no longer anything to stir the imagination. However, he contained his bitterness long enough to wish me well in my new venture and he sent me his love.

Eight

It was a day of snow and high winds when I finally left England for the sunnier land of Egypt. I took the overland route across France, joining a ship at Marseilles bound for Alexandria and the Far East, and as we neared Alexandria, I stood with my eyes peering into the distance for the first sight of land. I went on quickly to Cairo, where I had a few days for sightseeing. Professor Dalton had informed my godfather that I should take the early train out of Cairo on the fourth day and he would arrange for me to be met at the railway station in Luxor; after that it was a short trip across the river, and another by car to the site somewhere in the Theban hills.

I could find little to convince me that I was actually in Egypt at last. Cairo was dusty and overpopulated: the modern part could have been that of any capital city, and the native part reminded me of the *Arabian Nights*, the Mamelukes and Caliphs. It was a city where tall, supercilious camels rubbed shoulders with dainty pattering donkeys ridden by men whose feet almost touched the ground. It was a city of proud Arab horses ridden by fierce-eyed men from the desert, a city of mosques and minarets, of decorated domes and fairytale elegance, of white stucco and brown *meshrebiyah* windows, a city of the thousand and one nights. Over it all was the potent, poignant scent of the Orient, the perfume of many spices, of myrrh and jasmine, but in me I sensed a deep disappointment at this city where so many races of both East and West mingled. I could have wept that her streets did not ring with the sound of chariot

132

wheels on stone and that the cries of the *muezzin* from his minaret had superseded the chanting of white-robed priests in lofty-pillared temples, but then gazing across the rooftops from my balcony overlooking the Nile, I became aware for the first time of three great pyramids standing at the edge of the desert, desolate and lonely, and instead of tears came an excitement greater than any I had ever known.

My godfather had insisted that I should stay at Shepheard's for the few days I intended to remain in Cairo, particularly as I was travelling alone. I was glad that I had followed his advice. The hotel was within easy walking distance of the museum and it was there I spent my first afternoon gazing rapturously at the things that had been discovered in the tomb of the young Pharaoh Tutankhamun. There was so much gold it became unreal, but I loved the jewelled crowns of two princesses that had been found and the many jewelled amulets and bracelets in the glass cases.

I was still wandering round the great halls when the bell sounded to tell visitors they should leave. I did not enter the room containing the royal mummies although there were a great many who did. I had no wish to gaze on the faces of long-dead monarchs and I was afraid of finding among them the face of one I had known. As I walked back to the hotel through the city streets I wondered what I would do if I entered one of those tombs cut deep into the rock in the Valley of the Kings, and if I would remember the day when, as Princess Tuia, I had followed my father on his last journey into the corridors of the blessed. I prayed that I would not make a fool of myself and earn the displeasure of Professor Dalton.

Immediately after breakfast the next morning I went to the hotel desk to order a taxi to take me up to the pyramids. There was a middle-aged gentleman making similar inquiries, an Englishman who, on better acquaintance, told me he was a retired Indian Army officer, and the outcome was that we agreed to share the taxi.

The route to the pyramids led along a broad avenue lined with villas, hotels and the zoological gardens, an avenue

133

that eventually led to the desert and the plateau on which the pyramids had been built. From the road they appeared suddenly over the rooftops, which robbed them of their height and something of their majesty, but at the base of the plateau my companion said, 'I think we should leave the taxi here. You will get a much better impression of their grandeur if you ride up to them slowly, so I suggest we either take a camel or a horse.'

I looked down at my skirt in some dismay and he nodded his head. 'I see what you mean. In that case I suggest we take camels. You sit on his back and put your leg round that little stump. It's rather like sitting side-saddle. I suppose you've done that at one time or another.'

I enjoyed my first camel ride. It was a far smoother experience than learning to ride a horse. The animal's great splodgy feet made little or no undulating impact on the road and the only thing I found difficult at first was controlling his head at the end of his long snakelike neck. He was not a very amiable beast, and hated anything or anybody to get in his way. On one occasion, the major's camel stepped in front of us, whereupon Napoleon, for that was my camel's name, stretched out his long neck and sank his teeth into the major's beast so that he shot forward without the slightest warning and the major had to cling tightly to the reins for several minutes before he was able to control him. The Arab running alongside us was highly amused. Evidently the same thing had happened a great many times, but I was glad I was managing to control my animal without too much trouble.

The major had been right. The view of the Sphinx and the pyramids as we approached them slowly was too magnificent to have been missed. These mountains, made out of stone by human hands, their dimensions perfect to the merest fraction of an inch, were quite rightly one of the wonders of the world. They soared heavenwards, great blocks of stone that had once been faced with smooth limestone, their peaks shining with electrum, built to house the remains of three kings of the Old Kingdom, pharaohs of unlimited wealth, power, and egotism.

My companion had entered the pyramid of Khephren but had been unable to persuade me to accompany him. I preferred to stay outside in the sunlight with the sweet, clean air of the desert all around me and the towers and domes and minarets of Cairo below me in the distance. From here I could see the Nile twisting and turning through lush fields of emerald green before the fields gave way to golden sand, and farther away I could see other pyramids, Sakkara and Abusir and Dashur. As I walked my camel slowly round the base of the second pyramid I was gripped by such a feeling of excitement that I urged him on, riding him so fast that we left the camel driver far behind. When at last he caught up with us where we waited for him, high on a ridge over-looking the desert, he was beaming from ear to ear.

'My lady ride camel good,' he said. 'You come again tomorrow, ride Napoleon again.'

'I'm afraid not. Tomorrow I must go to Sakkara.'

'I too can go to Sakkara, lady can ride camel round Sakkara.'

'No, tomorrow I must take a horse and I shan't have much time. I have someone to meet there.'

'I have nephew, him good boy, he has nice horse for lady to ride, very nice horse, most beautiful Arab horse.'

'Where does your nephew live?'

'At Hawamdieh. I tell him to meet most beautiful lady on West Bank, he will be there with horse, you see. His name is Ishmail and horse's name Emir. Nephew very well off, had good education, speak many languages. He no need to work for living, his father owns much land, but he like to lend horse to lady and practise his English.'

'How shall I know that your nephew will agree to meet me?'

'I tell him tonight, he be there, near ferry on West Bank. On the tomb of the Prophet and the word of Allah I swear it.'

'Very well, I shall wait for him on the West Bank opposite Hawamdieh at nine o'clock. I will wait ten minutes only. If he does not come then I shall look for another horse.'

'If Ishmail not come I find some other who will take you.

I arrange only good horse. You ride horse like you ride camel?'

'Rather better, I hope.'

He beamed again. 'We go back now, my lady. Gentleman will have left pyramid and be looking for us.'

I turned Napoleon round but we had not gone far when we saw the major on his way towards us.

'I'm jolly glad you didn't go in there, my girl – it's dark and narrow and at one place we had to get down on all fours and climb up a steep incline. Besides, there are bats down there, nasty furry smelly little things.'

'That's one reason why I cried off,' I said. 'Is there much to see?'

'Two big chambers with great stone sarcophagi in them, but there's no evidence that the pharaoh was ever buried in the pyramid. In any case, I expect it was robbed in antiquity. Fancy doing the museum in the morning?'

'I'm sorry, I have to go to Sakkara in the morning and I spent most of yesterday at the museum. You should go, there are some wonderful exhibits.'

'Oh yes, I'll go, but I'm sorry you can't come with me.'

I had no definite arrangement to meet Ahmed Sadek but I didn't want the major with me at Sakkara. I guessed that he was lonely. He was a widower returning home to England after service with his regiment in the Punjab and I felt sorry that I could only offer to be his companion for a brief afternoon.

Descending from our camels at the bottom of the plateau, we bade our smiling camel driver farewell, after he again reassured me that I could depend on Ishmail to accompany me to Sakkara.

On reaching the desk at the hotel to pick up my keys, I was informed that I had had a message – a telephone number to ring at Luxor. The number was that of the Winter Palace Hotel and I was to ask for a Mr Mike O'Hara.

It took only a few minutes to find him and his first words took me by surprise.

'You've had a reprieve, Miss St Clare,' said a deep, rather musical voice. 'Professor Dalton's had to go off to another

site and he'll be away from here for two weeks. I suppose
you were coming by train?'

'Yes, the day after tomorrow.'

'Is this your first visit to Egypt?'

'Yes.'

'Instead of the train, why not take one of the river boats?
You'll see a great deal more, get acclimatized and arrive
in Luxor in a week's time. Your hotel will make all the
arrangements and one of us will meet you on your arrival
if you can let us know the day and time.'

'But are you sure the professor won't mind my doing
this?'

'He's not going to know, is he? And we can manage
without you until then.'

'I should like to do the journey by boat, I would see so
much more.'

'Well, why don't you? You'll not be putting anybody out,
we are constantly in Luxor for supplies. I shall probably be
the one to meet you.'

'Thank you, Mr O'Hara, you're very kind.'

A whole week on the river watching the pattern of Egyptian life pass by. The thought of it filled me with delight,
and inwardly I blessed Mike O'Hara for thinking about it.

I left Shepheard's in a taxi the following morning heading
for the West Bank where I hoped to find Ishmail waiting
for me. A raft of sorts plied across the river bringing men
and women and even animals from Hawamdieh, and the
driver stopped the taxi quite close to the ferry point. A
crowd of young men squatted on the floor playing some
game with small counters, and to my relief I could see that
a group of horses, camels and donkeys stood close by. I paid
the taxi driver what I owed him, and almost before I had
closed the door of the taxi a young man stepped forward,
saying, 'I recognize you anywhere, my lady. My uncle, he
say most beautiful English lady he had ever seen wish for
me to take her to Sakkara. I am Ishmail.'

I shook hands with him. He was a most presentable young

137

man, wearing European dress apart from the burnous round his dark curly hair.

'You wise to go to Sakkara early,' he said smiling. 'Later too many tourists and too hot. This is Emir, he very good horse, thoroughbred.'

My eyes lit up at the sight of him. There is nothing quite so beautiful as an Arab stallion and this one was no exception. He was milky white and he looked at me out of liquid brown eyes sheltered by enormous long lashes. I allowed Ishmail to lift me lightly into the saddle, adorned with princely trappings. He mounted another horse, equally beautiful, and I was amused at the way he allowed her to prance and cavort, well aware that they made an enchanting spectacle.

'How long you in Cairo?' he asked as we rode along side by side.

'Only three more days, I regret to say.'

'You go home then?'

'No, I am going to Luxor. I have come here to work.'

'You not look like lady who works. At what do you work?'

'I am going as an assistant to Professor Dalton at Thebes.'

'You Egyptologist then?'

'I hope to be.'

'My uncle say you go to Sakkara to meet someone, your lover?'

I laughed. I might have known Ishmail's poetic, romantic mind would think it was a lover I was going to meet. 'No, Ishmail,' I said smiling, 'I am not going to meet a lover. I am going to meet Mr Ahmed Sadek, I hope.'

'You hope! He does not know that you go to meet him?'

'No. We have never met but I hope to find him at Sakkara. Do you know him, Ishmail?'

'Oh yes, I know Mr Sadek well. He very good Egyptologist, as good as your Dalton man. He now director of Cairo museum.'

'I'm very glad to hear it. It is nice to have an Egyptian on the board of directors. How well do you know him?'

'I lend him my horses. He knows my father.'

'Then when we get to Sakkara you will be able to take me to him?'

'Of course.' His young, good-looking face split into a smile. 'You will light up his day, my lady, you will make him forget all those old dusty mummies. He will find you as sweet to the nostrils as honeysuckle.'

I laughed again. 'Oh, Ishmail, I was listening to flattery like yours when I was just a little girl.'

He laughed with me, and then as we came to the end of the dusty, narrow street, if one could call it a street, he pointed ahead to where another pyramid rose in giant steps from the sand. 'See, my lady, the pyramid of Zoser. Now we are at Sakkara.'

We rode across the sand until we stood beneath the Step Pyramid, gazing up into the brassy blue of the sky.

'Oldest building in the world, this pyramid,' Ishmail was telling me. 'Older than the pyramids of Giza, older even than the Sphinx.' I looked upwards and all around me. I had the weirdest feeling that I had seen this pyramid before, but in the days when the desolation of the desert was hidden by temple buildings and gardens, when lotus blossoms floated on a calm blue pond, and peacocks walked across the lawns instead of noisy donkey boys and their animals.

As we rode across the sand, uneven with rocks and stones that had once formed parts of buildings, Ishmail pointed out to me other things he thought I should see. 'That is pyramid of Unas, not so grand as Step Pyramid, not made so well, and there are tombs here, my lady, marvellous tombs showing nobles hunting in the river and dancing girls, many dancing girls.'

'Yes, I have read about them, I hope to see them for myself one day.'

'You go to Thebes, you see other, bigger tombs. Pharaohs' tombs. Once this very great country, great empire, you know that?'

'Yes, Ishmail, I know.'

'Once Egypt owned all Palestine, all Libya, other countries a long way from Egypt. Mighty pharaohs fought great wars, brought home much treasure. You will see this history

139

on the temples and tombs in Thebes. Perhaps one day Egypt will be like that again.'

'I hope so, Ishmail, I hope so very much.'

He smiled, well satisfied, and for a while we walked on in silence. We had come to a long colonnade where we were stopped by a young archaeologist who came towards us, holding up his hand. 'I'm sorry, madame, but you can come no further. Excavation work is going on here.'

'I am hoping to find Mr Ahmed Sadek. Can you tell me if he is working here?'

'Yes, he is over on the south wall, but I believe he is very busy right now.'

'I have only three days in Cairo before I go south to join Professor Dalton. It is imperative that I see him.'

Something of my urgency must have shown on my face because he said, 'I will take you to him, madame. Perhaps you would remain here with the horses,' he added to Ishmail.

I dismounted and after a brief smile in Ishmail's direction, answered by a fatalistic shrug of his shoulders, I followed my guide along the colonnade where native workmen and Europeans were busy digging in the sand. At last we came to a square chamber where a tall man wearing a red tarboosh stood in the midst of a crowd of young men who listened while he pointed out carvings on the wall. My guide approached him, said a few words, and they both looked in my direction. The tall man was too far away for me to see the expression on his face, but from his hesitancy I did not think he was pleased at the interruption. However, he came towards me and as he got nearer I could see that he was frowning. Somewhat uncertainly I went forward to meet him.

'Mr Sadek?' I inquired briefly.

He nodded curtly.

'I'm sorry to interrupt your work but it is important that I speak to you. My name is Kathryn St Clare. I am Professor Ensor's goddaughter.'

The frown became slightly less pronounced, and taking my hand he bowed over it gravely.

140

'You have a message for me from Professor Ensor?' he asked.

'No, but he knows I intended to find you. Can you tell me if it will also be possible to speak to Mr Strickland before I leave Cairo?'

He stared at me in some surprise. 'Strickland! I very much doubt it, Miss St Clare. He is not well, I doubt if he will see anyone.'

'But you know where he is?'

'I do, but he wants no visitors. He would not thank me for taking you to him.'

'Is he in Cairo?'

'He is near Cairo. Why are you so anxious to see him?'

'I badly want to talk to you both. Professor Ensor brought home an amulet you had discovered in a tomb somewhere in the Theban hills. This amulet is very important to me.'

His stare became more intense.

'I am sure there is nothing we can tell you that the professor has not already told you. You found the amulet of interest, then?'

'Yes. I have it here.'

I hunted in my bag and brought out the amulet wrapped in thin tissue paper. When I held it out to him, he seemed reluctant to take it.

'You are superstitious about the amulet, Mr Sadek?'

'Superstitious, no, but it is like no other I have seen, and I have reason to believe that it was because of that amulet that the priest was buried alive.'

'It is the talisman of Set, is it not?'

'Yes, the god of evil, the lord of the underworld. You have studied Egyptology, Miss St Clare?'

'Yes, but I have still a great deal to learn.'

'St Clare? Your father is not Alexander St Clare, by any chance?'

'Yes, do you know him?'

'I have met him several times. I would have thought your interest would be centred round his work in China rather than in Egypt.'

'I have no desire to work in China. Mr Sadek, I don't

141

know how much Professor Ensor told you, but speaking to Mr Strickland and yourself is so very important to me. I can honestly say that, at this moment, it is the most important thing in my life. If you will take me to him, I promise not to be a nuisance if he is ill, but all I ask is that you give me that chance.'

He stared at me searchingly for several minutes before he replied. Then, as if making up his mind suddenly, he said, 'Where are you staying in Cairo?'

'I am at Shepheard's.'

'I will go there at nine o'clock this evening and will look for you in the residents' lounge. If it is as important as all that, Miss St Clare, perhaps you will be there.'

'You can depend upon it, Mr Sadek.'

He bowed, and wishing me good morning he strode back to his waiting pupils.

I had little appetite for my evening meal and promptly at a quarter to nine I was sitting opposite the door in the residents' lounge in a position where I could see everybody who came. I had not been there many minutes when the major entered with his newspaper, and made a beeline for me.

'All alone I see,' he said brightly.

'But not for long. I am expecting a friend,' I said, hoping he would take the hint and find another table.

'Oh, I see. Well, sorry, m'dear, I'll sit over there, don't want to be a spoilsport,' he said, laughing heartily.

Promptly at nine o'clock Ahmed Sadek strode into the lounge and came over to my table.

He was a striking man in his European clothes and bright red tarboosh and a great many eyes were trained upon him as he crossed the room. He was very tall and slender, and he walked with a quiet catlike grace.

'Allow me to tell you what I propose we should do,' he said, as soon as we had exchanged greetings. 'I know where John Strickland is but he may refuse to see you. I try to see him once every week if that is possible, to make sure he has food and fuel and decent clothing. Sometimes he will not

142

open the door and I know that the demon which pursues him night and day has overcome him. Another night he may receive me almost like his former self. We shall not know until we arrive at his door whether we face the John Strickland I know or the demon that drives him to destruction.'

'My godfather told me that he drank too much, that it had been his downfall for a great many years.'

'Yes, that is so. We each have our own private demons that drive us mercilessly on, and drink is John Strickland's demon. With some it is women, with others drugs, with some it is gambling, and with others it is fear of the unknown. I wonder which has been your particular demon, Miss St Clare?'

'Perhaps after this evening I shall be able to tell you.'

'Perhaps. With me it is work. I must sift and probe and, now and again, as with that amulet, I go too far and it would have been better if I had never begun.'

'Have we far to go?'

'Not too far, but it is outside the city walls. I have a car waiting outside. We shall journey through the old part of Cairo, which I don't suppose you have visited yet.'

'No, but I'm sure I shall find it very interesting.'

'It is interesting, but it is a beauty shadowed by great poverty. In that part of the city are beautiful mosques and buildings, sad deserted gardens and narrow twisting streets where the goldsmith and the silversmith ply their trades. You could not go there alone, which is a pity for that is the real Cairo, not this pseudo-modern city with its European hotels and fashionable shops. The Cairo we shall see tonight is the way it was in medieval times, when the banners of Saladin swept under the archways beyond the citadel, when the sultans and the caliphs held court in her palaces.'

'Cairo is an Arab city, Mr Sadek. I have been to Baghdad and to Basra, I recognize those two cities in Cairo but I have not as yet found Egypt.'

'You will find Egypt on the river, at Abydos and Dendera, at Thebes and Abu Simbel. Come, we must go.'

A chauffeur-driven car waited for us outside the hotel and

Sadek took his seat next to me. We spoke little during our drive through the modern city, and it was only when we drove through the great arched walls and into the old part of the city that he began to point out things to me. Mosques and palaces, narrow twisting streets where craftsmen worked at their trades in holes cut into the wall, lit by flickering lamplight. How I would have loved to have left the shelter of the car to explore those dark winding alleyways! Great bowls, filled with all the spices of the Orient, stood side by side on the pavement, and fruit and sweetmeat stalls were open to the night sky.

I exclaimed with delight at the sight of a water carrier and another selling sherbet, and again at an old man surrounded by a crowd who stood entranced as they listened to the story he was telling them.

'I suppose there is a fortune teller as well,' I said. 'How can it be possible to read someone's fortune in a few grains of sand?'

He smiled, showing white even teeth in his dark face. 'The sand is unimportant, but the man himself is no doubt a student of human nature. He knows that a young girl desires news of a lover, a young matron hopes for a child, and old people a fortune in their old age.'

'Then he deceives us.'

'I'm afraid so.'

We laughed together in the darkness of the car. I suddenly realized that here the streets were less well populated and considerably darker.

'We are outside the city walls now,' he said. 'In a little while we must leave the car and walk. There is no traffic in the streets which we must tread.'

'He lives here in this dark silent place?'

'No. We must walk some little way.'

He tapped on the glass that separated us from the driver and the car drew to a halt. As I stepped down from it I was more than grateful for the full moon which turned even this desolate place into something approaching normality. There were no lamps along the deserted streets and no lights from the windows of the houses. Only a weird uncanny silence

144

prevailed so that the sound of our feet on the cobblestones seemed unnaturally loud.

'Where are we?' I whispered, glad of his arm beneath my elbow.

'This is the City of the Dead. You have never heard of it?'

'Yes.' I had read of it but I had never expected to find myself walking its streets in search of an Englishman and, dismayed, I asked, 'Surely Mr Strickland cannot live here?'

'I am very much afraid that he does live here.'

I cannot describe the streets and buildings we passed. Decrepit houses lining long dismal streets, unlit and empty, where the wind moaned mournfully stirring the dust that had settled over the centuries. I started with a cry in my throat at the strange howls that came from a side street and my companion held my arm closer.

'Are they dogs?' I asked him fearfully.

'Pariah dogs perhaps, or jackals. Come, they will not harm you.'

'There are no lights in any of the houses.'

'Of course not. They are tombs.'

In spite of the comfort of his arm I was desperately afraid of the loneliness and the silence, of the sense of decay and corruption. Still we walked on and I asked him anxiously, 'Why don't the police patrol these streets?'

'They do when they are looking for vagrants and evildoers. You need not worry, I would not come down these streets unarmed.'

I stared at him with wide frightened eyes but he seemed unconcerned, and I swallowed hard to disguise my terror.

We came at last to a still more narrow street leading off the one we had walked down from the car, and he whispered, 'We are nearly there.'

Only a little way along this street he paused and I could see a pale flickering light shining through the cracks in a door.

'Stand behind me,' he whispered, 'I don't want him to see you until I am sure he will receive you.'

I did as he asked, waiting with chattering teeth as he

rapped on the door. There was no immediate reply and he knocked again, more urgently this time. 'Strickland,' he said, 'Open the door, it is Sadek here.'

I heard shuffling footsteps and then the sound of bolts being drawn back. A chink of light appeared in the doorway, then the door was opened wider and I gasped at the spectacle of the man facing us. He was unkempt, his hair reaching his shoulders, and there was several weeks' growth of beard on his face. He peered at us out of glazed bloodshot eyes, and when he saw me, he started back with a muttered curse, but Sadek put his foot in the door to prevent him from closing it.

'John, this is Mark Ensor's goddaughter. Will you talk to her?'

'No, no,' he muttered. Then he started to cry, and the sound of his sobbing distressed me even more than his appearance had done.

'Please, Mr Sadek, it doesn't matter,' I said urgently. 'I can see he is in no fit state to talk to anybody.'

Turning back towards the doorway, he said, 'You have sufficient food, John?'

Strickland nodded, and when he attempted to close the door this time, my companion made no effort to prevent him.

'Come,' he said to me, 'we must go back, we can do no good here.'

We made our way back the way we had come and I was very glad to see the car waiting for us across the deserted street. I was trembling and Sadek's concerned gaze brought the hot tears to my eyes. He allowed me to cry in the corner of the car without attempting to console me. By the time we reached the hotel, I was reasonably composed and he said softly, 'You must have a warm drink before you retire for the night, and try not to think of what you have just seen.'

'You are asking an impossibility, Mr Sadek. I shall remember what I have just seen for the rest of my life. Please come into the hotel with me, please, there are so many questions I need to ask.'

146

I had no idea of the time, and consulting his watch he said, 'It is very late. Are you sure you want to ask those questions tonight?'

'Yes, I am.'

'Very well then, we will have coffee and you shall ask your questions, but I warn you my answers will not erase the memory of what you have seen tonight.'

How normal and comfortable the hotel lounge seemed after the trauma of our visit to the City of the Dead! We sat opposite each other with a small marble-topped table between us on which a tray containing Turkish coffee had been set. I watched Sadek's slender tanned hands pour out the coffee. He handed a cup to me and urged me to drink it at once, and the hot sticky confection warmed me and brought colour into my pale face.

'Now,' he said leaning forward a little. 'Ask your questions, Miss St Clare, and I will try to answer them.'

'Tell me a little about the place we visited tonight.'

'At one period in the Middle Ages, a terrible plague afflicted Cairo so that its inhabitants died by the thousands, and as the corpses were too numerous to be carted to cemeteries, people were buried in the houses in which they had died. The ravages of the plague were so severe in the part of the city where we were tonight that it was entirely deserted by the living and henceforth became known as the City of the Dead. Later, a new city rose between the citadel on the east and the Nile where it flows past the island of Gezira on the west, and this now is the heart of modern Cairo.

'After the plague had passed, the richest citizens who had survived found that they had two houses, one in the new city and one in the City of the Dead, so the practice arose of using the City of the Dead as a cemetery. More bodies were buried beside the victims of the plague in the old family mansions there until the custom became such a well-established one that the government decreed that every Muslim family in Cairo must own a burial house in that quarter.

'It is now suburbs which stretch away into the desert, the queerest suburbs imaginable since a present-day purchaser

147

of a site need do no more than lay the foundations of a house and build an outer wall about three feet high. The result is acres and acres of land covered by long, straight streets intersecting each other every few hundred yards and composed of thousands of partially built houses differing only in their state of completion and design.

'It is a grim and desolate place even by day as no one ever goes there except funeral processions and an occasional sightseer – apart from one night in the year when the surviving members of each family occupy their house and spend the night in prayer for the departed.'

'What would we have found behind the façade of those houses?'

'Arab tombs, nothing more.'

'And Mr Strickland lives in a house that is also a tomb?'

'That does not worry him. He has spent his life working in tombs, ancient Egyptian tombs which are, of course, palatial in comparison, but where else would he live while he is possessed of his demon drink? If he lived in the old city at any one of a hundred cheap lodging houses, he would no doubt be robbed, perhaps even murdered for the few things of value he possesses, and none of the European hotels such as this one would admit him for a moment in his present state.

'He has lived in my house from time to time, and when he is sober he is an intelligent, delightful companion, but at those other times, he is worse than any animal, he is a disgusting sight.'

'His pride was hurt tonight. I wish with all my heart that we had never gone,' I said unhappily.

'Yes, it is unfortunate that we saw him on one of his more terrible days. I fear it is too late for John Strickland. His demon has pursued him for too many years and now it has almost destroyed him.'

'Do you believe that the mummy of the priest you found in the Theban hills had any effect upon him?'

'Yes, I am sure it had. Strickland is a strangely sensitive man, something of a mystic perhaps. At the time, the mummy made a deep impression on him, as well as the disappointment. He was so sure there was another tomb close by but we did not find it.'

'Professor Ensor told me that you had originally been working with Professor Dalton in the Valley of the Kings. Is that why you both left him, because you thought there was another tomb near where you found the mummy?'

'Yes. One afternoon Strickland saw one of the workmen trying to sell a trinket to a German tourist. We both knew this German well, he spends a great deal of time in Egypt and pays good prices for articles he can smuggle out of the country. We chastised the workman and he confessed that one of the men from his village had given him the trinket to see if he could dispose of it nearer civilization. He had promised the German to bring other pieces of jewellery, so that night John and I went to the native village to see the man. He was frightened, knowing it is now illegal to offer authentic antiques to casual tourists, and he brought out other objects he had found. We tried everything to shake him but he was adamant that he had found them in the sand. There was no doubt about their authenticity.'

'What sort of things, jewellery?'

'Yes, a woman's jewellery. Earrings and amulets, quite beautiful. Obviously the workman didn't know the value of them but he did know they were real. The outcome was that John and I decided to go further on and look around for ourselves. Dalton was furious and entirely scathing, even when we showed him the trinkets. You will find out that, although he is a quite brilliant man in his field, he is also vain and reluctant to give credit for anything he has not discovered for himself. As you know, all we found was the otherwise empty chamber with the priest's mummy, and it is unlikely the jewellery came from there.'

'You still think there is something there, though, don't you?'

'Yes. But after we found the mummy, the workmen, who are very superstitious, refused to go near the place. We had no diggers and the weather was becoming increasingly hot. John was drinking again, and I decided it was time we returned to Cairo.'

149

'Do you have any of the trinkets?'

'I handed them in to the museum as soon as I arrived back in Cairo, all except one amulet which O'Hara has. He's a dependable sort of chap and he said he would take a look round for himself whenever he got the time. I don't know what he can do without the workmen, but I've no doubt he'll try.'

'Mr O'Hara telephoned me to say I should go by river boat to Luxor instead of by train. Apparently Professor Dalton is away from the site for about two weeks.'

'That is a splendid idea and it will enable you to become acquainted with the real Egypt. You know, Miss St Clare, the Nile is Egypt and Egypt is the Nile. Cairo is just another Eastern city even if it is the largest in Africa. Egypt, the real Egypt, is something quite different.'

'Yes, I know.'

He was looking at me intently, his dark eyes questioning, and I felt strangely drawn to him. His was the sort of face I had seen in my dreams under striped linen headdresses or princely crowns. His profile was severe yet perfectly proportioned, his eyes deep-set behind long dark lashes, and I thought that, if he had been wearing ancient Egyptian dress instead of European clothes, he could have been any one of those figures I had seen adorning the walls of the temple in my dream. It was difficult to tell his age. His hair was blue-black and shining, but there was a sprinkling of grey in its darkness. Suddenly he smiled, making me blush painfully when I realized that I must have been staring at him.

'I am almost painfully like my ancestors. I know it because I have been told it a great many times, but I can assure you, Miss St Clare, I am very much a creature of my generation, while you perhaps are not.'

I was startled by his perception and I began to tell him about myself. I had never before felt quite this urge to tell anyone about those things that had haunted my life, and he listened without interrupting me until the tale was told.

I looked at him, expecting derision, amusement perhaps, tolerance even, but he seemed unsurprised by my story, almost as though every day of his life he listened to young

150

English women telling him that they had lived before as royalty in his land. Somewhat bitterly I said, 'You think my story is pretentious. I am sorry.'

'On the contrary, Miss St Clare. I am intrigued by it. If you had said you once lived as Cleopatra or Nefertiti, I should have been amused. But how much do you know of Egyptian history?'

'I have been studying it, but I knew nothing when I had my first dream.'

'Your father never talked about it?'

'Never. The first I knew of Egypt was shortly after the tomb of Tutankhamun was discovered. We were in Mesopotamia at the time and I was eight years old. As soon as I saw those pictures in the newspaper I became aware of a tremendous excitement and that night I dreamed for the first time about this ancient princess. I saw the temples and the river, things that were not mentioned in the newspaper, where only objects they had brought from the tomb were shown. There have been times when I thought I must be going mad to dream such things, so I shall understand if you scoff at my dreams.'

'You forget that I am a Muslim. It is part of my faith to believe that we justify our existence through many lifetimes, so why should I scoff at dreams that show pictures of another lifetime, even if they were conjured up by a few pictures in a newspaper? I know that this can happen – it is one of the most interesting experiences one will ever know – to walk down a road and suddenly realize what will be round the corner, the curious desolation and inexplicable mystery of such a feeling. Scientists give us reasons but men of faith know differently.'

'But could they have happened in reality, the things I have dreamed about?'

'I am sure they could. The ancient Egyptians were the most inbred people on God's earth. The pharaoh was more than a king, he was a god, and he was not necessarily the eldest son of the pharaoh before him. To make doubly sure of the throne, therefore, he must marry the royal heiress who was the eldest daughter of his predecessor and his great

151

royal wife, the queen. You know as well as I that in some cases this meant that they were brother and sister, but it was not quite so bizarre as it seems, since as children they would have had little contact with one another. They were brought up in separate establishments and perhaps did not meet until they were practically adults. It is entirely feasible that the daughter of a secondary queen would not be allowed to marry the reigning pharaoh however much they loved each other.'

'Do you think I am right to have come to Egypt to try and search for the truth?'

'Ah, that I do not know. The truth is elusive and particularly so when all this happened so long ago. Looking for lost tombs is bad enough; searching for lost emotions and tragedies is even more difficult.'

'But I am right to try?'

He did not speak for several minutes but sat looking down at his hands resting on the table in front of him, his brow puckered, his face formidably thoughtful. At last he raised his head and looked straight into my eyes. 'Yes,' he said. 'I think perhaps you are right to want to know the truth, but if you do not find it, the disappointment might be almost more than you can bear.'

'But not more than if I never made the attempt?'

'No, perhaps not. One day, perhaps, you will tell me if you have been successful in finding what you are looking for.'

He rose to his feet and I walked with him towards the entrance of the hotel which overlooked the broad sweep of the river. A broad promenade stretched along it, sheltered by trees, well lit and as modern and uncomplicated as the Thames embankment, yet I knew that across the river lay those narrow twisting streets and, beyond them, the City of the Dead. I shivered a little, and as though he could follow my thoughts, he said, 'It has not been a happy introduction to the city of Cairo, but if you will permit me to be your guide on your last day here, I should like to show you a city you will remember for the rest of your life.'

'Oh yes, Mr Sadek, I should like that very much.'

'Then tomorrow morning we will take advantage of Ishmail's most excellent horses and ride out towards Memphis. We must go early before the place is thronged with tourists, and in the afternoon you shall see all Cairo before you from the top of the citadel.'

I thanked him enthusiastically and watched his tall, upright figure walk away from me into the night.

He came for me early before I had finished breakfast, and I thought how attractive he looked with his sleeves rolled up over slender brown arms, wearing riding breeches and a white open-necked shirt. I, too, was equipped for riding and soon we were on the road beside the river heading for Sakkara. We had no difficulty in finding Ishmail, who greeted me with laughing eyes and smiling lips, waiting until he could speak to me without Ahmed Sadek hearing him.

'I lend you Emir, my lady. You tempt Mr Sadek away from his temple, him very lucky man.'

I laughed, happy in the golden morning with the prospect of an excellent guide. Ishmail stood in the centre of the road waving after us as we cantered away. All around us was Egypt's big sky and beyond the narrow strip of emerald green, the great rolling dunes of the Sahara. In those first moments it seemed we passed the most extraordinary mixture of ancient and modern life marching side by side, or rather, I should say, the East marching with stately tread, while the West whirled by in motor cars and electric trams. Ahmed rode Ishmail's beautiful mare well and I gave myself up to the enjoyment of riding a fine, fast horse again.

Here and there on our road towards the desert, we had to pause to allow past herds of buffalo cows and flocks of goats as black as their Nubian shepherds. We met Bedouins sunburned as ripe chestnuts, Arabs almond-tinted and proud of mien, and always there were camels, camels soft of foot and evil-eyed, supercilious as only camels can be with a mighty disdain for the present day.

We raced our horses across the soft sand under a sky as cloudless and blue as an Alpine lake, and at last when we paused, breathless, where we could look out across the desert with the shapes of the pyramids against the horizon, we laughed in pure enjoyment at our feeling of wellbeing and our delight in the golden, glowing morning.

When I got my breath back, I said, 'How familiar one grows with pyramids. I suppose most people think there are only three, but look, they stretch for uninterrupted miles as far as Memphis.'

He nodded. 'I think they look more impressive when one sees them like this as an entirety. Perhaps we should go back now if you want to see Cairo in the late afternoon. You will need to change out of your riding habit and wear something cooler.'

It was later, when the sun had passed its zenith, that he escorted me through the streets of the Cairo he loved. Here I discovered the city of the caliphs, the city of Saladin and of *The Arabian Nights*. Cairo, the city of white, pattering donkeys and blue-shirted *fellahin*. Hot, dusty and noisy, a city obsessed with life, whereas so much of Egypt was so terribly obsessed with death.

Together we explored her mosques and the streets of her bazaars where silversmiths and goldsmiths worked patiently at exquisite Oriental jewellery. We walked in the Esbekiyeh gardens and watched the swooping wings of the kites and falcons which find their Eden there. With shining eyes I watched the life that flows and loiters along the wide pavements which are the lounging place of the black Sudanese fortune tellers, the dark-browed Persian turquoise vendors, the perambulating barbers, and the sherbet hawkers.

With Ahmed Sadek I climbed the citadel hill, where memories of Saladin rise up at the sight of his walls and even Cairo is forgotten, obliterated by the might of the pyramids on the outskirts of the city, alone in the solitude of the desert.

'I always think the citadel of Cairo has one of the most beautiful views in the world,' Ahmed said softly. 'It is so much more beautiful than it really is, which sounds absurd. In reality, only squalor and poverty exist in those narrow

154

streets, yet when you look at the city from here, it seems as though some divine hand had passed over it and made this world fair enough for the kingdom of heaven.'

'It is the light,' I said, 'that deceptive, bewildering Egyptian light. Surely there is no scene more unique, no sight more Oriental than the tombs of the Mamelukes in the evening sunlight. It is amazing, it is both weird and enchanting!'

He nodded, appreciating my mood, 'Yes, Kathryn, but this is Egypt! Exquisite only in her hours of amazing light, exquisite when you are not so near as to see her disorder.'

We walked without speaking until we reached the apex of the citadel high above the dark medieval city, piled up on its ramparts and towers and bastions, elegant with its minarets and fairytale dome, and I marvelled again at its beauty.

'Come with me and I will show you something which its builder can only have planned,' he said, pulling me away from the parapet. He pointed to where, through the white columns of the loggia, I could see, in the far distance, the pyramids framed between the arches.

'Was it happy chance, or did its builder, the great Mohammed Ali, wish to gaze through the arches of his new colonnade across the stretch of the years into the eternal past?' Ahmed said softly. 'Those pyramids, which he would so unhesitatingly have destroyed to build his barrage!'

The man beside me was a modern Egyptian and a Muslim, yet I was aware of his standards of honesty and integrity in the midst of a corruptible society, and I sensed in him a great love for his native land. As we turned away, I thought to myself, oh, Mohammed Ali, it is the light that makes your mosque a jewel in midair, it is the light that wipes out all that is ignoble, all that is unfitting, and leaves only what is sublime.

I had been only three days on the river but every golden morning and every silver night had been a time of enchantment. Surely I had always known the monotonous move-

155

ments of the sand and the graceful waving of the palm fronds, and hadn't my ears always heard the chants of the slender brown-limbed men as they pulled up their water buckets at the shadoofs which riddled the banks as closely as sandpipers' nests? It seemed to me that Egypt had gone on like this since the beginning of time and would continue to do so until time itself ceased to exist.

Nothing could interfere with or stop her eternal and unvarying monotony, yet I felt I could go on watching it until the day I died and never weary of its sameness. It was the true spell of Egypt, that sameness which was never the same, that monotony which was never monotonous and which had nothing to do with the pomp surrounding the ancient courts of the pharaohs or the monuments they had left for posterity.

I loved it all. The soft pearly dawns when a spider's web caught between the branches of an oleander captured all the colours of the rainbow, strung out like a jewelled pendant where the branches bent into the water. Then, before the river came to life, the flashes of blue where the swallows dipped and darted across the surface of the Nile. I loved the age-old chanting of the fishermen as they worked at their nets and the songs the boatmen sang as they waited patiently at the barrages.

The inundation had left pools of cool clear water through which rose dark green palm groves, and above them towered tall limestone cliffs, while at other places along the river, the desert sand came right down to the banks of the Nile.

I knew now why the ancient Egyptians had worshipped Ammon in the form of the sun. Egypt is dominated by the sun – from the first moment when it thrusts pale, tentative fingers into the morning mist, until each brilliant day comes to its end and the clarity of the light fades, leaving the wild splendour of the sunset in the western sky. After the heat it was surprising how quickly the days cooled and the first stars were lit as if by some unknown hand, yet on and on sailed the white paddle boat, feeling its way through wide expanses of orange and black, for the tones became deeper

156

and deeper and more and more tragic after the pale lemon and turquoise left the sky.

I was not anxious to reach Luxor. I would have been happy to spend the rest of my days living in the dreamlike world of the river, and yet, like the river of life, it bore me remorselessly on, to the morning when from the prow of the boat I saw the ruins of Karnak rising majestically into the sky. I was oblivious to the crowds that had surged to the side of the boat to get their first glimpse of the temple, I was only aware of the broken pillars and crumbling pylons, and yet Karnak was tremendously alive, nothing, not the centuries nor the effect of the elements could destroy her overwhelming majesty. The boat sailed on, past hotels and villas, their gardens and palm groves lining the river's banks, and then I was looking at the temple of Isis and its rose-coloured pillars that rose gracefully behind the landing stage.

I had collected my belongings earlier so that I would not miss one minute of our entry into Luxor, but even so, I was one of the last to leave the boat. Before me walked another Englishwoman, wearing an old-fashioned sun helmet and carrying an umbrella. One of those intrepid women that England produces from time to time, who march from country to country armed with sketch pads and travel guides, invincible in their eagerness to travel on small means and prompted always by enthusiastic determination.

A man standing at the end of the gangplank went up to her, raising his hat, but after the few moments' conversation she went on and he continued to scan the passengers leaving the boat. I smiled to myself. This must be the man who had come to meet me, and he obviously expected my father's daughter to look like the woman who had just left the boat. As I approached him, I smiled and, astonished, he stepped forward and said tentatively, 'Miss St Clare?'

'Yes,' I answered him. 'You seem very surprised.'

'Astonished, actually,' he said, recovering himself.

'I saw you speak to the lady who has just left the boat. Evidently you believed she looked the part of an Egyptologist better than I do.'

He grinned at me disarmingly. 'Gracious, was my surprise as obvious as that? My name is Mike O'Hara. Please call me Mike, everybody does.'

'Then you must call me Kathryn. How do you do, Mike.'

I held out my hand which he took in a firm clasp and I looked up into cheerful blue eyes in a tanned, attractive face. He had removed his rather disreputable hat and I could see that his hair was fair and bleached by the sun.

'You're a sight for sore eyes,' he said, smiling. 'Wait until the other chaps see you. They've been speculating about what you'd look like.'

'I'm sure they have reached the conclusion that I would be a female counterpart of my father and something of a bluestocking.'

'Something like that,' he admitted.

He relieved me of my luggage and indicated that we should move on to the next landing stage.

'We might as well get back to the site. I'm sure you don't want to hang around Luxor with this luggage, and I'm hardly dressed for entertaining a lady at the Winter Palace. There'll be plenty of other opportunities for you to come into Luxor and the ferry's already on its way over.'

On the ferry he kept up an endless flow of conversation, mostly about Luxor, the site, and the men I would be working with.

'Has Professor Dalton returned yet?' I asked him.

'No, next week some time. In the meantime I'll introduce you to the others, show you around, and tell you a little bit about what you'll be doing. Enjoy your stay in Cairo?'

'Very much.'

'I suppose you went to the museum and saw the pyramids, everybody does that. Get out to Sakkara at all?'

'Yes. I went there to meet Mr Ahmed Sadek. You know him, of course.'

He stared at me curiously for a moment. 'Yes, I know him well, charming chap. How do you know him? I didn't think your father dabbled in Egypt much.'

'He doesn't. Professor Mark Ensor is my godfather, he asked me to look him up.'

He laughed. 'I see. Now we can understand why Dalton took a girl. He usually hasn't much time for women on the site, says they're all tears and tantrums. Actually you're the first woman we've had here at Thebes.'

'I don't usually go in for tears and tantrums, Mike.'

'No, I'm sure you don't. You mustn't let Dalton get to you, Kathryn. He'll try to show you how little you know, particularly as you're St Clare's daughter and because Professor Ensor recommended you. Don't let him needle you. We've all had it at some time or another.'

'I have been warned about him.'

'And you still wanted to come.'

'Yes, it was very important to me. I don't intend to be a disturbing influence, I'm here to work, hopefully to the exclusion of everything else.'

'One usually hears sentiments like that from women who are anxious to get over a love affair, or women whom love has unfortunately passed by.'

'You can't understand that?'

'Oh, believe me, I can, but aren't you a little young to adopt a philosophy of all passion spent, fear no more the heat of the sun, etcetera?'

'There are times when I don't feel at all young. You'd be surprised how very old I do feel.'

'May I just say it doesn't show?'

He was smiling down at me and instinctively I warmed to him without any feeling of that attraction that I had felt for David. He looked away and pointed towards the West Bank and the gaunt purple hills that rose starkly beyond the sand and the edging of emerald green.

'I'm glad you're wearing trousers,' he said. 'We shall have to go the rest of the way by donkey. I suppose you won't mind that?'

'Of course not. How stark they are and yet they're so beautiful!'

'Yes, but wait until you really see them. Not a blade of grass, not a tree or flower, nothing but the overwhelming heat that seems to bounce back from the cliffs. Not even a bird unless it's a hawk looking for the odd lizard. Those

159

valleys are like the end of the world, or some old forgotten planet.'

'Perhaps the ancients felt they were appropriate. It was the end of the world for those who built their tombs there.'

He nodded. As the ferry was about to land, there was no time for further conversation. A group of donkeys waited above the path in the charge of a smiling youth and I followed Mike to the gangplank and the steps which led up to the path.

The donkey boy came forward to meet us and Mike passed over my luggage. 'Take your pick,' he said. 'They're all quite docile, and Talek here will see that your donkey doesn't run away with you.'

The boy came forward, a broad smile on his face.

'You take this one, my lady, he very special donkey. I choose him for you, his name Hassan.'

The donkey he brought forward was snow-white and his neck was adorned with a blue halter from which dangled tiny tinkling bells.

He lifted me into the saddle and Mike mounted a larger animal, then we set off along the long dusty road towards the rocky cliffs ahead. We rode in silence and I was glad of it. Behind us at some little distance I could hear Talek singing, but Mike seemed to understand that I wanted to absorb the scenery without conversation. As the green fields planted with bamboo and sugar cane gave way to sand and the hills came nearer, I couldn't have spoken for the tightness of my throat. The hills seemed to close in upon us until they towered on either side and the sandy road wound ever onwards, desolate and breathtaking.

Here and there, paths ran up the cliffs and I became aware of holes gaping wide on the rockface. I pointed them out to Mike, asking, 'Are they tombs we can see up there?'

'Yes. The entire valley is riddled with them. Empty now, of course, and robbed in the ancient days, perhaps even by the men who built them.'

'But this is not the Valley of the Kings?'

'Not yet, but you will recognize it as we approach it. Let your imagination have full rein and you will be able to see

160

those funeral processions with all their pomp going into this most desolate of places.'

I did not need to use my imagination. Long before we reached it I knew what I would find around the bend in the road and I thought about Ahmed Sadek's words to me in Cairo, the curious desolation and inexplicable mystery of such a feeling. I had dreamed of this land for many years, and I had lived in Egypt for only a week, but this was the first time I had felt in all sincerity that I had passed this road before.

Mike rode up to me, and in a voice little more than a whisper, he said, 'I knew you would be awed by it as I was. The first time I came to work in this valley, I felt that I had always known it, but of course such a notion must have come from seeing photographs of it. I'm no mystic like Strickland. I look for proof, and when I do not find it, I still don't attribute things to the supernatural.'

'It must be very nice to be sure, always to believe that there is a normal, mundane answer to your questions.'

He looked at me sharply. 'I take it you are not so sure?'

I decided to ignore the question and said instead, 'Like you said, no place on earth has been more photographed. Where do the royal tombs start?'

'Right up there. Some of them are quite inaccessible without ropes and ladders. They have all been opened and plundered, but tourists are not allowed to enter a good number of them because they are unsafe.'

'And the ones tourists can enter?'

'They are nearer the paths, well lit and ventilated and with no fallen bridges or death-traps originally planned for unwary tomb robbers.'

'Are some of the best-known tombs inaccessible?'

'Yes, but there are also some that are very easy to get to. Seti I's is the largest and possibly the most beautiful. One day you must visit Abydos. Seti built his temple there, and of all the temples in Egypt, the reliefs on the walls of Abydos are the most beautiful.'

'Shall we be working directly in the royal valley?'

'No, and what's more, we wouldn't get much done if we

161

were. The place gets crowded with tourists, even in the summer months when quite honestly it is far too hot. We are working in a side valley which leads off this one. There are a host of royal tombs above us but they are closed to the public for obvious reasons. Do you know anything about the work you will be doing?'

'A little. Professor Ensor explained it to me. I shall be copying reliefs and hieroglyphics and reassembling pottery and perhaps jewellery. Does that mean you're finding things all the time?'

'I'm afraid not. I only wish we were.'

'But I believe John Strickland and Ahmed Sadek found the mummy of a priest quite recently as well as some trinkets.'

'So you know about that also?'

'Yes. I saw the amulet they discovered with the mummy.'

I felt his eyes upon me but I made myself look straight ahead, trying to remain as unconcerned as possible.

'I didn't know Ahmed Sadek had the amulet.'

'He doesn't. John Strickland gave it to Professor Ensor and he showed it to me.'

'Really?'

I stole a look at his face but was unable to read anything from his expression, so in some desperation I went on, 'Where is the mummy now?'

'Still in Strickland's workroom, I suppose. It should be replaced in the tomb and sealed.'

'Couldn't you do that?'

'It isn't my affair.'

I had been told by both my godfather and Ahmed Sadek that they had left matters in Mike O'Hara's hands, so why wasn't it his affair? I could feel that he didn't want to talk about it but I didn't know whether it was because he wanted to be the discoverer of a tomb if there was one or because he too felt superstitious about this unknown mummy and the sense of evil which surrounded it.

We rode in silence and, from the frown on his face, I guessed his thoughts were on other matters. When the silence became more than I could bear, I said nervously,

162

'Can you tell me a little more about the people I shall be working with?'

The frown vanished instantly, and he smiled apologetically. 'I'm sorry to be such a silent companion. I'm afraid I was thinking about something else. There are only five of us including Dalton and myself. There are two young men straight from university. One of them, Alan, arrived last week, the other is Ian, he's been out here about a year. Then there's old Professor Anthony. He's been out here for years, never goes home to England because he has no family there. In the summer months he goes to Greece or Italy but, come September, he's back here on any site he can find.'

'What are the living conditions like?'

'Fairly primitive, I'm afraid. You'll be sleeping under canvas and then there is a large communal tent and a workroom. We have a gang of workmen with us and two Arab servants who cook for us and attend to the daily chores. Does it sound too terrible?'

'No. I was brought up in Mesopotamia until I was nine years old in similar surroundings.'

'Oh yes, of course. And how does your father feel about this?'

'He isn't very pleased with me. If I had to go into the field of archaeology, he would have preferred me to go out to work with him in China, not here in Egypt with Professor Dalton whom he doesn't care for very much.'

He laughed, and for the first time, I realized how attractive his face could be. He stirred no strong emotion in me – I could look at his face dispassionately, as I believed I would look at men's faces for the rest of my life – but I felt I would like this man's friendship.

'We turn off here,' he said. 'The path gets narrower and steeper but in a few minutes you'll be able to see our site.'

Nine

I had been in Egypt for just six months but I never seemed to have had another life. The uncanny desolation of these valleys had eaten into my soul, making every hot dusty morning and every cold starlit night seem like a year of my life. In all this time I had only been twice into Luxor: the first occasion had been with Mike to collect my mail and some supplies, the second because it had been my birthday and the two younger archaeologists had insisted that we go to a ball at the Winter Palace. A glance at myself in one of the mirrors in the corridor of the hotel had filled me with dismay. The sun had bleached my hair, replacing the bright colour with platinum, and my skin was tanned so that my eyes seemed even more startlingly blue. Alan and Ian had both brought dinner jackets with them, anticipating that they might find some sort of nightlife in Luxor, but I had left my ball gowns at Random Edge, and it had been only because they had been so insistent that I had bought a kaftan. The Arab who had sold it to me had waxed lyrical about the colour of my eyes, insisting that I choose a colour that would do them justice, so that in the end I had bought a deep-blue watered silk one that was heavily embroidered with silver. After a bath in scented soapy water and a visit to the hairdresser, I had felt as though I was once more suitably attired to enter the land of the living.

It had been heavenly to dance and listen to music, joyous to find admiration in men's eyes even when I had believed my heart was immune to such things, but for that one night only I had returned to the twentieth century and had revelled in its gaiety.

164

I got on very well with Alan and Ian who were about my own age, but considerably less so with Professor Dalton. There were many times when he treated my presence with veiled sarcasm, when he would refer to my father and say, 'Of course there is no need for me to explain such things to Miss St Clare. She will know all this from her father.'

When I denied this, he would say, 'Of course, I had forgotten that your father has been consistently wrong about Egypt.' Nevertheless, he insisted on his quiet little jibes, and Professor Anthony said to me, 'Take no notice, Kathy, he's jealous of your father, perhaps because he never got a knighthood and your father did. The man's miserable and eaten up with envy – that's why he's taking it out on you.'

I grew very fond of Professor Anthony, who called me Kathy from our very first meeting. He was a kind, gentle man who seemed to live in his own quiet, dreamlike world of the past, although he did have a touch of impish humour, mostly levelled at Professor Dalton.

Mike O'Hara proved helpful on all matters concerning my work but he kept his distance. He never joined us on our walks when the work was done for the day and the nights were beautiful under the starlit sky. He preferred to stay in his tent and read or argue with the two older men in the large tent which served as a common room. At times I would find him staring at me, but when my eyes met his, he would look away quickly, concerning himself with other things. Sometimes he would ride off on his donkey and I could only suppose that he was riding to the site where John Strickland had found the mummy.

I had never thought that one day I might quarrel with Mike O'Hara, but one afternoon I saw that he was saddling his donkey so I walked over to him and asked, 'Are you riding anywhere in particular?'

'No.'

'Would you mind very much if I came with you?'

'I'd prefer it if you didn't. The paths are very stony and uneven, and haven't you work to do?'

I stared at him, surprised at the hostility in his voice, and with the colour flaming in my cheeks, I said, 'I've been

165

walking and riding on stony uneven ground for a very long time. I'm not a piece of china that might be broken.'

'Nevertheless,' he persisted, 'I have work to do where I am going and I don't want disruptions of any kind.'

I was angry at his rudeness, and tossing my head, I snapped, 'I'm sorry I asked. You can be sure I shall never make a similar request,' and, with my head held high and deep resentment in my heart, I marched away from him towards my tent. I knew that he was staring after me but I didn't turn my head, allowing the flap covering the entrance to fall into place behind me.

I avoided him as much as I could for days after that, until one day he pushed several letters into my hands which he had collected that morning in Luxor.

I thanked him shortly and went to sit outside my tent to read them. One was from my father, short and to the point. He informed me that great finds were being made in China and that he had engaged several extremely able archaeologists to assist him in his work. He hoped I was well and sent his love. It was clear that he was still angry at what he termed my 'desertion'.

The other letter, from Serena, was postmarked weeks before. I was aware that my fingers trembled uselessly as I struggled to open it. She informed me that she was now practically recovered from the effects of her fall and that she and David hoped to marry before leaving for the Sudan. She added that perhaps we would be able to meet on their return journey if I was still in Egypt.

I felt a dull empty ache in my heart. I don't know what I had expected, but of course it was right that David and Serena should marry. I had renounced him of my own free will so the feeling of regret must surely be illogical.

Often in the early evening Professor Dalton would lecture us about various temple sites on which he had worked and on the whole I enjoyed these talks. On one such occasion he passed round photographs showing an obelisk they had come across in the desert several miles from Luxor and

166

which he was convinced had been on its way to stand outside the temple of Ammon at Thebes. To my surprise I found myself disagreeing with him violently, at first unable to believe that it was my voice telling him that he was wrong and that the obelisk had been intended for a far smaller temple dedicated to the goddess Hathor in memory of a secondary, much loved queen.

I was suddenly aware of the deadly silence in the tent, the embarrassment of all those present, and my own acute disbelief at my temerity. Even while he had been speaking to us, I had seen that obelisk lying on an immense barge drifting down the centre of the Nile, propelled by many boatmen with ebony black skins, the hot sun shining on their bent backs as they manoeuvred the barge towards the shore. My memory at that moment had been so potent that the tent and its occupants had ceased to exist. Instead I had been standing in the company of other young girls, all robed in virginal white and carrying long-stemmed white lillies, and with us had stood eight white-robed priests surrounding a dais on which rested an effigy of the goddess.

Standing on the platform of his gold chariot, the Pharaoh had waited to receive the obelisk. I could see the purple plumes on the heads of the horses and the gold of his armour fashioned like the wings of birds, and I had remembered how proud I had felt to be his daughter, awaiting the obelisk which he had caused to be carved out of the living rock in honour of my mother.

I was dragged back into the present by the sound of voices, all speaking at once, all anxious to cover the gaping silence, and I stared around me stupidly until I met the professor's narrow glittering eyes, snapping under dark beetling brows while his voice lashed me with sarcasm. 'Of course I had forgotten that we had with us the daughter of Sir Alexander St Clare. I should have known better than to try to teach her anything of Egypt when, no doubt, her father has already instructed her in everything she needs to know. Why don't you take my place here, Miss St Clare, and I will sit with the others? We must listen to this young lady who can tell us so much about the past that she appears to know so intimately. Come here, young lady, the floor is yours. We shall not make similar mistakes in the future.'

To suit his action to his words, he walked from behind his table and went to sit in front of it with Professor Anthony. As for the others, they were looking anywhere but at me. I jumped to my feet, saying, 'Please excuse me,' and ran unseeing from the tent.

I ran along the narrow lane between the giant cliffs without seeing them and it was only when I reached the Valley of the Kings that I paused, looking round me with dismay. In the distance the last load of tourists were being shepherded into their coaches ready for the drive to the point where the ferry would take them across the river to Luxor, and at that moment I had no wish for company, preferring instead to climb the cliffs to where I could see down the length of the valley, with my back resting against a rock.

I do not know how long I sat there, but I saw the shadows lengthen and the sky become a fiery furnace in the western sky. The cliffs shimmered in colours of purple, crimson and rose and the air grew cooler with the setting sun, but still I sat, straining my eyes along the valley, visualizing those funeral processions of old with their royal pageantry, the court dignitaries and chanting priests, seeing the heavy gold coffin borne on sledges, hearing the crack of whips and the rumbling of the chariot wheels and, above it all, the wailing of the mourners as they came nearer to the royal tomb.

I sat with my arms around my knees staring into the encroaching darkness. Suddenly I heard the sound of a rock falling down the cliff-face and next moment I felt someone sit down beside me, taking my hand gently.

'Whatever made you talk to Dalton like that, Kathy? You're probably quite right but you should know by this time the sort of man he is.'

I turned my head to stare at him. It was Mike calling me Kathy and holding my hand, Mike whose gentleness brought the hot stinging tears into my eyes, Mike who took me in his arms and let me sob out my distress against his shoulder.

He didn't speak again until the sobs subsided, then with something of the humour I had seen in those early days of our acquaintance, he said, 'He's hopping mad. You're going to have to apologize, my girl.'

'I know. I don't know what came over me, but it seemed logical to suppose that, if the obelisk was found in the Eastern desert, then somewhere close by there must have been a temple. Why was it discovered so far away from Karnak?'

He smiled. 'The supposition sounds healthy enough, but why didn't you put it to him like that instead of saying so adamantly that he was wrong?'

'I don't know. What do you think he'll do?'

'He'll make it hell for you, Kathy, he'll never miss an opportunity to take you down, but he won't get rid of you. He won't cut himself off from the pleasure he's going to get from hurting you every chance he gets.'

'I don't think I can bear it.'

'Oh yes, you can bear it, my girl. You'll sit there with a mask of polite indifference on that lovely face of yours and let his sarcasm wash over you, and when he's most scathing and bitter, you'll think what a little man he is and how much you despise him. In the meantime, go along to his tent and eat humble pie. Say it, even when you don't mean it.'

He was gripping my hands tightly in his and some of his strength seemed to flow into me so that I looked at him gratefully. 'Oh, Mike, I'm so glad we're friends again. I never wanted to quarrel with you.'

'It was my fault, I'm as bad as Dalton. I knew as soon as I'd left you what a boor I must have sounded, but I'd had a few words with him that afternoon and I suppose in a way I took it out on you.'

'I thought you and he got along famously.'

'No, we don't. We'd had words about the site Strickland and Sadek were working on. I want to have the mummy put back in the tomb and re-sealed, he wants it brought down here with all the rest of Strickland's stuff. If the mummy comes here, the workmen will leave. There are no people on earth more superstitious than these desert people who have lived around these valleys all their lives. They are all descendants of the ancient people who built the tombs and then robbed them. They have no compunction whatsoever about stealing from the dead, but this mummy that Strickland found is something different. They regard it as evil and they know quite well that the amulet Strickland found on the mummy belonged to the god Set. They can't have lived here all these centuries without knowing something about the ancient beliefs. All their lives they have been surrounded by texts of the Book of the Dead and they know very well that the lord of evil would only figure prominently in something that was at one time considered sinful.'

'But the mummy has lain in these cliffs for centuries. How can its discovery affect any of them?'

'I'm not an Arab workman, Kathy. I only know that the men won't go near the place and that we'll have trouble with them if Dalton brings it here.'

'You have seen the mummy?'

'Yes.'

'Does it frighten you?'

'No, it doesn't frighten me, it makes me immeasurably sad. It is wrong that anybody should look upon a face showing so much agony. Agony and grief like that should be private, even after three thousand years or so.'

I was gripping his hands so fiercely that I could feel their steely slenderness, and hoarsely I asked, 'Was there nothing in the tomb to say who this man was?'

'Nothing.'

'Have you no thoughts about who he might have been?'

'I think he was once a priest, and probably a priest in the temple of Ammon. I believe he may have stolen the amulet in order to procure something outside the normal run of a man's desires, but what that was I have no idea.'

'What sort of things could he ask from the god Set?'

'The death of some other human being, perhaps. I don't know.'

'Ahmed Sadek told me that both he and Strickland thought there might be another tomb close by, but they had been unable to find anything. They said they had left matters in your hands.'

'I told Dalton about the jewellery they had found, I told him I wanted to excavate up there, but up to now he's pooh-poohed the whole idea. At the moment my hands are tied. The workmen refuse to return to the site and there's nothing I can do alone. When I have the time I ride up there and take a cursory look round. There must be some reason why that priest's tomb was built where it is, and there is no denying that the jewellery is the real thing.'

'May I see it?'

'I don't see why not. Come along to my tent after dinner tonight, but right now you should go along to see Dalton and crawl if you have to, or your life is going to be a misery for the next few months.'

'I'm not very good at crawling.'

'But I've heard that women are very good at pretending. Believe me, it will be worth it.'

He rose to his feet, pulling me up after him, and together we walked down the narrow slippery path towards the wider dusty road below. On our way back we met Professor Anthony coming towards us. He stood in the middle of the road waiting for us and he smiled gently, no doubt taking in my tear-stained face and Mike's protective hand under my arm.

'Are you all right, lassie?' he inquired solicitously.

'Yes, thank you, professor. I'm on my way to apologize for my bad behaviour. Is there a chance he might forgive me, do you think?'

'Oh, there's a chance, lassie, when he's made you squirm long enough. You'll find him in the workroom. I think we've all decided to give him a wide berth this afternoon.'

I hurried on and left them to follow more slowly. It was dark in the tent after the glowing sunset outside. Professor Dalton sat at a long table on which were spread pieces of ancient papyrus which he was looking at through a magnifying glass. He deliberately ignored me when I entered the tent and continued with his work, and I stared at the wispy hair which covered his narrow skull until I could have

171

screamed with frustration. I must have stood there fully fifteen minutes before he raised his head and peered at me short-sightedly through his steel-rimmed spectacles.

'What do you want, Miss St Clare? Can't you see I'm busy?'

'I'm sorry, professor, but I have come to apologize.'

'Apologize for what?'

'Contradicting you in front of the others. It was quite unforgivable of me. I should have known better.'

He stared at me through narrowed eyes for several seconds, then he said, 'I expected I might have trouble with you when I agreed to take you. You have all your father's disregard for fact. He always believed that fact was wrong and he was right, but he was proved wrong about Egypt, wasn't he, Miss St Clare? Probably that is why he has never been back here.'

'It has nothing to do with my father, Professor Dalton.'

'But you are like him.'

'I'm not in the least like him. I have come to apologize for my conduct earlier today and I shall do my best to see it doesn't happen again, sir.'

'I have no complaint about your work, Miss St Clare, indeed I have had excellent reports on it from both Professor Anthony and Mr O'Hara. Confine your words and thoughts in future to the things you know and do not argue with or contradict those who know more and have considerably more experience.'

His eyes returned to his work and I realized my brief audience was at an end. I left his presence, still smarting from his words. I disliked him intensely. I thought him a mean-spirited little man who was eaten up with his own importance, an envious man who was reluctant to forgive me for my father's success. Then my sense of humour came to my assistance and I smiled to myself. There was a grain of truth in his remarks about my father, but there was no doubt about it, my father could have cut him down to size even if I never could.

*

172

Over dinner that evening it was the turn of Professor Anthony and Mike to come in for some of Dalton's ill humour.

'I'm having that mummy brought down here tomorrow,' he informed Mike tartly. 'I see no point in Strickland's things being left up there. They should be collected together and brought back here. There's nothing up there for him to find, always supposing he was in a fit state to find it.'

'We should consult Ahmed Sadek before anything is removed,' Mike said practically. 'He was in this with Strickland and we know that he is working at Sakkara.'

'They were both assigned to me, so with or without their permission I can order their camp to be taken down. I'll get some workmen up there tomorrow with orders to disband the site. The mummy can be brought here until I decide what is to be done with it.'

'Why don't we simply put it back in the tomb and re-seal it?' Mike asked logically. 'What can it possibly tell you if we keep it here? Besides, none of the workmen will touch it.'

'The workmen will do as I tell them. Such superstitious nonsense! I mean it, O'Hara, I'm not having you going up there when you should be working here. There is no tomb to find. If the men have been peddling jewellery, it's something that was found a long time ago, not just recently.'

Mike didn't answer him and Professor Anthony began in his usual gentle fashion, 'Why don't we all take a look round one afternoon? Strickland was a good Egyptologist even if he was a little unorthodox, and Ahmed Sadek is dedicated to his work to the exclusion of everything else.'

Dalton fixed him with the same stony stare he had levelled at me only that afternoon. 'Strickland hasn't been a good Egyptologist for years – you know for a fact that Sadek's carried him. No, I've made up my mind. The site is to be disbanded and the mummy brought down here. If the workmen won't bring it then some of you will have to go.'

He rose from his chair to indicate that the discussion was at an end, and without another word, he left the tent. There was a short uncomfortable silence and then Professor

173

Anthony said, 'You're not happy about it, are you, Mike?'

'No. I think we should consult Sadek before doing anything about it.'

'And you're unhappy about the mummy?'

'I think it should be put back in the tomb. It's a sad, sorry mummy, it should be left in peace.'

I looked at him quickly. His sensitive face was troubled and I knew that he cared about this mummy. My eyes smarted with unshed tears and I thought to myself that it was time somebody cared. If it was the mummy of Ptahotep, as I firmly believed it was, the caring had come too late. In that dim shadowy past, too few people had cared for him, least of all that proud princess who had used him and discarded him as easily as she might have discarded one of her sandals. Mike's eyes met mine across the table and it was almost as though he knew, as though at that moment something passed between us, too intangible for words.

The two younger men had joined in the conversation now. Mike looked away and it was as though I was suddenly released from bands that had bound us momentarily together.

'I suppose we shall have to bring the mummy down,' Alan was saying. 'The workmen won't touch it. Where's Dalton going to put it? I don't fancy having my dinner with that thing standing in the corner.'

'We shall have to put up a shed down here and leave the mummy in that,' Mike said practically. 'If the workmen know it's here, they'll go back to their village and that's the last we shall see of them.'

'I'll give you a hand tomorrow to bring the stuff down here,' Alan said. 'Suppose we do it at night after the men have gone home?'

'We can try it, but have you ever tried keeping anything from them? The orderlies will tell them. Anyway it's Dalton's decision, let him sort it out.'

They left the dining table and went to sit around the stove. The nights were intensely cold and the stove was always lit in the evenings. The two younger men settled down to write letters while Professor Anthony made himself comfortable in his favourite chair, preparing to doze a little. Mike, however, came over to me, saying, 'Come along to my tent and take a look at the jewellery. Dalton doesn't know I have it, nor do the others. I promised Sadek I wouldn't let any of them see it for the time being.'

I followed him into the night, glad of the warm jacket round my shoulders. It was a night potent with mystery. The wind blew along the valley stirring the dust and the dark blue vault above us was blazing with stars that seemed so near I felt I could reach up and gather them into my hands. From the workmen's village we could hear the barking of several dogs, unnaturally loud in the overpowering stillness, and I felt an overwhelming desire to stay out in the open where I could savour fully the mystical quality of the night. As though I had spoken the words out loud, Mike said, 'The night's too beautiful to go inside just yet. Would you like to walk a little way?'

'Oh yes, please, Mike, I was about to suggest it.'

'We'll keep to the centre of the path and walk towards the Valley of the Kings.'

We walked in silence for most of the way, but it was a companionable silence, almost as though neither of us wished to dispel the haunting potency of the shadows that came and went as the silver bright moon slipped behind clouds in a sky like dark blue velvet. Desolate enough in the sunlight, the valley seemed more so in the cold light of the moon and I found myself thinking of the endless rock tombs that lay all around us, on whose walls, never meant for the eyes of the living, were depicted the life of an entire civilization. The carved and painted figures in their perpetual pageantry revealed all that time had tried to hide. The sowing and the reaping, the Nile's flood and fall, the labour of the scribe and artisan, the hunting of the lion and the spearing of the fish, birth, marriage, war, festival, and death. On those walls still crept the slave and stalked the pharaoh, and there too still sat the stylized queen, proud and lovely, receiving gifts which did her homage.

Here and there along the royal valley, small fires glowed where the guardians of the tombs sat out their long and

175

weary night, and I wondered if they too were thinking about the whole force of the ancient cult of the dead and the horror of corruption which was suddenly brought home to me in this ancient valley. I thought about the pharaoh lying in state in his palace, stuffed with balsam, cassia and myrrh, and then the last terrible journey across the river and along the dusty road between these towering cliffs, through tomb passages and chambers, through antechambers and across bridges guarded by ponderous trapdoors of stone until, at last, in the farthest chamber, the mummy was left in its solid gold coffin tricked out with gold and jewels. In the heavy dry air, alone, the image of the dead king on the mummy case for ever stared at the ceiling, awaiting in vain the dispensation of Osiris and an end to mortal claustrophobia.

I shivered and Mike tightened his hand under my arm.

'Are you cold? Would you like to go back?' he asked solicitously.

'No. It's this place. It takes such a hold on me. I can't help thinking that we are probably walking through the greatest monument to wasted human energy that time has spared. What a bitter waste it has all been!'

'Yes,' he agreed, 'but think what an aristocracy this valley represented in its heyday! Probably the most exclusive society in the world, for the pharaohs, at once both kings and gods, preserved their distance even in death. Here no lord or commoner by art or flattery could gain an entrance: royalty were privileged to await alone a summons that never came.

'If they had not been spared the realization of it, how bitter would have been the deception of these kings who, for a lifetime, had carefully planned to exchange the pomp and pleasures of earth for the finer ones of heaven. And think of their queens in that other valley, wrapped in gold leaf and chastely coffined. Surely they must have presented a galaxy of beauty and imperial grace unparalleled in courts above ground, but there were no movements and no voices. No opportunity came to unfold their jewelled charms in that endless pleasance of gods and kings that they had so assiduously promised themselves.'

176

His voice, barely above a whisper, held my attention as no other voice had ever done, and I wanted him to go on, speaking to me of the things that had coloured my life. As if in answer to my unspoken prayer he said, 'Unfortunately the resurrection of these kings and queens was altogether different, colder, more sudden and brutal than they had anticipated. The robbers came. Trapdoors were forced, lights, hurrying feet and plebeian profanity came echoing into the chambers. The gold went and the jewels and the alabaster. They were roughly shaken from their expectant immobility. The wrappings were pulled from beauties with the same eagerness as if they had been snatched by lovers. The mummy cloths of kings were painfully torn off, like bandages from wounds.'

His voice was bitter and I stopped and turned to face him. 'Oh, Mike,' I murmured. 'You care so much. I thought it was all science with you, that the ancient Egyptians had ceased to exist as people. I'm so glad that you care.'

'Yes, I do care. Have you never thought, Kathy, how strangely ironic it is that these tombs should be the end of persons who believed the next world to be as real as this and who confidently laboured half their lives to enter it in a manner befitting their station?'

'Then you believe that there is nothing, that whatever we do in this life, good or evil, giving joy or pain, is all simply snuffed out like a candle on the day we die?'

'I don't know. What else can one think in this most awesome place? What do you believe?'

'I think we pay, but not in some wonderful utopia where we might expect all our sins to be suddenly forgiven. I think we pay here.'

'I have known a great many sinners, and, believe me, they have not paid. They have escaped retribution remarkably well.'

'But in other lifetimes, perhaps. I spoke of these things to Ahmed Sadek and he seemed not to think them foolish.'

'Sadek is a philosopher, he is also a Muslim. The theory of reincarnation would not sound strange to him.'

'But have you never felt that you have said words before

177

and done things before? Have you never looked at another human being and believed that you have known him for thousands of years?'

'Have you?'

I was glad of the night, glad that the silvery moonlight hid from him my blushing face, and reluctantly I turned back without answering him.

'You haven't answered my question, Kathy. Those who have such theories call it "far memory" and I have never argued against it, but where are we to find the proof? Not in dreams, because they have no substance in the light of day, not even in hope, because so many ordinary hopes are doomed to disappointment. Like I told you once before, I must have proof, I can't accept a theory if there is no proof to substantiate it.'

I could not tell Mike my story, not yet at any rate, and the feeling that he would not understand made me feel suddenly quite vulnerable and alone. As though he sensed something of my disappointment, he took hold of my hand and with laughter in his voice, he said, 'Come and look at the jewellery, but I must warn you it isn't much. You'll probably be disappointed, but you might be able to tell me if you wore it long ago in the temple of Isis to celebrate her festival.'

I joined in his laughter and lengthening our stride we returned to his tent where he unlocked an old cash box.

'Here it is,' he said after rummaging for a few seconds. 'Sit here near the lamplight and tell me what you think of it.'

My first reaction was a feeling of acute disappointment. I was holding in the palm of my hand a piece of jewellery shaped like a bird's wing. It was made of turquoise and the edges of the feathers were chased in gold. I turned it this way and that and the frown on my face deepened.

'I told you it wasn't much. Now you're disappointed,' he said.

'What was the other jewellery like?'

'There was an amulet, a quite beautiful thing representing a hawk, and part of a bracelet set with turquoises and agate.

178

What do you make of what you're holding? I thought you might know, being a woman.'

'It isn't complete. Do you suppose it's broken off an amulet?'

'It may well have done. So you can't help me?'

'I didn't say that. May I borrow it until morning? I promise I won't lose it and I'll give it back to you when the others aren't there.'

'Take it by all means, but don't stay up all night trying to unravel the mystery. Care for a nightcap before you retire?'

'No, thanks, Mike, I think I'll go to my tent now. But I would like to go to the other site tomorrow if the rest of you are going.'

'Of course, there's that wretched camp to break up and the question of the mummy. You don't want to look at him, do you, Kathy?'

'No, I don't. I couldn't bear to look at him.'

He walked with me to the larger tent where lights were still burning and I went on to my own tent where I lit the lamp and sat studying the broken piece of jewellery. I got out a piece of paper and started to draw, and as I drew, it all suddenly began to take shape. It was part of an earring with the wing following the contours of the ear, the head of the bird resting on the lobe and the other wing drooping down. After drawing the side of a face, I soon placed the earring in position. I was filled with such a strange feeling of excitement that it took all my willpower not to go running from my tent to show Mike what I had done.

My camp bed was comfortable but I lay for a long time listening to the soft wind sighing along the valley, my thoughts busy with the events of the day. Why had I never talked to David as I found I could talk to Mike O'Hara? With David it had always been the urgency of our love that was so important, the brevity of our time together, the ecstatic surrender, and the despair and pain of parting when we wanted so much more. But we never talked, and now I found myself wondering if he talked to Serena, if she knew

179

all his secret longings and the innermost desires of his heart. Things I had never known.

I was aware of the activity long before I had completed my toilet, and looking out of my tent, I saw that a group of boys with their donkeys had already gathered on the path. I hurried down to the large tent where we ate breakfast to find that everybody except Professor Dalton was already there. I sat down next to Ian and asked, 'Are we really going up to Strickland's camp?'

'Yes, the old man said he wanted it done today. It's a case of taking down the tents and the huts and collecting any other material they might have left up there.'

'Will it be difficult to bring it all down today?'

'I shouldn't think so. The huts are sectional and the tents are no problem. Are you coming?'

'Yes, I don't want to stay here with Professor Dalton on my own. I'm not exactly his blue-eyed girl.'

'Oh, but you are, Kathy, his beautiful blue-eyed girl. Even Dalton can't have escaped that.'

'You're flirting with me, Ian, and I'm sure that if my eyes had been bright scarlet Dalton wouldn't have noticed.'

It was easy to flirt with the two younger men and to laugh with them about things I couldn't have laughed about with Mike. I felt that I could treat both of them like brothers.

As soon as I left the tent, the donkey boy who had met me on the first day came forward, bringing Hassan for me to ride.

'We wait for you specially, my lady,' he said, his boyish attractive face split with an enormous smile. He fished inside his loose, bright blue robe and brought out an exquisitely carved green alabaster vase. It was only about four inches high but the smoothness and feel of the alabaster in my hands made me exclaim with delight.

'But this is beautiful, Talek!'

'My brother, he make it especially for you.'

'It is exquisite. Why should your brother make things for

me? He's never met me. Besides, he could get money for it in Luxor.'

'I tell him it is for most beautiful lady I have ever seen. My brother very romantic, great poet, love beautiful things. He would rather give to you than get money for it from big fat ugly lady.'

He spread his arms wide and made a face by blowing out his cheeks. I had to laugh at him, in spite of his unkind words about some unfortunate tourist.

'It is kind of your brother to make it, Talek. I shall always treasure it, but I feel I must give him something for it.'

'No, he would not take. I tell him you are lady who loves Egypt. People come here and shake their heads, they see only poverty and mosquitoes, they not see Egypt's beauty.'

'I know, they see her ruins and forget what they must have been like centuries ago. I do love Egypt, you were right to tell your brother that. I am glad you are to come with me to the other camp.'

'I do not come with you, my lady, you go with English gentlemen. I wait here until you return with Hassan.'

'But why don't you come? You came with your donkey to Luxor.'

'That different. I go with you to Cairo, to Aswan. My lady, I go with you to the moon, but I not go to other camp.'

'Why not?'

'I not go near mummy. He not *mafish* when he go in there, not dead.'

'You are right, the poor man was buried alive, but I can assure you that he is quite dead now.'

'He not *mafish* because him evil man, evil place up there. You go, lady, and Talek say prayers to Allah for your safe return.'

'Oh, this is all silly superstition. The mummy will not harm you.'

He looked at me sadly out of his liquid brown eyes. 'You will see, my lady, none of the workmen will go. Bad place, bad people buried there.'

'It didn't stop some of the workmen from looking for jewellery there.'

181

'That before they discover mummy. I wait here, my lady. Hassan very good donkey, he not know you take him to evil place.'

Mike came striding towards me asking if I was ready.

'I'm ready, but Talek refuses to come with me.'

'None of the native workmen or the donkey boys will come. You can hear them muttering among themselves from here.'

'Can we manage on our own?'

'We'll have to.'

'Do you think they would have gone with Ahmed? After all, he is an Egyptian.'

'He's an educated Egyptian. These men are Arabs and riddled with superstition. The sooner we get going, the sooner we shall accomplish what we're going for.'

I followed him along the lane. The two younger men were already mounted, Alan on a decidedly frisky animal that he was having great difficulty controlling, much to the amusement of the donkey boys. I was surprised to see Professor Anthony attempting to mount a donkey at a mounting block they had brought for him, and Mike went forward to help him. The portly professor looked far from comfortable on the animal's back, so I decided to keep him company on our ride to the other camp.

As my donkey fell into step beside his, I said, 'I didn't know you intended to come with us, Professor Anthony.'

He smiled at me rather ruefully. 'Consider the alternative, my dear – a day in the company of Dalton. Normally I can stand it when the rest of you are around somewhere, but alone, no, thank you.'

We rode through silent groups of glowering natives, but none of us looked back and soon we were climbing towards the camp high up on the cliffs at the end of another valley. The sun poured down on us even though it was still very early, and I saw Professor Anthony mop his brow several times, his face strained.

The camp proved to be a much smaller affair than ours, consisting of two sleeping tents, a work hut where I assumed the mummy was kept, a smaller hut for eating, and one which contained a chemical toilet. They had left the camp in something of a hurry, and Strickland's notes were still spread out on a small table in his tent.

'Perhaps you'll collect together all the small things, Kathy,' Mike said, 'the notes and the cooking utensils, the bedding and anything else you find. There's a hand-cart at the back of the larger tent. We'll have to put the big stuff on that and try to harness the pack animals to it. The mummy will have to go back on that.'

'Will you put him back in his coffin?' I asked, shuddering a little.

'It's the best way to carry him. The coffin is made of cedarwood so there won't be any problem with weight.'

I tried to read Strickland's notes but the writing was largely illegible. They were written in the form of a diary telling which day the mummy was discovered, the day the workmen left them, but sometimes the writing became so blurred and small that I had to put them aside and get back to stripping the camp bed and piling everything up outside the tent.

We ate our packed lunch in the shade of the cliff. It was a silent meal, as though the weirdness of the place with its desolation and uncanny stillness prevented normal conversation or laughter. As soon as the meal was over, Mike said, 'Well, I think I'll get back to work. Perhaps one of you will give me a hand in the tent.'

'Is there anything I can do?' I asked hopefully.

'You can help us load up later, Kathy. If you want to have a look at the tomb, it's up there. You can just see the hole in the rock.'

My eyes followed his pointing finger and Mike said, 'You're not superstitious, surely? Would you like somebody to go up there with you?'

'No, I'll go alone. It isn't superstition that makes me hesitate.'

I scrambled up the rough path until I came to the entrance and looked into the passageway. It was the hottest time of the day and the sun struck the rock and lit up the passageway so that I had no need of the torch I carried in my shoulderbag. It was slippy on the rock and once or twice I had to put my hands on the wall to stop me from falling, but at last I stood in a plain square room, unadorned except for the places where the chisels had hollowed it out. It was more like a cave than a chamber, and I shivered in spite of the heat. A lump rose in my throat as I thought about that man they had left here to die without any prayers for his soul's survival, and without even a name to say who he was.

I walked back the way I had come and sat outside the tomb on the rocks, staring along the valley. I was not seeing the valley, however; I was remembering my dream when I had seen Ptahotep standing in chains in that most awesome of temples, his face calm, his eyes closed almost as though his soul was already far away from the punishment they intended for him. But what of the princess? I did not know if Ipey had made for her that last potion or what they would have done with her when they found her dead. A strange feeling of excitement washed over me, and I leaped to my feet and stared around me with a fast-beating heart. Suppose they found her dead. Her body would have had to be embalmed and spend its forty days in nitrate. A princess who had been guilty of suicide would not have merited a tomb in the royal valley, but they could have brought her here, and because Ptahotep had aided her in her sin, they could have brought him here also so that they might spend eternity together. I was convinced that I was right and yet whom could I tell? Mike would look at me with amused tolerance, and even Professor Anthony would regard me as fanciful.

I could see Ian sitting on a rock puzzling over the notes I had left in John Strickland's tent. I waved to him, feeling sure he would put them aside and join me on the cliff path. Predictably, in a few minutes he stood beside me, saying, 'Are you afraid to go in alone?'

'No, I've been in. There's nothing to see except the marks of chisels on the rockface. Whose was this other tomb Strickland and Sadek expected to find?'

'The owner of the jewellery, I suppose. Strickland didn't

talk much, he was a bit of a loner, but Sadek thought the jewellery had belonged to someone of note. The poorer people were content with mummy beads and largely went to their tombs unadorned.'

'Why would the jewellery be found out here?'

'It probably wasn't. The workmen probably know where the tomb is and have access to it. It was only when the mummy was found that they became frightened. They have no compunction about stealing from the dead, but this mummy was "no *mafish*" when he was put in there, so they feel now that they are stealing from the living.'

'Can't they be made to say where the tomb is?'

'You try it, Kathy. They'd lie and stare you in the face. You'd never shake them.'

'So as soon as we take the mummy down to our camp, they will start thieving again from this tomb, and whatever still remains in it will be peddled round the tourist sites and sold for next to nothing?'

'It looks that way, doesn't it?'

I was angry at his complacency, angry that those greedy brown hands should be tearing jewellery from the body of a princess who had perhaps once been me, and I marched down the cliffside with Ian tearing after me, saying, 'Hey, hold on a minute! Now what's got into you?'

I turned to face him. 'We've got to stop them stealing from that tomb, Ian. We've got to think of something.'

'But we don't know for certain that there is a tomb.'

'There is, there must be. Have no other mummies been discovered near here?'

'Yes, about a year ago. The mummy of an old woman in a shallow tomb down there in the sand. She was probably a slave or simply a peasant woman. They evidently hadn't thought her worthy of a coffin, she was discovered in the sand which had preserved her body the way that the sand preserves most things in Egypt. As soon as it was subjected to the air, it simply disintegrated and nothing was left except dust. Nothing was found on the body, no amulets, no jewellery, nothing.'

'Were you here when it was found?'

'No. It was just before I came here. Anthony told me about it.'

'Ipey,' I murmured to myself.

'What did you say, Kathy?'

'Nothing, I was just thinking aloud. I must talk to Mike. Is he very busy?'

'He's in the tent where the mummy is. I rather think they're putting it back in its coffin ready to bring out here.'

'I'm not going in there. I don't want to look at the mummy. I'll wait and talk to Mike later.'

'There he is now,' Ian pointed. 'If you hurry you might just catch him before he goes back.'

I ran along the road and clambered over the rock. Catching Mike's arm, and with my words rushing over one another, I managed to gasp out, 'Mike, we can't take the mummy back, we've got to leave it here or they'll go on stealing from the tomb.'

He stared at me as though I had taken leave of my senses, then he put his hands on my shoulders and said, 'What is this? What are you talking about?'

'You've got to listen. There is another tomb round here, the tomb of a princess, and we've got to find it before any more jewellery is stolen.'

'There is no tomb. If there was, don't you think Strickland and Sadek would have found it?'

'They didn't look long enough. Don't you see, if the mummy goes with us the robbers will just come back to steal the jewellery in the princess's tomb.'

'What princess?'

Desperately I hunted in my bag for the piece of paper on which I had drawn the earring, and handing it to him, I said, 'That is no ordinary person's earring. It belonged to someone of wealth and position.'

'But we don't know where it was found. The workmen said they found it in the sand but Egypt is covered with sand. Look around you, Kathy, these cliffs are honeycombed with tombs, it could be one of a thousand and we don't

186

really know where to start looking. Strickland and Sadek were here for almost two years. Don't you think they would have found it if there was one to find?'

My sense of disappointment was so intense that I could have wept, and seeing my disconsolate face, he put his arm round my shoulders and said gently, 'Don't mind so much, Kathy. Jewellery has been stolen from these tombs for centuries. We can do nothing to stop it.'

Miserably I went to rejoin Ian on the rocks below. 'You don't look as though you had much joy with Mike,' he remarked evenly.

'No. I suppose one day somebody will find the tomb, and it'll be empty and the body broken up like all those others they found.'

'I expect you're right. I think I'll go into the tent and see if they want any help. Coming?'

'No, I'll wait out here. Call me if you need me.'

I sat in the shade until the sun moved round to the west and the tones in the sky began to change. From palest turquoise the sky was now pale mauve with, here and there, a streak of rose, and the valley below became dark and mysterious, lit only by the tints in the western sky.

Ian and Alan came out of the large tent and began to assemble the hand-cart. They struggled with makeshift ropes to harness the two pack animals to the cart. After all this, they returned to the tent and in a few minutes the four of them came out carrying the coffin. The wood had been bleached almost white with the years and they seemed to have little difficulty in placing it on the cart, finally roping it to the sides so that it would not slip.

It was a strange, ill-assorted procession that trooped along the valley in the fading light, burdened as we were with large packages, riding weary donkeys, and trundling between us the cart bearing the mummy of the priest. At the end of the journey I was relieved to see that the mummy was placed in a wooden hut some little way from our communal tent and my sleeping tent.

*

None of the workmen was present and it was fully an hour before the boys came to retrieve their animals. They came silently, with frightened eyes, looking behind them at shadows peopled with menace conjured up by their own fears. Talek took Hassan's reins without his customary smile.

'You will tell your brother how much I appreciated his gift, won't you?' I said to him.

'Yes, my lady, I will tell him. You bring mummy here to camp?'

'Yes, but there is no need to be afraid. He will not harm you.'

'You go from here, my lady, you go back to Luxor, I take you today.'

'My work is here, I have to stay. Do you know where the workmen found the jewellery that was offered to the German tourist?'

'I know nothing of such jewellery, my lady. I only donkey boy, I not know about tombs.'

'But you will find out for me, won't you Talek? Otherwise I will ask the mummy's spirit to find out where it was found and who were the finders. You know as I do that he was the guardian of that tomb and now it has been violated.'

He was looking at me with frightened eyes and I was sorry that I had to play on his superstitious nature after he had been so kind. 'You will tell me what you discover, won't you Talek?' I said meaningfully, and with a brief smile I left him staring after me.

He was the last to leave the site, and I watched the donkey boys straggling along the dusty road pulling their weary beasts behind them. At that moment Alan came towards me. 'The workmen have all gone, Kathy, even the two orderlies. We'll have to rustle up a meal for ourselves. Are you any good as a cook?'

When had I ever cooked? From the age of nine I had been cosseted and waited upon so that now I doubted if I could even boil an egg, let alone cook a meal for five grown men. I felt useless as a woman. Cooking a meal was something I could have done if I'd had the right sort of upbringing. Fortunately the two younger men were more than equal to the occasion and I watched admiringly as they peeled potatoes and made stew with the workmen's simple cooking utensils. Although I served the meal and cleared away afterwards, I couldn't help saying to Mike, 'I feel ashamed of myself. I felt so helpless watching them preparing this meal, but my grandmother had a houseful of servants and I never needed to do things for myself.'

'It's not your fault, Kathy. I expect you thought you'd marry some man who would keep you in the style to which you'd been accustomed.'

'Perhaps I did. There were always plenty of them around, but I didn't want the men who wanted me.'

'You preferred the one who wanted somebody else.'

'Why did you say that, I wonder?'

'It was something you said on the day you arrived. Don't you remember, all passion spent, etcetera? I thought then you were trying to get over an unhappy love affair, but I don't suppose you want to talk about it.'

'I could try. He was engaged to my cousin before we met but it didn't stop us falling in love with each other. He was going to tell her but then she had an accident on the hunting field and it wasn't possible. I came out here because I thought it was the best thing to do. I'd always wanted to come to Egypt, I'd always been terribly interested in things Egyptian, it wasn't simply a case of trying to get over a disappointing love affair.'

'I see. But I suppose your cousin will recover. What then?'

'I don't know. I left them together, perhaps that's how they were meant to be.'

'And you?'

'There is no me. It's over. One day I may tell you the whole story, but not yet. You might laugh about it and I couldn't bear that.'

'I can't believe that I would laugh about anything so serious as a broken love affair.'

'Not that perhaps, but there's more.'

'Then I'll wait until you can bear to talk about it.'

I watched him walk away, striding easily up the rocky

cliff path, the afterglow gilding his bleached hair. I was glad of Mike's friendship, and since our walk along the royal valley, we seemed to have drawn somehow closer together. I did not want him to fall in love with me, or I with him. I believed at that moment that, young as I was, I never wanted to feel again the agony and pity and power of love, but I needed this man's friendship and I respected him too much to lose it.

That night over dinner Professor Dalton complained bitterly about the missing workmen, and Mike, sterner than I had ever seen him, said, 'Surely you knew what would happen as soon as the mummy was brought here? It would have been far better if we'd put him back in his tomb, he'd have kept the workmen away from other finds too.'

'What other finds? Those tombs have all been robbed and plundered centuries ago. Even Strickland realized that when he returned to the base.'

'Strickland came back because he was ill. Besides, you never listened to Strickland or Sadek, and the jewellery is coming from somewhere.'

'The jewellery has probably been in the possession of some family for years. Those people in the village are the descendants of generations of tomb robbers, and over the years small pieces of jewellery will have been trotted out to supplement their living. They're not stupid. They daren't risk bringing it all out or the authorities would seize it.'

'Well, I'm not entirely satisfied. In the meantime, what are we to do about the mummy? They'll not come back while it's here.'

'They'll drift back for money. Even those people can't live on fresh air.'

'I think you'll find they're more terrified of superstition than hunger. No doubt they'll move on to the tourist sites and peddle more jewellery to people who don't know its value.'

'Then we must warn the authorities and have them keep an eye on them.'

'Always supposing we can find a member of the authorities who doesn't expect to take a rake-off.'

I could hardly believe that this was really Mike arguing with the Professor and using the same argument I had used with him only that afternoon.

'You are particularly cynical this evening, O'Hara. I know you didn't want to break the camp up or bring down the mummy, but this attitude that we can trust nobody doesn't say very much for your affinity with these people, or your desire to work among them.'

'Oh, come on, Professor, you know better than that. When has there ever been a time when pharaoh wasn't sold for balsam, the shinbone of a king sold for a few pence in the market, the hand of a princess that men would once have died to kiss kept in the folds of a filthy robe and brought out to show to awed women tourists? Few of these men have any real feeling for the past. They'd sell their grandmother for a few shillings if they could convince some tourist that she was a genuine antique.'

'But those men like you, Mike. You get on so well with all of them,' I couldn't help protesting.

He looked at me sharply but I did not miss the bitterness in his eyes. 'Don't think I haven't great sympathy for them. For years they've been subjugated, at almost every period of history the rulers of Egypt have been the country's worst enemies. Everybody has taken from Egypt, the people of this land have invariably been under the heel of some despot or other. Is it any wonder they have raised a race of men who live by their wits and see nothing wrong in stealing from those who were their masters?'

'There were good pharaohs as well as bad,' Professor Anthony protested mildly.

'Of course, but think of those others. How many rulers wasted the energies of a hundred thousand men to build one pyramid with all the physical exhaustion that was the price of that building? I'm not disputing that there were good pharaohs, but the history of the pyramids was repeated in a thousand temples and tombs, and the situation was worse under foreign rule. It seems to me that only the British did anything for Egypt. At least they brought back a new pride to the people and a desire to work for their country.'

191

'I remember reading that, under Persian rule, the labour of a whole city was devoted to keeping the wife of the Persian governor in shoes,' Alan stated.

'Yes, and it was worse under Roman rulers. They stripped the pyramids of their limestone to make their villas on the banks of the Tiber. And the Arabs only brought wholesale corruption to the people,' Mike said harshly.

'Well, I propose to go to my tent where I have work to do and leave you to your arguments,' Professor Dalton said, and with this he strode out of the tent, knowing that he was likely to lose any argument he entered into. Mike was singularly annoyed about something and his annoyance was making him strangely dogmatic. I had never seen him in quite this mood before.

Professor Anthony chuckled to himself after Dalton had left. 'You've got him rattled, Mike,' he said smiling. 'I suppose it's his decision to break up that camp that's brought this on.'

'Yes. We've no workmen and no servants, thanks to him. We might as well pack up and go home. We'll get precious little done here.'

'I agree, but perhaps they'll trickle back in ones and twos. After all, they need to eat.'

'Perhaps,' he said mournfully.

I fell asleep quickly. Normally I lay for some time thinking about the events of the day, but as soon as my head touched the pillow I must have slept. I have no idea what awakened me, but suddenly I was sitting up in my bed, staring towards the flap of my tent. I strained my ears for any sound but there was none, and it was still dark. No moonlight invaded my tent, but all the same I was wide awake. I groped for my torch in my bag beside the bed, switched it on and looked at my watch. It was just half past three. I had been in bed almost five hours.

I lay on my back, listening, but there were no further sounds, and annoyed with myself that I had awakened so suddenly, I turned on my side in an attempt to sleep. It was impossible. I felt quite sure that out there in the darkness someone walked around the camp, and although I am no braver than the next person, I shrugged my shoulders into my dressing gown and went gingerly to the tent flap. The darkness was intense, but it was the stillness that oppressed me most, the thing about Africa I had never thought about. The silence of the desert struck my ears, it almost thundered at me. I had never imagined that the stillness of a world totally without life could be so oppressively full of sound. It was only in the desert that I could picture the world before any living thing was created, and the world after all living things were dead.

Slowly I moved out of my tent and along the path that led towards the other tents. My eyes were now becoming accustomed to the darkness and I was aware of shadows and the overwhelming burden of a past hoary with years, both around me and above me. The sky was a deep blue velvet dome lit by stars, the most friendly thing in that raw African night, but even as I crept forward I heard the ring of a stone tumbling down the cliff-face and I knew that, ahead of me, somebody else walked in the darkness. I peered in front of me but I could see nothing. Suddenly I remembered the mummy lying in his cedar coffin in the wooden hut on the cliffside. I looked up but I could see nothing, and angrily I told myself that surely I had not expected to see the form of a mummy walking in front of me, trailing his bandages in the dust? This was the twentieth century, and not even the mysterious magic of an Egyptian night could make me believe anything so fanciful.

Again I heard a sound, this time above me, but try as I would I could see nothing. I was mindful to call out but I didn't want to waken the others sleeping in their tents in case it was only a prowling dog, and there was nothing of value to steal in our camp, at least as far as the village people were concerned.

I could hear another noise now, a sound as though water was splashing on the ground, yet I knew there was no water in this most barren place. I cried out with amazement as my eyes were suddenly blinded by light and I realized that, above me on the cliff path, the hut in which the mummy lay was ablaze from end to end and the sparks were flying upwards into the night sky.

I stood transfixed, looking at the largest bonfire I had ever seen. Tinder-dry by the sun, the wood blazed fiercely, and the mummy, enshrouded in its bandages, and centuries old, would by this time be little more than a charred piece of nothing in the glowing hut. I could not have prevented it, nor could I believe that one of those villagers would have been desperate enough to have overcome his ancient fears and find the nerve to come up here in the darkness and set fire to the hut. I ran back to my tent, but almost immediately I was aware of voices and I knew that the others were awake. I left my tent to find them standing in a small group looking at what was left of the hut and then I saw Mike walking towards us down the cliff.

It was too dark for me to see the expression on his face, but immediately he joined us, he was besieged with questions from the others. He gave perfectly logical answers to them all: he had left his tent because he had thought he had heard a noise; he hadn't seen anything, he was on his way to investigate when the hut went up in flames. After all, hadn't I left my tent for those very same reasons? But although the others seemed to accept his answers, somehow I could not. For one thing he was completely dressed, so that ruled out any idea that he had left the tent in a hurry, and for another, there was the tremor in his voice and his desire to leave matters until the morning. When morning came, he would have collected himself sufficiently to go about the business of looking at the charred remains of the hut with equilibrium.

I was sure that Mike himself had set fire to the hut, but why? Was it so that the workmen would return, their fears gone, or was it because he felt that that long-dead mummy should find some peace? I didn't know, but I was determined that one day I would ask him.

Ten

I slept no more that night but lay on my camp bed staring up at the ceiling waiting for the dawn. There are no dawns like Egyptian dawns. In the east the sky would be a delicate pink blending into grey, like the breast of a pigeon, and then suddenly it would come magnificently, strident and glowing, shining on the obelisks and pylons of the temples, stirring up the mist on the river, turning the western hills into cliffs of purple. Long before this I was dressed and outside the tent, walking towards the charred remains of the hut on the cliffside. It was just a burned-out pile of rubbish; nothing remained to show that once there had been the body of a man waiting in his cedar coffin for another part of his eternal journey to take place.

I turned away sadly, and although it was not yet completely light, I could hear the sound of voices and shuffling footsteps, and round the bend in the road I could see the workmen coming, followed by the donkey boys with their animals. I wondered at that moment if I could have been wrong about Mike having set fire to the hut, but then I remembered that, from their village, they would have seen the glow in the sky and they would no doubt have sent a scout out to reconnoitre.

I returned to my tent with the intention of finishing the letters I had started to write so that they could all be taken into Luxor. I opened the drawer to take out my writing paper when my eyes fell on the alabaster vase that Talek had given me the day before. I had not had time to examine it then, but now I took it out and, going to the flap at the entrance to the tent, I scrutinized it carefully in the light.

I was conscious of a strange feeling of excitement as I turned it this way and that. I would have staked my life that this was no new thing fashioned by a modern man with a smattering of knowledge about ancient things. The vase was old and very beautiful. I was familiar with the hieroglyphics that the natives copied, ill formed and haphazard, but those on the vase were exquisite, the alabaster so delicate that a light put inside it would easily glow through. I sat on the edge of my bed holding it in my hands, delighting in its cool smoothness.

Bursting with impatience I sat through breakfast listening to the desultory chatter of the others, waiting for Professor Dalton to leave the table. I did not want to say anything in his presence. At last Mike rose to his feet, saying to anyone who cared to listen, 'I want to go into Luxor today. Do any of you wish to come with me?'

Ian said that he did; he had letters to post and wanted to buy shaving soap and perhaps make a telephone call. Mike looked at me but I merely shook my head saying, 'I have some letters, if you don't mind taking them.'

I followed him out of the tent and with some urgency said, 'Mike, please come to my tent for a moment. I have something very important to show you.'

'Let it wait until tonight, Kathy. I want to catch the early ferry. I need to telephone Sadek before he leaves for Sakkara.'

'You are going to tell him about the mummy?'

'Yes, and the breaking up of his camp. He should be told, there are things that belong to him and Strickland. Perhaps he'll try to get here some time in the near future.'

I could tell he was impatient to be gone and already Ian was waiting for him with two donkeys and their boys.

I asked Professor Dalton's permission to visit one or two royal tombs in the area, having done very little sightseeing since I arrived, and he gave instant permission. I suspected he did not wish to have me around for the rest of the day.

I made sure that I had a torch with me as well as fruit pastilles and aspirin, then I walked to where the boys waited with their donkeys. Immediately Talek saw me he came running, dragging Hassan reluctantly behind him.

'You wish to ride, my lady? You go to Luxor?'

'Not this morning, Talek. I'm not quite sure what I am going to do.'

'I take you to Deir-el-Bahari, see temple of great Queen Hatshepsut, see Colossus of Memnon. I take you to Valley of Queens.'

He was evidently overjoyed at the idea of spending a day in my company. His dark brown eyes bubbled with laughter, his mouth smiled widely showing perfect white teeth, and I couldn't help thinking what a splendid example he was of young Egyptian manhood.

'Did you thank your brother for the beautiful gift he sent me?'

'Of course. My brother very clever, he make many beautiful things.'

'What does your brother do?'

'He work for government, in antique factory. He make heads of kings, alabaster work, scarabs, cartouches. You say and Abdullah make.'

'And yet I hardly think he made the vase you gave me yesterday.'

His eyes met mine and shifted. I had seen the first flutter of fear in them.

'Come, Talek, I know I'm not a very good Egyptologist like Professor Dalton or Mr O'Hara but I do know that the vase you gave to me was never produced in any factory. It is very old, probably over three thousand years old. I want you to tell me where you found it.'

'I tell you, my lady, Abdullah make it. I tell him I work for beautiful English lady and he say he will give me gift for you, he very clever workman. Talek would not lie.'

'Oh, Talek,' I said, making my voice sound disappointed, 'I had thought I could trust you. Now I shall have to give that vase to Professor Dalton because I am aware of its value and he will have to inform the authorities.'

'As you like, my lady. If you not trust Talek, he inform authorities in Luxor, they tell you truth.'

197

'Not Luxor, Talek. He will send for Mr Sadek and he will know who is speaking the truth.'

I rode on, staring in front of me, and he hurried his stride, almost running to keep pace with me. I could see that his eyes were wide and frightened but I deliberately appeared unconcerned.

'You not send for Mr Sadek, lady, you give vase back to me and I tell my brother what you say. He get into very bad trouble, I get into bad trouble if Abdullah give real vase. He not know vase real.'

I fixed him with a stern eye and said, 'Talek, I don't know if you knew the vase was real or not, perhaps you gave it to me in good faith. But you know where these things are being stolen from, and now that the guardian of the tomb is no more, you know that more things will be stolen. Mr Sadek will need to be told. This must be the tomb he was looking for.'

'No, no, my lady. No tomb. All old tombs up there, discovered long time ago, all robbed long time ago. No new tomb.'

I looked at him sadly. If my appeal for the real truth did not work then I would have to feign sorrow. 'You disappoint me, Talek, for I had thought you to be a truthful boy, a very honest boy, and I had intended to speak to Mr Sadek about you, to tell him that, thanks to you, we now knew where the tomb was to be found and that it was your honesty that led me to it.'

'If you tell him that, lady, I am a dead man.'

'You are afraid of the men who visit the tomb?'

'Yes. We poor people, work very hard for little money. If I told, they would take Hassan away from me, take away Abdullah's licence to work in antique factory, we would have nothing.'

'But there is such a tomb, Talek, the tomb of a princess?'

'Yes.'

He hung his head and looked at the ground. I felt a great surge of pity for Talek and others like him who all through the ages had had to live on what they could steal from the dead, but at the same time I felt angry. It was as though,

198

once again, I was two people, the modern woman who could afford to feel pity for these people who had lived for centuries under the heel of some master or other, and the princess, surrounded by the things she had loved in life, knowing that bit by bit and piece by piece those precious things were being stolen.

'Will you and your brother show this tomb to me?'

'My lady, we dare not.'

'If you do not, Talek, then I shall keep the vase and show it to Mr Sadek when he comes here, but if you show the tomb to me, I shall tell him that I believe I know where it is and that I discovered it accidentally when riding in the area. You can trust me, Talek. No blame will fall upon you or your family.'

'I have to ask Abdullah. He may not agree.'

'When will you be able to let me know?'

'Tonight.'

'When tonight?'

'After dark. I will meet you where the two valleys meet. I will whistle, like this,' and to demonstrate he gave a long, low whistle, looking at me closely to make sure I understood.

I nodded. 'If your brother agrees, bring him with you and we will go to the tomb tonight. I will say nothing to the others yet, I promise.'

'If my brother will not come, what then, my lady?'

'Mr O'Hara has gone into Luxor this morning to telephone Mr Sadek. No doubt he will come here soon, so you see, there is very little time.'

He nodded miserably. 'You want Hassan for day? I go now to see brother.'

'I will take good care of him. I will ride up to the old camp. If I am seen up there they will no doubt think I'm doing a little investigating on my own.'

'Tomb very high up on cliffs, my lady, you must climb.'

'You mean the entrance is on the cliff-face?'

'We not find real entrance, we dig shaft and it bring us to passage in tomb. Very difficult to get in there, not fit for lady.'

I rode Hassan all the way to where we had broken up

199

John Strickland's camp, and after tying him to a rock, I clambered up to the cave where they had discovered the mummy. I had the strangest feeling that I was being watched, that more than one pair of eyes was trained upon me from across the valley, but I concentrated on examining every inch of the wall of the cave in case there should be something the others had overlooked. I was convinced that I was wasting my time – both Strickland and Sadek had known better than I what they had been looking for – but the faint hope lingered that some memory from the past would come to aid me in my search. Needless to say, it did not.

As I climbed upwards towards the gaping holes in the rockface, I knew these ancient tombs would be empty. In one of them I found a roll of mummy bandages and some broken pottery, but their original occupants had long since been deprived of whatever valuables they had been buried with, and no doubt the mummies had been broken up by thieves.

It was late afternoon when I finally rode back to the site, meeting Professor Anthony taking his short constitutional along the path.

'What, no donkey boy?' he remarked smiling.

'No. Talek was generous today, he allowed me to borrow Hassan and go off on my own.'

'How far did you get?'

'I went up to the other camp and had a look round at the old tombs.'

'Thought you might find Strickland's tomb and surprise us with it?' he asked astutely.

'How could I succeed where so many more competent Egyptologists have failed?' I replied casually. 'Are Mike and Ian back yet?'

'No, I expect we shall only be three for dinner this evening. The others are still in Luxor.'

I was glad. It meant that I could return to my tent immediately after the meal. There would be no earnest discussions over the coffee cups, no invitations to saunter under the dark jewelled sky. Secretly I could go with Talek

alone to the tomb so that, in the morning, I could surprise
them all by showing them where it could be found.

That I was doing something foolishly naïve and stupid
never occurred to me. I had never been able to see danger
until it was too late.

In my tent that night I took my torch and two new batteries
in case the light gave out. I also took gloves in case we had
to scramble down ropes which might hurt my hands. I had
asked one of the servants to feed Hassan and now I went to
where the donkey was patiently waiting for me along the
path.

I held my breath several times as my shoes struck stones,
standing quite still to listen in case one of the others came
out, but nothing happened so I led the donkey away, not
daring to mount until we were well clear of the camp. I rode
in the centre of the path, my eyes now accustomed to the
light. It was a dark, moonless night and the shadows from
the cliffs seemed to bear down at me, enclosing me in some
sort of cavern, blotting out the horizon, but the donkey
trotted quietly on, sure-footed and heading for the path
where the valleys divided.

It was lighter where we reached this point because we
were not so enclosed, and almost immediately, like a silent
white shadow, Talek was by my side, accompanied by
another figure whom I looked at curiously.

'You are Talek's brother?' I asked him.

'Yes, Abdullah.'

I took out my torch and shone it into his face. He was
taller than Talek and considerably more swarthy. He
stepped back, blinking in the sudden light, but even in that
brief moment when I saw his face clearly I knew that this
was no Talek. His look was sly, his eyes cunning in his dark
bearded face, and for the first time I began to feel afraid.

They had with them another donkey which Abdullah
rode, allowing Talek to trot behind us. He was silent on the
journey, and turning to Talek, I asked, 'Does your brother
speak English?'

201

'Only little, I speak better.'

'What did he say when you asked him to accompany you?'

'He not like, my lady. He angry that I told you tomb there, he say this dangerous journey.'

Silently I agreed with him. It had been an act of foolhardiness for me to come alone with these men, but the need to prove something to myself had been much stronger than any sense of danger.

'I will keep my promise, Talek,' I told him quietly. 'Ahmed Sadek will be here in a day or so and I have told Mr O'Hara that I am going with you and your brother tonight.'

'You tell Mr O'Hara this?' Abdullah said sharply, proving to me that even if he did not speak much English, he had no difficulty in understanding it.

'Of course, you don't suppose I would make this journey without telling the others where I was going?'

'Then why not he come with you?' he asked sharply.

'Because of my promise to Talek, but you need have no fears that we shall be unobserved in case of accidents.'

He muttered something under his breath but we rode steadily on and I began to feel a little happier with the situation.

'You were unwise to give that vase to Talek, Abdullah. Surely you must have known I would recognize it as being genuine?'

'I not give to Talek, he stole.'

'I see. Then you are angry that we are making this journey?'

He didn't answer me but continued to ride by my side in silence. Turning to Talek, I said, 'Your brother speaks better English than I had thought he would. Is he trustworthy, do you think?'

'Oh yes, my lady.'

'You realize that if I am not back at the camp by morning they will inform the authorities that I was with you and your brother. There will be many questions asked and by that time no doubt Mr Sadek will have arrived in Luxor.'

Talek merely nodded, and with further misgivings I rode

202

on, although by this time I was feeling decidedly sick with worry about my chances of returning from this adventure unscathed.

We reached the site of the old camp and Talek murmured, 'We should dismount now.' Pointing with his finger he said, 'We go up there, my lady, much climbing to reach shaft.'

They climbed like monkeys, hitching up their long, loose jellabas and pulling me up after them. I did not dare look down the steep rockface but kept my eyes deliberately trained upwards, relying mostly on Talek's strong slim hands to hold me. At last we stood on a narrow ledge and I was grateful to see that a thin crescent moon rode high over the cliffs. I could see the valley below us and, in the distance, lights in what I supposed was the workmen's village. We came to a large rock and, underneath it, a small hole, barely large enough for a man to creep through.

'Hole dug by jackals,' Talek explained. 'That way tomb found.'

We crept in on our hands and knees and I was surprised how bitterly cold it felt compared to the night outside. I switched on my powerful torch and could see that we were in a cave the size of a large room that had been hollowed by hand, the furthest part being entirely free from drift-sand. My heart began to race as my eyes fell on row upon row of hieroglyphics. Talek took my hand and pulled me into a narrow passageway, pointing with his hand to a hole in the ground and a pit of such dense blackness I could see nothing beyond the gaping hole.

'Do we have to go down there?' I asked, my voice trembling even though I clenched my hands fiercely together in an effort to calm my fears.

'We have rod, tie rope to it, then we go down.'

I watched them drag the rod out of a corner of the cave and I held my torch while they tied the long rope to it. Then, without looking at me, they placed the rod in position over the hole with the rope dangling downwards. I shone my torch into the blackness while Abdullah descended, placing his bare feet against the smooth sides of the well and vanishing into the blackness. At last the rope ceased shaking and a faint shout came rumbling up the well to announce his safe arrival. From far below a small light appeared and I realized that he had probably found a supply of candles which were kept down there to aid the tomb robbers in their silent search.

Talek held the rope, indicating that it was now my turn to descend into that inky black darkness. Never had I been more grateful for the gloves I had had the foresight to bring, but, even so, my hands hurt agonizingly before I felt Abdullah take the rope from my hands, shaking it so that Talek would know that he could begin the descent.

I was miserably aware of my sore knees and shins which had at times dangled helplessly against the rockface, and I dared not take off my gloves to look at my smarting hands. The light from two candles illuminated a narrow passage. Talek came down hand over hand like a sailor, and finally we all stood staring at each other in the flickering light. I wondered if my face registered the terror I was feeling.

Abdullah went first, and then, horror of horrors, I heard the squeaking of bats. The next moment they were all around us, in my hair, touching my face, and I heard myself screaming while the two men hit out at them, muttering strange Arabic curses at their persistence.

'Bats only in this place,' Talek consoled me, 'none in chamber.'

I covered my head with my hands and followed them. The shaft we were in had been dug to catch unwary tomb robbers, but the enterprise of that jackal had turned it into an entrance to the tomb. I recognized the obvious arrangement of the trapdoor through which we were entering and with my torch I could now see that we were in a chamber, the walls of which were decorated with the figures of gods and goddesses. There were prayers and supplications for the journey of the soul through the corridors of the blessed until at last she was accepted into the chamber of the gods in the land of Amenti. I supposed some of these painted figures represented the face and form of the deceased, but they were so stylized that they were just like hundreds of others that I had seen on the walls of the tombs I had so far visited.

Around me was a scattered collection of funereal equipment arranged in higgledy-piggledy haste. Tall jars in the form of *ashabti* figures, a chariot embossed with the wings of birds that had been thrown broken into a corner, and vases of alabaster crumbling now and obviously disdained by the tomb robbers.

'Can we get into the burial chamber itself, Talek?' I asked him in a whisper.

'No. No way out of this chamber, only by way we come. Burial chamber still sealed, Abdullah say.'

My heart gave a wild surge of relief even though I had little faith in anything Abdullah said. Then remembering, I said quickly. 'Was it here that the jewellery was found?'

'Yes, my lady, in the dust, in corners.'

'You are telling me the truth, Talek?'

'Oh yes, my lady, my brother not lie, by all the names of Allah he speak the truth.'

'Then we can go back.'

'You not want to take anything, you just come to look!' he said, staring at me in dismay.

'Why, yes, Talek. I want nothing from here.'

I shone my torch over the walls searching for a cartouche, but I could find none. Somewhere there was another entrance but now at least I could tell the others where to find the tomb.

I turned round to find that I was alone in the chamber, and from ahead of me I heard the raised voices of Talek and Abdullah. They were quarrelling, and with something like fear, I approached them, feeling quite sure that they were quarrelling about me. Abdullah was glaring at me.

Their raised voices echoed hollowly round the chamber. I had thought I understood Arabic reasonably well by now, but they were speaking in some form of dialect that was difficult to follow. I watched helplessly as Abdullah grabbed the rope and began to hoist himself up. Talek struggled with him, trying with all his might to pull him down from the rope, but with a vicious lunge the older man struck out, felling Talek to the ground where he lay still after striking his head on the stone floor. I too tried to grab the rope, but

205

with a thrust from his foot, Abdullah sent me staggering away, and now he was climbing rapidly upwards, leaving me staring after him with a terrible fear in my heart.

Talek was moaning at my feet, and when I knelt beside him, I could see the dark bruise at the side of his face. His eyes were open, looking dully round the chamber, then with a sharp cry he pointed to where the rope was being dragged upwards. Although I reached for it, I had no hope of catching it. I could hear Abdullah dimly cursing to himself and then there was silence. He had left us in the tomb and I had no faith that he would come back for us.

All sorts of emotions troubled me in those first few moments: rage that Abdullah had left us, coupled with amazement that he should leave his brother in this plight even if he showed no compassion for me, and anger at my own stupidity in thinking I could trust him and at my audacity in believing that I could succeed in finding a tomb that more experienced archaeologists had failed to find. I had been guilty of the most reckless folly in going to the tomb with Talek and his brother without leaving a note of where I was going.

I thought about the night ahead of us. Suppose they didn't miss me until the morning. They would search the cliffs, fearing that I had gone walking and perhaps fallen and injured myself. When they failed to find me, they would go to the workmen's village, but if any of them knew of my fate, they would stick together like leeches rather than say what had happened to me. None of them would be willing to jeopardize their livelihood.

What would happen when the candles went out? I had matches in my bag and I had a torch but the thought of lying in that dark tomb filled me with terror, and already in my imagination, the air was becoming stale and thin.

I looked at Talek sitting with his back against the wall and exasperation filled me so that I snapped angrily, 'Your brother is evil, Talek. How dare he leave us here? Surely he doesn't intend to leave you here to die?'

He shrugged his shoulders, that fatalistic shrug of the

Oriental which says so clearly that today is today, tomorrow is in the hands of Allah.

I stared at him, obsessed by my anger, then a strange sort of pity took its place. It was my fault that Talek was in this situation. He had brought me here because he liked me; it was not his fault that his brother had proved to be such a traitor.

'We must conserve the candles, Talek,' I said briskly. 'I have matches to relight them and I have a torch, but I propose we only keep one candle burning at a time. Heaven knows how long we must remain here before they find us.'

He looked at me sadly out of his large brown eyes and shook his head. 'My lady, do not set your hopes too high. If Abdullah has replaced the stone perhaps they never find us. Already they have searched long for this tomb.'

'Your brother will be made to tell them where we are. Mr O'Hara will see to that.'

'My brother will leave Luxor, go to Aswan or some other place. He dare not stay here.'

The prospect that we would not be rescued was one I refused to contemplate. Talek's voice was fading and I could see that he was nearly unconscious; the wound in his head must be throbbing painfully. I reached into my bag and found my eau de cologne and proceeded to bathe the wound gently. 'It will smart, Talek, but it will be better afterwards,' I consoled him.

I sat beside him on the cold stone floor, hugging my knees. 'Oh, Talek,' I said savagely. 'At this moment I wish I were that long-dead princess. Your brother would not have dared to do this to her, and if he had she would not have been afraid to exercise a terrible revenge. It seems to me that too much civilization is a dangerous thing.'

He stared at me but he did not know what I was talking about. I went about extinguishing the candles, apart from one which stood flickering against the wall, then I settled down again beside Talek to wait. We would not know when morning came; in this tomb in the bowels of the earth, sunrise and sunset would be as one.

Talek slept but I was determined that I would stay awake,

however strong the compulsion to close my eyes. The minutes dragged on and the stillness which descended on my brain rendered me acutely aware of the stillness which had descended on my life. The world with its noise and bustle was now as utterly remote as though it did not exist. No sound, no whisper came to me out of the darkness. Silence is the real sovereign of the ancient Egyptian tombs, a silence that began in prehistoric antiquity and which no babble of visiting tourists can really break, for every night it returns anew with awe-inspiring completeness.

I felt the powerful atmosphere of the tomb, and the passage of time deepened it, enhancing the sense of the immeasurable ages which enveloped me and made me feel that the twentieth century was slipping away. A strange feeling that we were not alone began to creep insidiously over me. I sensed that something animate and living was throbbing into existence. It was a vague feeling but a real one and it was coupled with the increasing awareness of the returning past.

Yet, nothing clear-cut or definite emerged from this vague general sense of an eerie life that pulsated through the darkness. The hours slipped on and, contrary to my expectation, the advancing night brought increasing coldness with it. Cold air was creeping into the tomb and my flesh began to shiver through the thin shirt I was wearing. My chilled flesh felt cold and clammy to my touch and I sat nearer to Talek for warmth. I had momentarily forgotten how the nights of Egypt could be bitterly cold.

Quite suddenly the spluttering candle went out and I felt again the cold breath of air on my face. I sat in the darkness shivering. I could no more have risen to relight the candle than I could have grown wings and floated upwards through that narrow hole above us. The all-encompassing darkness began to press on my head like an iron weight.

The shadow of uncalled-for fear flickered into me. I brushed it away impatiently, but to sit in the encroaching coldness of the tomb required all the moral fortitude I possessed. I thought about snakes and scorpions emerging from their timeless holes, moving silently along the floor.

With a little cry I jumped to my feet before I realized that it was only in my imagination that I heard their writhings across the stone floor.

Shadows began to flit to and fro in the shadowless room and gradually they seemed to take more definite shape. Age-old spirits seemed to have crept out of the neighbouring necropolis, a necropolis so old that mummies had crumbled away inside their stone sarcophagi, and the shades that clung to them made their unwelcome ascent to the place of my vigil.

Somewhere in the centre of that still thing which was my body I knew that my heart beat like a hammer under the strain. The dread of the supernatural, which lurks at the bottom of every human heart, touched me again. Fear, dread, horror persistently presented their evil visages to me in turn and involuntarily my hands clenched themselves as tightly as vices. My eyes were closed and yet these grey gliding vaporous forms obtruded themselves across my vision, and always there came with them an implacable hostility and feeling of menace.

I felt that I was going to die as they came nearer. Monstrous elemental creations, evil and fiendish, gathered around me and afflicted me with unimaginable repulsion. In that haunted darkness I lived through something that I felt sure would leave a remembered record behind for all time whether I was rescued from the tomb or not, yet the end came with startling suddenness. The malevolent ghostly invaders disappeared into the obscurity from which they had emerged, into the shadowy realms of the departed, taking with them their trail of noxious horrors. My half-shattered nerves experienced overwhelming relief. It was as though the god Set had done his worst. Suddenly I became aware of a new presence in the chamber, a friendly benevolent one who stood before me and looked down upon me with kindly eyes. Something clean and sane seemed to have come with it, soothing and calming me, and gradually it took shape, a tall man in long white robes with the gleam of leopard skins about his shoulders and the staff of a high priest in his hands. In that moment I ceased to be me, and

209

once again I was the Princess Tuia gazing into the eyes of the high priest of Ammon and silently asking his forgiveness for that ancient sin which had followed me down the ages. He reached forward and held out his hand and I felt the brush of his fingers on my hair.

Then I was alone in the chamber with Talek asleep beside me.

For a long time I sat gazing before me as I tried to piece together the events of the night. I felt incredibly calm. I refused to believe that those dreadful shadows and the vision of the high priest had only been figments of an imagination brought to life in a state of dreaming sleep, and now the cool air playing on my face gave me hope. Abdullah had not replaced the stone above the hole dug by the jackal. Groping in my bag I found my torch and shone it on the face of my watch. It was almost seven o'clock and I knew that it was morning. My throat felt parched and dry so I made myself slowly suck a fruit pastille, then I shook Talek gently until his eyes opened.

'It's morning Talek, they must come for us soon.'

No such optimism showed in his face but he took one of my sweets and I told him that his brother had not replaced the stone.

'How you know that, my lady?'

'Can't you feel the cool air? It was very cold last night, the cold draught must be coming down the shaft.'

I made myself talk normally to my companion, asking about his life, his ambitions, his family, until he caught hold of my wrist fiercely, and my heart leaped with hope as he rose to his feet and stood below the shaft with his eyes and ears straining upwards into the darkness. I stood beside him listening but I could hear nothing, and in despair I said, 'Oh, Talek, don't do that to me, I can't hear anything.'

He cautioned me to silence, then hoarsely he bellowed up the shaft and imbued with his enthusiasm I added my voice to his. Dimly I could hear men's voices, and clutching Talek's arm, I said, 'It could be your brother, Talek, come back for you.'

I felt afraid as I remembered Abdullah's dark shifty eyes

and his determination to leave me behind, and as though he sensed my fear, Talek said, 'I never leave you, my lady. I only go if you go also.'

The voices were nearer now and we shouted until we could shout no more. Then to my utmost delight I recognized them as English voices and my hopes soared. Suddenly a light shone down the shaft and I heard Mike's voice saying, 'They're here, we've found them. Kathy, is that you?'

'Oh yes, Mike, I'm here. Talek is with me. You'll need a rope.'

They moved away but I knew they would be back. Hope filled my heart like a benediction and already I was feeling the sun of my arms, seeing the golden, glowing morning and the deep blue Egyptian sky above me. Talek, too, had recovered his high spirits and was looking upwards expectantly.

A rope came down and Mike's voice called down to me, 'Can you manage to climb up, Kathy, or shall we pull you up?'

'A little bit of both, please, Mike.'

It had been bad enough on the downward journey, and the mere thought of dangling on that rope which stretched upwards into the darkness filled me full of terror, but gritting my teeth I reached for it. I hauled myself up, painfully and slowly, every inch causing me so much pain in my hands and on my battered legs that I could have cried with it. At last I felt my shoulders taken in strong hands and I was pulled through the hole in the rock. I stood in Mike's arms, taking in great gulps of air.

He put me aside after a few moments and went to help Alan and Ian pull Talek to safety. We were out on the ledge, my eyes blinking in the strong sunlight, with the morning air clean and sweet around us after the dust of centuries we had been breathing below. My limbs ached painfully and my hands felt as if they no longer belonged to me, but I was aware of a great exultation as I thought of what I would be able to tell Mike later.

With Mike leading the little procession we slid and scrambled down the cliff path and there to my relief I found

211

Hassan and a group of other donkeys waiting to take us back to the site.

As Mike helped me to mount, I saw for the first time that his face was set and angry, and some of my high spirits seemed at that moment to desert me. He was angry with me, and rightly so, but as our eyes met I was conscious of the relief he felt underneath his anger, and taking hold of his hand I said, 'Oh, Mike, I have so much to tell you, don't be angry.'

'You can tell me all about it later, Kathy. In the meantime you must get some rest. You can tell me tomorrow.'

'But I don't want to tell you tomorrow, I want to tell you now. It's important.'

'Tomorrow, Kathy.'

With a brief nod he left me to mount his own donkey and I could have wept with frustration and some other emotion I refused to acknowledge.

My bones ached wearily as Hassan trotted along the rough-hewn path towards the valley. When we reached our destination I was helped from his back and stumbled wearily towards my tent. There I stared with dismay at the great red weals which the removal of my gloves laid bare. My legs too were in a sorry plight, black-and-blue bruises and here and there blood-raw where the skin had been torn away. I couldn't bear the bedclothes to touch them so I contented myself with sleeping on top of my bed. I didn't look at my face or my hair. It was Mike, shaking me into wakefulness, who brought me back into the land of the living.

I stared at him through half-closed eyes, dimly aware that he was hurting my arms as he gripped me, and I moaned dismally, wishing he would let me lie back so that I could go on sleeping.

I heard their voices, Mike's and the two boys', then I heard Professor Anthony's voice saying as if from miles away, 'Is she awake? Is she all right? She looks as though she's been battered and left for dead.'

I felt cool water on my forehead and I moaned a little as one of them took my sore hands, exclaiming anxiously at the state of them.

'Kathy,' the voice went on, more soothingly this time, 'Kathy, wake up. We must attend to these poor hands of yours.'

I opened my eyes, dimly aware of several anxious faces staring down at me, then whimpering a little with the pain of my bruised limbs, I tried to sit up.

'No,' the voice said, 'don't sit up, just lie still while I look after your bruises.'

It was all coming back to me now, the tomb and the hole in the cave, the bats and the long terrible night, and I heard my voice babbling while they stared at me in silence. Then Mike bathed my hands and my bruised legs with soothing lotion, only occasionally looking at me in a worried fashion until I firmly believed he thought I was demented.

Ian handed him a glass to which Mike added two tablets, pressing it into my hands saying, 'Drink it all up, Kathy. You'll feel much better next time you wake up.'

I took it like a child, allowing him to push me back against the pillows. My eyes searched his face, looking for the anger that had been there before. The last thing I remembered before I floated back into unconsciousness was that the anger had gone.

I awoke to golden sunlight flooding my tent and the normal sounds of men's voices and kitchen sounds, occasional laughter and the dismay of finding that my watch had stopped. Gingerly I sat up and put my feet on the floor. I still ached, but less, and the pain in my hands seemed to have miraculously disappeared. I struggled to rise, reaching out for the portable mirror on the cabinet, then I cried out with dismay. My hair was a mess where frantically I had brushed the bats aside, and my face devoid of makeup showed a blue bruise over my forehead and a cut at the side of my chin.

I was still staring at my reflection when the flap opened and Ian came in. A delighted smile spread over his face and he immediately called out to someone outside: 'She's awake

213

at last, and looking at herself in the mirror. She must be better!'

Alan and Mike joined him and, smiling, Mike said, 'You look more like yourself this morning, Kathy. Feel better?'

'I think so. I have just managed to stand on my feet. What time is it?'

'Just after nine. You've been asleep all of twenty-four hours so you should feel better. Now you can have breakfast and tell us what happened, and no more talk of some tomb you thought you'd found.'

'But I did find it, Mike. I went with Talek and his brother,' and I proceeded to tell them from start to finish every single episode of my adventure, except for my experiences with the shades in the dark tomb. These I would keep to myself for the rest of my life. They were disapproving of my rashness but they were excited, too, as I went on to tell them about the chamber filled with vases and furniture, even though much of it was broken and crumbling, and the gold chariot with its beautiful decoration of wings. When I explained that it had been discovered because a jackal had dug his hole over the mummy pit, they could hardly contain themselves in their anxiety to go there.

'We must wait until Sadek gets here,' Mike said firmly. 'This is his tomb, his and Strickland's. If Dalton knows about it he will take full credit and that would be unfair.'

I didn't want Dalton to have any part of it. I didn't yet know whose tomb it was, but if it was who I hoped it was, I couldn't bear to think of Dalton's thin fingers prodding and exploring, dissecting with cold dispassionate fingers the body which had once been so beautiful and which had embraced both life and death with such ardour.

Dalton did have the good grace to ask if I was fully recovered and I was glad to know they had not told him the reason for my indisposition. He merely believed I had been suffering from a migraine and he was not sufficiently interested to inquire further. I doubt if he even noticed my bandaged hands.

Talek returned with Hassan and I was relieved to see him looking none the worse for his experience in the tomb. I asked after his brother but he merely shrugged his shoulders, saying that Abdullah had gone to Aswan and he did not know when he would return.

'I have told them about the tomb, Talek, and Mr Sadek is coming here tomorrow. You can rest assured they will not make public your part in this but you will be rewarded privately.'

He beamed from ear to ear. 'Thank you, my lady. Perhaps Talek could buy other donkey, that way twice as much work.'

'I'm sure their gratitude will run to another donkey.'

'Perhaps even camel? But no, donkey better for tourists, camel they no like so much.'

I laughed at his cheerfulness, remembering how desperate we had both been only a short time before.

Ahmed Sadek arrived shortly after lunch, urbane and courteous, treating Dalton's ill humour with Eastern tolerance.

'I suppose you want Strickland's notes and the other things we brought down from your camp?' Dalton said.

'His notes, yes, the other things can remain here.'

'I suppose you both realize that it was a wasted effort,' Dalton said scathingly.

'On the contrary, we would have been there yet had it not been for Strickland's illness.'

'We both know the extent and cause of that illness,' Dalton said sarcastically.

'Yes, it is sad. All men cannot greet life's disasters with equanimity. Strickland drinks, but he has remained a gentle man without bitterness or jealousy. Many of us could learn from John Strickland.'

He was looking at Professor Dalton with narrowed eyes and there was a gleam in them that afforded the rest of us a certain satisfaction.

Dalton did not linger in the communal tent, and as soon as he had gone, Mike instructed me to tell Ahmed Sadek all that I knew. Ahmed was not a man given to outward excitement, but I could tell by his shining dark eyes that he was enthusiastic.

'You'd better start work there as soon as possible,' Mike said. 'At least before any more articles are taken from the tomb.'

'I will return to Luxor and telephone the man who is working under me. They can continue at Sakkara without my help. Here, I shall need workmen and one or two of you to help me. What about Dalton?'

'We needn't inform him of the part Kathy has played in this. I think it would be best if you simply went up there with some diggers, informed him of the discovery, and let the rest fall into place,' Mike advised.

So that was how it was. For long days we didn't see Sadek but he got his workmen, and if they were angry and frustrated that their tomb had been discovered, he was very much their master. Dalton was visibly infuriated and made life difficult for the rest of us, but by the end of the hot summer months he decided to disband the camp and go home for what he termed a well-earned rest. This left us free to join Ahmed Sadek, which we all did without exception. We had worked through the hot dusty months of the Egyptian summer; the winter would soon be upon us and winters in Egypt are like perfect English summers but considerably more predictable.

They were still removing articles from the chamber I had already seen and had not yet made an entrance into the burial chamber itself. I was not allowed to swarm down the rope into the dark passageway so I had to contain my soul in patience labelling the things they brought out of the tomb and assembling them in some sort of order for packing and ultimate transport to the museum in Cairo. I worked on them unemotionally, for most of them were broken. Only the chariot with its exquisite design of wings brought an ache to my throat. It had never figured in my dreams but, repaired, it would be a beautiful thing and I could imagine some proud Egyptian beauty handling the reins of her spirited prancing horses, racing them across the hot sand.

One morning, while I was busy making tea, Mike burst into the tent, his face flushed with excitement.

'We've found the real opening to the tomb, Kathy. Tomorrow, with a bit of luck, you'll be able to enter it the way it was intended.'

'Can I come with you now?' I cried, already halfway out of the tent.

He held me back. 'Tomorrow, I promise. The seals are still on the doors. We shall have to try to open them from the inside. We've no idea where they are placed on the cliff-face.'

I couldn't sleep that night for excitement, visualizing the gaping hole on the cliff-face and praying that I would find it accessible. The morning seemed to drag on, but shortly before lunch, Alan came into the tent, saying urgently, 'We've got it open. Come on, Kathy, don't bother with lunch.'

I ran out of the tent and followed his hurrying figure towards the cliff, surprised that he didn't climb higher up the path. Instead he went to the cave where they had discovered the priest's mummy. I called to him but he merely turned round, beckoning me to follow. I entered the mummy cave uncertainly, surprised to see them clustered round a wide entrance on the far wall. They immediately stepped back to allow me to see into the passageway beyond.

'But why here?' I asked. 'Why not with the other entrances on the cliff-face?'

'I think that was where the entrance was originally planned, but then they decided to dig this chamber and set the entrance to the tomb further back,' Ahmed Sadek explained, watching my face with dark inscrutable eyes.

'Do you know whose tomb it is?' I asked fearfully, longing to know yet desperately afraid.

'From the cartouche on the door it is the tomb of a lady named Mutemwa. She was obviously a lady of some standing, to judge by the care that was taken in disguising the entrance to her tomb and by the things we have taken from it so far. She may well have been a vizier's wife or the wife of some court official or nobleman.'

217

My disappointment was so intense that I could have wept and my knees shook so that I had to lean back against the rock wall. I was aware of the sympathy in Ahmed Sadek's eyes and wished fervently that I had not told him of the dreams surrounding the princess which had coloured my life.

At length I found my voice. 'When will you open the burial chamber?' I asked.

'There is another passageway and chamber to be cleared, so it will probably take one or two days. As soon as we have it open, you shall see it.'

'I wonder why they put the mummy of the priest in here,' Alan said curiously, 'particularly a priest who had been buried alive.'

'Perhaps he and the Lady Mutemwa were guilty of an indiscreet love affair,' Ian said in an attempt to be humorous. 'Her husband probably found out and this is where they both ended up.'

Nobody laughed, and I think they were all at that moment remembering the expression on the face of the mummy whose tomb this cave had been.

I felt deflated, it was almost as though all my life had been a lie, even the feeling that I had loved David at some time in a far distant past, and now I was unsure of everything. Was I merely a silly romantic fool, obsessed with daydreams and unreal illusions, shaping my life to make them fit, refusing to realize that dreams were as insubstantial as wishes? Why couldn't I be more like Mike, always asking for proof, refusing to believe anything unless the evidence stared him in the face?

All day I was morose and miserable, setting out on my own to prowl down the valley, anywhere away from the sound of laughter and excited conversation, divorced completely from the enthusiasm of the others.

I was on my way back to the site when Ahmed Sadek came striding down the road to meet me.

'You are disappointed?' were his first words.

'For me, yes, for you and Mr Strickland, no. I've thought about him so often, living in that awful place, sick and tormented by his unseen demons. I'm only disappointed because I've been such a fool, allowing my dreams to shape my life. I thought about the mummy of the priest and made him into Ptahotep, the old woman they found I felt sure must be Ipey, and this tomb the tomb of the princess. It all seemed so definite and now none of it is true.'

'Just because this doesn't happen to be the tomb of the princess you dreamed about doesn't necessarily mean that your dreams have been futile. This valley and the others like it are riddled with tombs, many of them undiscovered,' Ahmed said. 'The fact that you made your dreams fit reality does not explain the many instances of unexplained happenings in the lives of a great many people, or that psychic forces are constantly at work even in this materialistic, mundane world. Try not to judge yourself too harshly just yet. I am not satisfied that this is the tomb of the Lady Mutemwa.'

'Oh no, please, no more false hopes, no more disappointments. I couldn't bear them.'

'I'm not trying to raise your hopes, Kathy, I'm only interested in finding the truth. The chariot we found in the antechamber, for instance, was decorated in a way that only the chariots of royal personages were decorated. We discovered a litter underneath the debris, a beautiful thing, and too large for the tomb robbers to steal because they would have had great difficulty in disposing of it without questions being asked. Many of those broken and crumbling things will be repaired and find their home in the Cairo museum. Even supposing the burial chamber reveals nothing, our time has not been wasted.'

'You think there is a chance that the burial chamber has already been violated?'

'I never expect too much, that way I am never unduly disappointed. Nothing in Egyptology is certain, that is probably why it is so fascinating to so many people.'

The hours dragged so that I could settle to nothing, waiting, always waiting. I saw little of the others since they only snatched at meals and disappeared immediately afterwards. Once or twice I walked up to the mummy cave but they were working inside the tomb and I had to retrace my steps, vaguely disappointed.

It was late afternoon on the second day when Ian came to tell me that they had broken into the burial chamber. Eagerly I asked, 'Has the chamber been robbed?'

'We haven't been able to see much, we've only just broken through, but there's an alabaster sarcophagus in there.'

'When can I see it?' I asked hoarsely.

'Probably tomorrow. Sadek wants to go on working tonight so I expect we'll make an entry wide enough to get in there before morning.'

I spent all night tossing and turning on my narrow bed, my ears straining for any sound so that I was ready to run out to meet them in case they returned to the camp. By first light I was up and walking towards the cliffs. An unnatural quiet seemed to hang around the valley and I stood still on the path, listening for any sounds from inside the cave. The silence was oppressive, and for the first time I began to wonder if they had returned to the tents while I had dozed fitfully as I surely must have done.

The sky above was pearly grey with, here and there, a hint of rose and already in the east there was a glow which heralded the sunrise. Making up my mind quickly I went into the cave and with determination in my heart I took the torch out of my bag and walked forward into the passage beyond. I knew the bats were above me, I could hear their rustlings, but I would not look at them. I went forward through the antechamber to where I could see the gaping hole ahead. It was wide enough for me to get through but I hesitated, listening. There was no sound. I was seized with such a feeling of dread that, for a brief moment, I felt suddenly faint, but I made myself go forward. I had come so far, I had to know.

I was in a large chamber supported by square pillars. The walls and the pillars were decorated with the figures of gods and goddesses, the ceiling was a deep midnight blue painted with stars, and in the centre of the tomb rested a large pale green alabaster sarcophagus, exquisitely carved. Apart from that there was nothing.

I stepped back, overcome by disappointment. Just then I felt somebody take my arm and I gave a strangled cry. I looked up into Ahmed Sadek's face, finding his eyes filled with sympathy.

'It is empty,' I said stupidly, and he nodded.

'Yes, Kathy, this is exactly how we found it. The sarcophagus is empty, we were too late.'

'But I don't understand. When was it robbed, in ancient days or recently?'

'It has probably been systematically robbed for years, first by the men who built it, then by their descendants.'

'But Talek and his brother told me the burial chamber had not been found.'

He looked at me pityingly. 'My dear girl, as soon as they knew the tomb had been discovered they would have removed everything that was left. I shall go to the village and interrogate the headman, but I shall discover nothing, you can be sure of that. The only time they did not take from the tomb was after the priest's mummy was discovered. When Dalton had it removed, back they came. I fear that inadvertently we played into their hands.'

'So we shall never know whose tomb it was?'

'Perhaps not. It was a woman's tomb, we can be sure of that from the paintings on the walls, and it was a woman who was entitled to wear the royal insignia on her headdress, but whether it was the Lady Mutemwa, or a princess, we may never know.'

I felt drained of all emotion. All the long, hot, dusty days they had worked painstakingly in the bowels of the earth with nothing to show for it, and now it was over. 'We found one thing, Kathy, of no value to the men who robbed this tomb but you might find it precious.'

He reached down inside the sarcophagus and took from it a small wreath of dried and shrivelled flowers and placed it in my hands.

For one moment I felt a wild surge of joy. They were the dried petals of the lotus flower intertwined with jasmine and mimosa. I wondered who had stepped forward at that last moment before they closed the alabaster lid and placed inside that small token of regard. The tears rolled down my face and fell on the fragile flower heads, mingling perhaps with other tears that had fallen upon them centuries before.

'Keep them if you like,' he said gently, but I shook my head and replaced them in the sarcophagus.

As I walked before him into the light of a new day, I began to feel more composed. It was over. No more would I find myself troubled by long painted green eyes that stared back at me from mirrors when they should have been my eyes. No more would I see her raven-black hair and proud exquisite face instead of my own which at times I had hated because it was not hers. Ahmed took my arm to assist me down the rocky path, and then I saw Mike coming slowly along the road towards us. He looked at Ahmed sharply, saying, 'She knows?' Sadek nodded and dropped tactfully behind to let Mike walk by my side.

'Don't be too disappointed, Kathy. It was always on the cards that we would find nothing. In Egypt one learns to live with disappointments of this kind.'

'I know, but I was so sure that this time it wouldn't happen.'

'Well, at least we've managed to salvage a few things of value. In a little while, when the experts have done their work, you will see how beautiful they once were.'

I looked up at him striding beside me in the early morning sunlight, and at that moment I felt very close to him. He smiled down at me and, taking my arm, he held it gently against him so that I could feel his strength and his warmth dispelling the disappointment in my heart.

'Mike, why did you set fire to the mummy?'

I heard his sudden intake of breath. More gently, I pressed home my question.

'I couldn't sleep that night, Mike. I went out of my tent and walked along the path. I was so sure somebody else was awake, too. I was down on the path below the hut when it went up in flames.'

'If you're so sure I did it, why didn't you say so when I walked back to the camp?'

222

'I knew you had your reasons. Besides, you were considerably agitated, quite unlike your normal self.'

'Yes, but that was hardly surprising when I had just destroyed a man who had lain unmolested for more than two thousand years. I was still obsessed with the feeling that all the ancient gods of Egypt pursued me and that a thousand mummies in a thousand tombs were crying out to them for vengeance.'

'But why, Mike?'

'I don't exactly know, except that ever since I first saw it, his face has haunted me. I found myself wondering why he had been condemned to suffer such a fate and I used to lie awake at night wondering how long they had made him wait before they put him into that tomb.'

I said nothing but I could have given him the answer. From the death of the princess to the day of her funeral it took forty days to embalm her body. They had given her the tomb of another so in those forty days they had hollowed out the chamber to receive the priest's mummy and set back the entrance to the princess's tomb. Those old priests had seen to it that, because they had sinned together in life, so would they spend eternity together.

'I'm glad you set fire to it,' I said fiercely. 'I'm glad nobody else is going to look at either of them, the priest or the princess. It is finished.'

Eleven

By early January the campsite in the Valley of the Kings and that in the other valley where we found the tomb of the princess had been taken down and disbanded and we were all in Luxor. The things we had removed from the tomb were in large crates and already packed on board the ship Ahmed Sadek had commandeered to take them to the museum in Cairo, and we were waiting to sail with her. At his suggestion we were to have two days in Luxor before the boat sailed and I was glad because I had seen nothing of Karnak or other temples, my life in Egypt having been confined solely to my work in the royal valley.

It was heavenly to bathe in softly scented water and have my hair pampered by scented shampoos and my skin softened by lotions and decent makeup. I purchased another kaftan for our celebration dinner at the Winter Palace Hotel and I revelled in the feel of smooth linen sheets on a real bed instead of my camp bed which had only proved comfortable because my bones had been so weary.

The future was uncertain and I felt inordinately sad when I realized that we might never all be together as a team again. Ahmed Sadek would resume his work at Sakkara and Ian had already stated his intention of joining him. Alan thought he would return to the valley with any expedition he could find work with and Professor Anthony decided he would go home to England. He was nearly seventy years old but, like he said, he would probably come back. He had gone home before, but Egypt with her magic had always called him back.

224

For some quite indefinable reason I had not asked Mike about the future, but the idea of parting from him filled me with so much regret I was afraid of it. I feared to admit even to myself that Mike had become special. Once before I had loved a man, believing that destiny had placed us together from the limits of time. I felt I must not think of Mike in this role. I had to go on believing that Mike was a new thing, a man of the present who would soon disappear out of my life to be replaced by others who in their turn would also disappear.

At sunset we had wandered as a group through the colonnades of the temple of Luxor, and stood in silent awe at the many lotus-headed columns, their rose-tinted splendour reflected in the waters of the Nile.

A lump came into my throat so that I hoped fervently that no one would speak to me or I would be lost. Surely I had always known those columns bathed in light, and the pink Theban hills which held back the limitless waste of the Sahara, and once more I was lost in their beauty.

It was Ahmed Sadek who broke the spell for me and I feel he did it deliberately. 'See, in the corner of the temple there, a Muslim mosque with its graceful minaret,' he said softly. 'One would not think it could have any place within the confines of a pagan temple, and yet I do not think it looks too incongruous.'

My eyes followed his pointing finger and I nodded silently. Then I felt him take my hand and gently press my fingers.

'Luxor is an enchanting place, Kathy. At all hours she is charming, in the blue of her midday and the rose tints of her early morning, but at sunset! Ah, at sunset, Luxor is unforgettable.'

That night in the dining room of the Winter Palace Hotel, we were gay, but it was a gaiety that was a veneer only. For me it covered a sadness that perhaps we should never again be happy as a group who had spent long months together in what must be one of the world's most desolate yet unforgettable places. In Cairo after a few days we would probably all go our separate ways and there was no guarantee that we would ever again experience the closeness we had known.

225

'Tomorrow we will go to Karnak,' Mike was saying. 'Early in the morning before the tourists descend on it, and again in the evening after they have gone.'

'Yes,' Ahmed Sadek agreed. 'We must see Karnak. Nowhere else in the world has so much wealth been spent on the ennobling and beautification of a great temple, in order to make it worthy of an imperial city.'

'What can it have been like in its heyday?' Alan said somewhat wistfully. 'Homer spoke of it as "Hundred-gated Thebes" and even now the sheer size and stature of the ruins make one feel insignificant and suddenly humbled.'

Silently I agreed with him when I stood, soon after dawn the following morning, looking upwards to where the columns and obelisks and pylons reached into the pearly morning sky. Its immensity overpowered me and I was glad that Ammon, the king of all the gods, was a human god and not one of the animal-headed ones of which the ancient Egyptians had been so fond.

Karnak, even in her ruins, was pregnant with the imperialism of the earth's first great civilization. I was dominated by the shades of all those mighty pharaohs who had walked her sacred halls and knelt in worship before the towering gods, and as we wandered from columned hall to columned hall, my thoughts refused to accept the figure of one outstanding god or pharaoh, but only the mighty whole. I was looking at what had been the imperial Egypt of the pharaohs, but it was Egypt in her ashes, spread before us and around us, and Egypt, clothed in her eternity, still lived!

We were walking in a museum whose roof was the sky and whose walls were the Theban hills. I knew that now and always I would carry in my heart her beauty and her sunshine, her sadness and her eternal majesty. Nothing could ever dim for me the pink of her hills and the gold of her light and the desolation of her former glory. Once I had dreamed of Karnak standing proud and beautiful on the Theban plain and of another life which had been a part of that majesty; now I felt I would only ever again dream of her ruins and accept that the past was dead and ruined with her.

I felt Mike's hand upon my arm and his whispered voice

226

against my ear. 'It is awe-inspiring, isn't it? Can you imagine the glory of this civilization that was already ancient when Greece was still unborn and there was no Rome on the seven hills?'

I nodded mutely, and he took my hand lightly and pulled me towards him. 'Let's walk on towards the sacred lake,' he said. 'From there you can see the reflection of the pillars in the water and perhaps get a better idea of the immensity of Karnak.'

I followed where he led, and when at last we paused on the far side of the lake, Mike spoke again.

'Can you imagine the festivals that took place on this lake? It was once linked to the Nile by a canal and along this passed all the sacred boats decorated with flowers. You can almost hear the chanting of the priests and the songs of the priestesses, you can imagine the pharaoh and his queen waiting to receive them. Nowhere on earth does history come so palpably alive as in the ruined halls of Karnak.'

I was caught by his enthusiasm, by his love for Karnak, and in a whisper I said, 'What must it be like in the moonlight?'

'We shall see it tonight. Under the moonlight it seems as though the ruins are whole again, and all the pillars stand upright as they were meant to stand, silent and waiting for the next act in her incredible story.'

I could have wept with disappointment when we returned to the hotel to be told that Ahmed Sadek intended to sail for Cairo immediately and that the others had elected to sail with him. It was Mike who told me that John Strickland was dying in hospital in Cairo and naturally Ahmed wanted to be with him at the end. The others were going to assist him with the findings from the tomb.

'But I shall go with you, of course,' I stated emphatically.

'No, Kathy,' Mike said firmly. 'I have a message for you also. Your cousin and her husband are at the hotel. They are expecting you to join them.'

'You have seen them?' I cried astonished.

'For a few minutes, they have only just arrived. I heard them asking for you at the desk and how they could get in touch with you. Naturally I told them that you were here in Luxor.'

I stared at him dully and he took my hand and held it in a firm grip.

'You have to face him sooner or later, Kathy,' he said sternly.

'Oh, Mike, I know, but I know I'm not in love with him now, I hardly ever think about him. Besides, he's married to Serena. Oh, why should they come just now? I wanted to go with you and the others to Cairo.'

He made me face him, holding my arms firmly and gazing deep into my eyes. 'It's no use telling yourself that you no longer love him when you are separated by time and distance. You've got to look at him and know you no longer love him, that it's really over, finally and irrevocably. Then and only then can you go on with your life!'

I was miserably aware that what he said was the truth, but in staying in Luxor to see David I was losing Mike. He had said nothing about the future and always between us was that strange uneasy feeling that he didn't trust me, his fear that I would hurt him.

I watched them sail on the afternoon boat, standing on the quayside until the boat disappeared round the bend in the river; then I retraced my steps towards the Winter Palace Hotel. I was so sure that I was ready to see David again in spite of that old enchantment that had kept me chained to him for so long. Now at last I could take his hand and murmur a polite word of greeting without that old sickening longing to throw myself in his arms. Mike was right, it was time I found out, and with a courage born of bravado, I stepped out across the road towards the gardens.

Before I reached the hotel one of the gardeners stepped forward and handed me a single, perfect red rose. He bowed, smiling with delight at my joy in his gift, and I thought to myself how courteous they were and polite, even the most menial of them. In this land where one is always aware of the past and the solemnity of the infinite, where time is so

228

unimportant and when tomorrow is forever in the hands of Allah, they behaved with a calm and simple dignity that acknowledged their past greatness and disregarded the long years of conquest and servitude.

My eyes filled with tears as I contemplated the tangled skein of my life and miserably I thought, we can never go back. We should never try to recapture the tenderness and magic of people or places we have once loved in case they are changed and our memories feel cheated and deprived. How much more foolish it was to go back to another life conjured up by dreams which was ethereal and insubstantial!

I had reached the terrace now and, with my heart in my mouth, I could see David coming forward to meet me. The sun shone on his dark hair, finding threads of silver that had not been there before. I could see that he was very tanned and incredibly handsome, walking with that lithe grace I remembered so well. He smiled, holding out his hand, and then I was walking beside him.

I thought I would have known in that first moment of our meeting if the past was truly dead or if something still remained to tantalize and tease me, but we were speaking formalities like two polite strangers. Then I saw Serena coming down the steps of the terrace to meet us. She looked pretty and relaxed in a cool linen dress, her slender arms tanned and warm golden lights in her soft brown hair. She put her arms around me and kissed me and I was glad that she was happy.

'We've so much to talk about, Kathryn,' she said. Then she turned to David. 'Do you think we could have tea out here, darling? It's far too perfect a day to eat indoors.'

'I don't see why not, I'll go and tell them.'

Alone with Serena I said reproachfully, 'Why didn't you tell me you were coming to Luxor? You were always a terrible correspondent.'

'But David said he would write. Don't tell me he didn't.'

'It doesn't really matter, only if Mike hadn't seen you at the desk I could have been on my way to Cairo with the others. Are you going back to the Sudan?'

229

'Yes, after a few weeks' leave in England. The man we met at the desk seemed very nice, attractive too. I always thought Egyptologists were all old and scholarly like Professor Ensor, not young and attractive like your Mike.'

'He isn't my Mike, Serena.'

'But he's nice?'

'Yes, very nice, they all were except Professor Dalton. I didn't get along with him too well but I expect some of that was my fault. Are you fully recovered from your hunting accident now?'

'Oh yes, but you can imagine my dismay when they told me my chief bridesmaid had gone off to Egypt and wouldn't be coming back for ages.'

'But you found somebody else? You always had lots of friends.'

'I didn't want my big church wedding any more. I couldn't face all the fuss and I was still a bit rocky on my legs. I couldn't have taken that long walk down the aisle with everybody wondering if I was going to make it. David and I were married quietly, and almost immediately afterwards we left for the Sudan.'

During the next few days I was constantly in their company and I could hardly believe that all that longing and passion was finally dead. I was missing Mike desperately. I missed his humour and the way his eyes crinkled attractively in his tanned face. I missed the lilt in his voice and his excited enthusiasm for ancient things, and I was wondering if he ever thought about me and was missing me too.

It was their last day in Luxor before going to Cairo and home. They had gone to the temple, and although they had asked me to accompany them, I had declined on the grounds of having letters to write. I sat in the gardens overlooking the river and the bleak Theban hills which rose in majestic crags to their summit, and I was thinking of those months when I had worked happily in the stifling heat, months which healed my tortured spirit and shattered pride, months that brought forgetfulness. It had been nearly two weeks since I had stood on the quayside watching the boat that had carried Mike and the others away from me and I had

230

not heard from him. Perhaps he didn't care what happened to me, perhaps already he was totally absorbed on a new site with a group of different people, and if he had cared for me at all, he was learning to forget me as I had learned to forget David.

I saw them sail in the late afternoon and received David's fleeting kiss without so much as a tremor. I sent my love to those at home, including Bridie, but Serena informed me that Bridie was no longer at Random Edge. She had disappeared again quite suddenly after my own departure for Egypt.

Serena saw nothing strange in her disappearance – after all, she had done it many times before – but I wondered about Bridie, particularly when Serena said she had complained that life was too dull at Random Edge after I had left it.

David and Serena stood together on the deck and I watched them until they were just two figures silhouetted against the setting sun. Thoughtfully I retraced my steps to the hotel. Seeing them standing there together seemed to me so essentially right and the final, irrevocable closing of a chapter in my life.

I stood on the terrace with my room in darkness behind me, thinking about those few emotional weeks when David and I had grasped love with greedy anxious fingers, believing that it was our right, no matter how much it might hurt others. Now I could only see the unimportance of those moments and the lost enchantment. The long calm years belonged to Serena, the steady, everyday joys and sorrows of living were for her just as they had once been for Asnefer, but this time I would not die, I would live, and somewhere in that great unknown I would discover my own destiny.

The night was soft and mellow, a night when the moon rode proudly in a sky lit by a myriad of stars, a night for love, and I was alone. Suddenly I made up my mind that I would go to Karnak. It would be deserted now, the last tourists having departed with the setting sun, and it would

231

be a place of fleeting shadows and vague uneasy ghosts, but I was not afraid. I had wanted to see Karnak by moonlight and that pleasure had been denied me. Now I would see Karnak alone.

The night was warm and I didn't feel the need for a wrap. I hailed a passing horse-carriage from the front of the hotel and directed the driver to Karnak. For a moment he stared at me as though I had taken leave of my senses, then he said, 'You go alone to Karnak, my lady? Karnak bad place, haunted place!'

'I'm not afraid, please take me there.'

'You go to meet gentleman, him lover, he protect you. Karnak good place to be with lover.'

'No doubt. Now please drive on.'

With a huge grin on his face, he turned his horse, encouraging it into a canter, and soon I was alighting from the carriage at the huge pylon gates. One of the guards recognized me as having belonged to an archaeological expedition, and with a bow he stepped backwards into the shadows.

I paid the driver of the carriage who grinned down at me and said, 'I see you are not afraid, my lady. Where is gentleman?'

'He will come.' I smiled briefly and turned away.

The silver night was almost as light as day. Mike had said that the ruins would look whole again in the moonlight, and as I stepped through the gate into the colonnades of the temple, I appreciated how true his words had been.

I stood in what was left of the great hall where, in my dream, I had seen a man standing silent and dignified, even though his wrists and ankles had been bound with chains, but now the chanting of the priests was stilled, the voices of the cheering crowds outside the gates were silent. The moonlight slanted through the pillars on to the broken stone floor. Once I heard the weird lonely cry of a bird or animal which brought a sob to my throat so that I shivered and turned away towards the lake.

I stared at the reflections of obelisks and pylons and a hundred pillars in the water, but all I could think of was that it was over, finished, the days of Karnak's glory, passed into limbo and with them all the profusions of old loves and ambitions and desperate hatreds. No more would those vast halls ring to the cheers of the crowds welcoming home a conquering army, or echo to the singing of the priests at a festival of the gods. Poor, sad Karnak, waiting like the pharaohs in their palatial tombs for the resurrection of the grandeur that never came.

A chill wind moaned along the colonnades, stirring the sand that had settled in the cracks on the floor so that it swirled and drifted down the passage before me. Suddenly I stiffened and held my breath. A man stood in the centre of the great hall of columns. He stood perfectly still, with the full moon silvering his hair, apparently deep in thought for he looked with unseeing eyes into the shadows, his expression immeasurably sad, as though he waited for something momentous to happen. I held my breath, but as though he knew I was there, he turned and as the moon fell upon his face, I gave a little cry. It was Mike.

I stepped out from the shadows calling his name and he came instantly towards me.

'Kathy! What are you doing here alone at this time of night?' he asked, staring into my face.

'I wanted to see Karnak by moonlight.'

'You could get lost here, it stretches for miles, you could easily spend all night trying to find the way out.'

'I could never get lost in Karnak.'

'You sound very confident, but other people have.'

'You were right, Mike, it does come alive in the moonlight. How long had you been standing there?'

'I don't know. Karnak has that effect on me, particularly at night.'

'What effect?'

'Sadness, a terrible indefinable aching sadness as though some tragedy in the past has touched me personally, as though it was still alive and potent.'

'I didn't think you believed in such experiences.'

'In the light of day I don't, but I could believe anything in this temple tonight.'

233

'Have you any news about John Strickland?'

His face grew sad in the moonlight, and taking my arm, he drew me towards the long colonnade which led to the entrance to the temple.

'Unfortunately he died before we reached the hospital, so he never knew about the tomb. We went to his funeral the next day – it is all so quick and final in the East – but it is sad he didn't know about the tomb, he had been so sure that there was one there. That reminds me, Kathy, Ahmed Sadek said I should ask you why you were so confident that we would find one. He said the time had come to tell me about it.'

I was reluctant. Mike with his disdain of anything supernatural, his impatience with superstition, but Ahmed was right, he had a right to know, and haltingly I began to tell him the story from that night in Mesopotamia when the dream had first come to me. The story unwound itself and I came at last to the night when I had stood in this temple with other dignitaries of the court, staring at the man bound in chains who seemed so unperturbed and calm, as though he had already cast off the shackles of mortality.

I had expected gentle mockery, doubt, and subtle derision, but looking into his eyes I found none.

'Did David ever know about your dreams?' he asked gently.

'No. I told my godfather because I could never have told my father and I had to tell somebody, and later I told Ahmed Sadek, because he's a Muslim and I knew he wouldn't scoff at such fancies.'

'And you expected me to scoff at them?'

'I think so.'

'And what part am I supposed to have played in your past that makes Ahmed Sadek think I should be told about it?'

'I think you answered that question yourself when you stood in the hypostyle hall of the temple tonight, Mike, and all those other times when you looked at me with uncertainty and distrust.'

'If any part of your dreams is real then it would seem I

234

had every right to distrust you, Kathy. Where is David tonight?'

'Oh, Mike, it really is over. They sailed for Cairo this afternoon and it was right that they should be together. I was glad for them, believe me.' I glanced up at him. 'I'm surprised to see you here.'

He looked at me keenly, and then he smiled, the smile that crinkled up his eyes in the way that I loved. 'Are you surprised, Kathy? Are you really surprised?'

I could feel my heart thumping painfully as he put his arms around me. I could feel the steady beating of his heart but his kiss was gentle, tender and promising and I felt a new warmth flooding my being as he drew me closer with increasing passion.

It had been no instant thing between us but it would be strong and binding. I felt it as surely as if he had put it into words, but we spoke no words as we walked through the gardens that skirted the Nile. A white felucca sailed towards the West Bank like a great white bird and in the silver moonlight the western hills rose dark and forbidding in the distance.

I had loved in this land before and I had suffered and made others suffer also, but now, with Mike's arms around me, warm and sheltering, it was like coming home, the end of a long and lonely journey.

Epilogue

The night before Mike and I sailed for England, Ahmed Sadek entertained us to dinner at his home near Heliopolis. We sat round the dinner table lit by candlelight and I felt extraordinarily happy as I looked at my friends and the man I loved. Ian and Alan teased us about returning to England, saying the ship would hardly have turned round before we were itching to get back, and Professor Anthony nodded sleepily over his brandy like a benign toby jug.

Our host lived in style in a white villa built on the edge of the desert. The scent of jasmine floated in through the open window, and from where I sat, I could see the pyramids rising majestically above the sand dunes. I was totally and ridiculously happy, but on this, our last night in Egypt, I was also aware of a feeling of sadness, like some haunting tune that refuses to go away.

In the last few weeks since I stood with Mike in the ruined halls of Karnak, we had explored together the slow pace of the river and revelled in its tranquillity. We have looked at the proud handsome face of Rameses set before his temple at Abu Simbel and at the face of Cleopatra standing with her son Caesarean on the walls of her temple at Dendera.

I studied her face under the ornate Egyptian crown and thought to myself that there were probably queens of Egypt who had been more beautiful but this was the woman whose passions had altered the destinies of the most famous men of her day, this gracious regal woman who had shed her voluptuous splendour over a tottering world.

We have been to Abydos and seen the most beautiful

reliefs in the whole of Egypt, standing within the white-walled pagan temple of Seti where legend has it that the goddess Isis at last buried the body of Osiris, and together we absorbed its peace and its gentleness. And now the time has come for us to go home.

I caught Ahmed's dark, long-lashed eyes looking at me through the candle flames and he smiled. 'Are you happy to be going home, Kathy, or are you simply happy to be young and alive and in love?'

'A little of everything, I think,' I answered him. 'It was Mike's decision to go home.'

'I know, and I have been wondering why.'

Mike smiled. 'Oh, suddenly I got a yearning for green fields and church spires over the hedgerows, long country twilights and rain. Even rain can be a blessed thing when one never sees it,' he said quietly.

'But what will you do in England? Your work is here,' Alan asked.

'We'll put down roots for a while,' Mike said, 'then we'll decide together where we want to go and what we want to do. I've got some land and a charming little house in Norfolk. I might even decide to turn myself into a country gentleman.'

They all laughed except Ahmed. He rose from his seat and walked over to the open window, then he went outside to stand on the terrace, looking across the desert. I think he knew that I would follow him.

He was looking at the pyramids shining ghostly white in the moonlight. Awed by their stark majesty, I was thinking that Joseph must have seen them shining smooth and unblemished when he was sold into slavery, that Moses must have seen them from the garden of the palace of the princess whose handmaiden found him sheltering in the bulrushes, and involuntarily I cried, 'They are so big, they make me feel small and insignificant beside their vastness!'

'And yet, Kathy,' Ahmed said gently, 'at this moment you are more important than they are for all their size, for you are alive and warm and lovely, while they are dead things, merely heaps of old stones.'

237

'But a hundred years from now, Ahmed, those stones will have changed hardly at all, while I shall be at one with eternity.'

'But what is eternity? I think it was Friedrich Nietzsche who wrote, "There will be one hour where for the first time one man will perceive the mighty thought of the eternal recurrence of all things." I think you have something for me, Kathy.'

'The talisman of Set?'

'Yes. Do you have it with you?'

I undid my evening bag and took out the gold and enamel talisman and his fingers closed around it.

'What will you do with it?' I asked him breathlessly.

'The river shall have it, where it is deepest and widest. And now I in turn have something for you.'

He felt in the pocket of his velvet smoking jacket and brought out a small parcel which he placed in my hands. It felt heavy and on opening it I found a solid gold bracelet fashioned in the form of a cobra bearing on its hood a royal cartouche. It was beautifully made, and as I held it in my hands, I became aware of a tightening in my throat like the ache of unshed tears.

'Where did you find it?' I whispered.

'It was brought to me by the headman of the village. I went to see him and threatened him with every dire thing I could think of if he refused to tell me who had plundered the tomb behind the mummy cave, but he disclaimed all knowledge of it. I parted from him in anger but that old rogue has worked for me often over the years and there is a strange sort of affinity between us. He brought the bracelet to me one night in Luxor, saying it was all that was left, that they had kept it only because it bore a royal cartouche and they were afraid that questions would be asked by the authorities in Cairo. That was not the real reason, of course. He knew I was angry and that I might refuse to employ him or his men in future. Now allow me to read the inscription for you.'

He stepped back into the light from the room behind us

and read softly, 'Ramaatra Tuia, by the gods beloved,' then he handed the bracelet back to me.

'By the gods beloved'! I was staring at him, wanting with all my heart to believe what he was telling me, that it had been the princess's tomb after all, and that all the anguished questioning and searching over the years had not been in vain.

'You see, Kathy,' he said to me gently, 'there are stranger things in heaven and earth. And now you can go home to England and forget about the past. It is over, that long weary journey which fate made you take, and that I think was the price you had to pay. Only the future is important to you now and Mike will make you happy.'

I slipped the bracelet into the pocket of my long skirt only just in time before Mike came out to join us.

'This is what I shall miss,' he said, 'the clarity of the sky, the nearness of the stars and the desert's stillness. I wonder if I shall ever get used to it, or if we will ever come back.'

He slipped his arm around my waist and held me close to him, Ahmed turned as though to leave us.

'I do not believe in saying goodbye to dear friends,' he said softly. 'Whether they return or not, I prefer to believe that the chain of existence will bring us together again and again, perhaps not in this life, but whenever it is the will of Allah.'

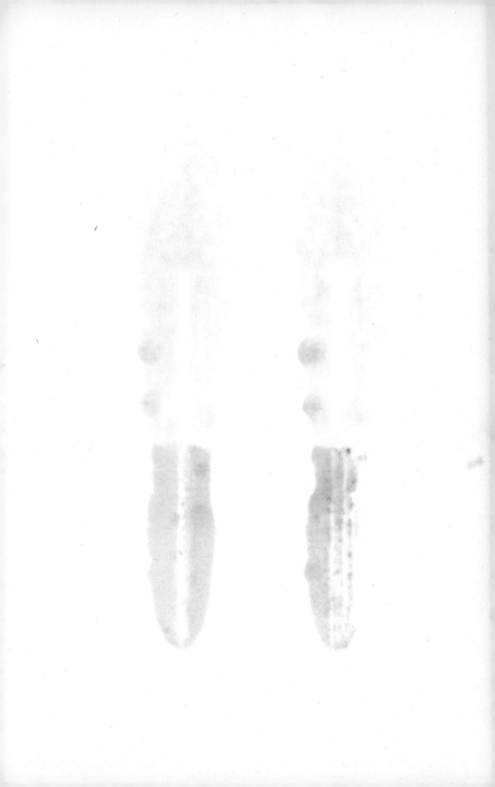

Hylton, S.
    Talisman of Set.